The Padre Phantom

To Paul

I hope you enjoy.

2016

DAVID HARRY

DISCLAIMER

Everything in this book, except for the establishments listed and a few local folks, is fictitious. The words spoken by the "real" locals, as well as any activities of the local businesses are, of course, also fictional.

LOCATION

The events described in this book are centered on South Padre Island, an island in the Gulf of Mexico separated from Texas by the Laguna Madre. A two and a half mile causeway separates Port Isabel on the mainland with the island. Every year the island is host to spring breakers kicking back from their studies in mid-March and to Winter Texans who migrate south to keep warm in the winter months. Despite what you might read in my books, SPI remains a safe and extremely friendly place to live, work, or vacation. Come on down. The sun, sand, and surf await you.

Printed in the United States and published by Hotray LLC

ISBN: 0988915073

ISBN -13: 9780988915077

DEBRA SUZANNE TANNENBAUM

January 25, 1967 – May 19, 2015

Daughter, Sister, Musician, Artist, Author

May her memory be for a blessing to all who knew her.

For a sample of Debi's writing, please go to:
https://youtu.be/nYpHjYTk90U

DEDICATION

To my daughter, Debra Tannenbaum, of blessed memory. You have left a hole that can never be filled. I love you now and forever. May your soul be bound up in the bond of life. You can rest knowing that the memory of you will bless me for all my remaining days.

Your loving father

TRIBUTE

We mourn the passing of my sister, Debi. But we also celebrate her life.

I have so many great memories of her: all of our sailing adventures that she loved (and hated due to being sea sick); our trip to England when she waited until the worst possible time to be airsick all over my mom's brand new London fog coat (yes, I found that extremely funny); the time in my aunt Ina's car (won't explain here, but that still cracks me up); the time we ate all of grandma Mollie's ice cream because we thought it would help her stay thinner; etc. etc.

She was a great sister, a terrific aunt, and the best daughter anyone could hope for.

We mourn for her even as we keep these great memories of her in celebration of her life. Be happy she touched our lives, rather than sad of her passing.

Dan

In Memoriam

Debi

If you told me we would say our last good-bye on Mother's Day...

I would not have believed you.

If you told me we would not get to celebrate another birthday or holiday...

I would not have believed you.

If you told me you would be gone tomorrow...

I would not have believed you.

If you told me you are now at peace...

I would believe you.

If you told me you are with Grandma Mollie and Grandpa Al eating a big bowl of fudge-swirl ice cream watching some Miami football...

I would believe you.

I know...you will watch over us ALL...

until we see you again.

Cousin Sheryl Tannenbaum Nevel

Debi
You were the Kindest, Loveliest, Creative, Tenderest, and most Beautiful person I have ever known. Family is a gift that lasts forever and I will always miss you.

This poem by an unknown author captures my feelings perfectly.

The moment that you left me, my heart was split in two, one side was filled with memories, the other side died with you.

I often lay awake at night when the world is fast asleep; and take a walk down memory lane with tears upon my cheek.

Remembering you is easy, I do it everyday; but missing you is a heartache that never goes away.

I hold you tightly within my heart and there you will remain; you see life has gone on without you, but will never be the same.

Cousin Missy Tannenbaum

NOTE ON THE SINGER RANCH

The Singer Ranch mentioned is a real place, once existing approximately twenty-six miles north of the present city of South Padre Island, Texas. Old man Singer's fortune, as the legend goes, was buried somewhere on the ranch, or in the vicinity of the ranch, when Singer and his family fled at the beginning of the Civil War. That much appears to be historically accurate. What is also accurate is that Steve Hathcock is an expert on the Singer Ranch, the Singer family, and the Singer treasure. The author has taken literary license with respect to the existence of fresh water wells on the property and, of course, their coordinate locations.

The potential structural discontinuity to the Port Isabel Causeway, as well as any potential involvement by *SpaceX*, as discussed in the book, is purely fictional.

SOUTH PADRE ISLAND AND PORT ISABEL ESTABLISHMENTS FREQUENTED BY JIMMY REDSTONE AND ANGELLA MARTINEZ

Almost Always Available Locksmith
A-Taxi
Beach House Vacation Rentals
Blue Marlin
Boy Scout Campgrounds

Café Kranzlers
Captain Donut
Coconuts
CVS
Dirty Al's
Dolphin Point

Harpons
Hilton Garden Inn
Holiday Inn Express
Island Clinic
Island Equestrian Center
Island Fitness Center

K's Jewelry & Beads
Laguna Bobs
Louie's Backyard
Paragraphs on Padre
Pan Am facility (Isla Blanca Park)
Parrot Eyes
Port Isabel Navigation District Boat Yard
Port Isabel Train Museum

Sea Ranch
Singer Ranch
Ted's
The Wave
Tom & Jerry's
UB Captain Kayak Rentals

Wanna Wanna
Wells Electronics
World Flavors Coffee House

Please don't forget to stop by and tell them Jimmy and Angella sent you.

ONE

With forty million in the trunk and the Texas border still seventy miles north, terror and excitement pulsed through my body in equal measures. The terror, of course, was attributable to my concern over bandits, especially bandits wearing stink'n badges.

The excitement was another matter altogether. Sex may be a close second, but money rules. It always has and always will. From my experience, money, the possession of it or its absence, is a person's single most important driver. And forty million, well, as an Illinois Senator once said, now we're talking real money.

I have always believed myself to be above the great wealth chase, but my excitement proved me wrong. Money is truly king without a doubt.

Closing on the border, my thoughts turned to the Mexican authorities and I had visions of forty million spread on the ground while the Mexican authorities figured out how to make it theirs.

Truth is, they knew how to make it theirs. Their debate would be what to do with my body. And that discussion wouldn't last more than a minute.

I called Tiny, my handler, and asked him to grease the skids. A few minutes after speaking with Tiny I knew the wheels of our government were turning because I received a call from Lucinda McNaughton, a Washington socialite and former Marine General. Although retired, she was still very involved with Homeland Security issues on a major scale. Her long-time lover, General (Retired) Maxwell Jamison, was the man the president always called upon to head up military operations in times of crises. Jamison took no prisoners.

Lest I get any ideas about the money, McNaughton quickly assured me the money belonged to the United States government and that I was to immediately deposit every penny of it in the *Marine Savings Bank* on South Padre Island where I currently lived.

I assured her I would.

"Every penny, Redstone," she had said. "No deductions for expenses, no meals, no gas allowances, no walking around money, nothing missing. All of it. You understand me?"

"I wouldn't dream of doing anything else," I assured her, despite me doing nothing for the past hours other than dreaming of what I would do with all that money.

"Just be certain you don't," was her parting shot before the phone went dead.

Tiny performed his job well, as he usually did, on both sides of the Rio Grande River. I was motioned through, first by the Mexican Border Police and then by two U. S. Border Patrol agents, even receiving a salute from them as I passed their station.

I drove directly to the bank and was immediately surprised when the senior Vice-President, a little man with a large mustache and an even larger attitude, informed me that I was not authorized to open an account in the name of the United States of America. I flashed my Homeland Security shield and that went nowhere.

No matter what argument I made, the little guy, who was wearing perhaps the only tie on the island, stood as tall as he could, sucked in his gut, and repeated, “I don’t care if you’re Homeland Security, the Governor, or even the frigg’n President, you’re not authorized to open accounts in the name of the United States. Is that clear enough?”

“How about if I open the account in my own name as trustee for the U. S. Treasury?”

“The only account you may deposit the money into is your own account, Mr. Redstone. Your own account, with your own name on it. No one else’s account. Nothing in trust for anyone else, unless of course, you have trust papers. I thought I made that perfectly clear.”

The little man wore me down. It took two hours while I painstakingly filled out more forms than if I had shot a man dead in cold blood at City Hall at high noon. Money importation forms. IRS forms. Immigration forms. Certifications of Non-Drug Related Activity forms to name just a few.

Of course, the bank didn’t have copies of all the forms and they had to access several government web sites to download them. There were even two forms from the Import/Export bank, whoever the hell they are. The Interstate Commerce Commission and the Federal Reserve had forms. Even the U. S.

Coast Guard required forms to be signed and notarized because the money came across a navigable river.

"How about if I just keep the money under my mattress?" I asked at one point.

"I wouldn't advise you do that, Mr. Redstone," the little guy answered, showing no sense of humor. "It would be most uncomfortable to sleep on and you might get hurt if a burglar learned of all that money."

If a burglar learned of the money? There couldn't be a self-respecting criminal in four counties that hadn't by now heard of the money. I was certain the entire city, perhaps the entire State of Texas, knew I had forty million in cash in my trunk. Banks don't have armed guards stationed in their lobbies anymore or I would have sent one of them out to the parking lot to stand guard.

Shooting a man dead at City Hall was sounding better all the time. The vice-president would be on the top of that list.

When the account was finally opened I had to carry all the money in by myself because as he explained, "I don't dare expose any of these good folks to the dangers such an amount of money presents, now could I Mr. Redstone?"

I kept asking myself why I was waiting for high noon at City Hall to shoot this guy.

When all the money was safely in their vault, the little guy said, "Sorry, Mr. Redstone, you won't be allowed to withdraw any of this without IRS written approval."

"Go get their approval," I barked. Not because I wanted any of the money, but because I was sick and tired of his rules.

"I can't do that, sir, until all these forma are signed, notarized, logged into our system and delivered to the various agencies. Then they have ten working days to process the paperwork. Sorry."

Good thing I hadn't brought my weapon into the bank.

Five hours later I had my first telephone conversation with an IRS agent who wouldn't take my word that the money actually belonged to my employer, the U. S. government. His position was based on the fact that my employer refused to take any responsibility for, or ownership of, said money.

But it was their money. It had come into my possession as the result of a successful—or so I would like to believe—operation in which my partner, Angella Martinez, and I played a major role. In concept, the mission was simple. Iran, or someone with nuclear bomb ambitions, was using a stolen piece of art, called the King's Cup, to finance the purchase of several nuclear accelerators. The accelerators would allow the Iranians to instantly have nuclear capability despite its agreement not to enrich uranium.

A uranium mine in Mexico was being used for the preparation of the accelerators but unfortunately for them Angella and I had encouraged the bad team to leave without the money transfer and without the accelerators. That's why the money—or more accurately, a substantial portion of the money—ended up in the trunk of the car I drove back across the border.

One thing is certain, the money is not mine—nor is it Angella's. However, had we headed south toward Panama, instead of north to Texas, I don't believe any agency of our government would have been unduly disturbed. In fact, I'm positive there would have been smiles all around—with the possible exception of the CIA.

Angella, who is usually deadly accurate in these matters, claims that if we had gone south our bones would someday be found in the jungle with extra holes in our skulls, the cash long gone.

Therein lies the problem. Despite what those in the know actually do know about the money, the official word is "What money?" Goes along with, "What operation?" And, "What King's Cup?" Some, such as the President's Press Secretary, if asked would even say, "We did what in Mexico?" Actually, given the way things were going, his response would be, "What Mexico?"

But once the money was deposited in the bank the forms took over and the IRS did what the IRS does. It pounced. Fifteen million, or about thirty-seven percent, is what they took from the account. And they took it by simply debiting my account at the bank within twenty-four hours of our first phone conversation. "As a deposit," the kind-hearted gentleman said when I called to complain, "against what you may ultimately owe."

The smile in his voice quickly faded when I just as politely informed him, in graphic terms, just what he could do with the money—and with the whole IRS. The result of my conversation was a courier at my door two hours later with a letter, duly signed by the head of the Brownsville IRS, containing a page of penalties I would face for non-compliance with any of their requests. The letter also contained five pages of procedures I had to follow in order to protest the IRS action. The kicker being the protest procedures only took effect after I filed my tax return for the year and the IRS made a final determination as to my tax liability. There was an added page informing me of the penalties for harassment. I was sure those penalties applied to my actions, not theirs.

I dialed the number on the letter and told the recording exactly, and I mean exactly, where the IRS could file their letter. Angella called from the kitchen, "Perhaps we would have been right in heading south. I like our chances with the CIA over the IRS."

"Can they tap an already tapped phone?" I called back.

"They'll be talking to each other, so many people are listening in on us. When the IRS is done with us we'll be lucky to own a phone." She came into the living room carrying a plate of cheese. "Perhaps that's why Tiny sent us the new communicators. Better start carrying yours. They're encrypted and he said not able to be monitored."

"What's even more important for the government, all messages in either direction are totally erased when read, or twenty-four hours after being sent, whichever comes first."

"Talk about missing e-mails." She kissed my cheek. "Back in a minute with the beers. You need to settle."

"It'll take a keg to wash away the IRS taste," I called after her. "Or two."

TWO

"Jimmy," Karen, the owner of *Ted's* restaurant said as she freshened my coffee, "such language. You'll scare away my customers."

"I'm the only one here." Indeed, this was one of those rare moments when *Ted's* was devoid of customers. It was already early afternoon and Karen was closing for the day.

"If they were here, they'd never return," she shot back. "Who were you talking to anyway?"

"The IRS, if you must know."

"About that money you deposited. In that case, I'd say go for it. Give 'em hell for me as well. Your lunch guests coming or not? The kitchen is closing and I need to get out of here. Been a long day."

I checked my watch. "Give them five. You know lawyers." In fact, Maria Cruz was always punctual. But this meeting included her client, Joy Malcom. And with Joy, one never knows what to expect. The meeting had been hastily arranged just thirty minutes ago and I only hoped it wasn't another dead body on the beach episode that Joy seems to always be involved with.

"So where's Angella this fine day?" Karen called from the cash register. "Haven't seen much of her lately."

"Cleaning the condo," I lied. Angella was plain tired of everyone grilling her on the money so she's at home catching up on the tons of paperwork bringing that money north has generated. Her throat was injured in that operation, so Washington has given her unofficial medical leave. Which only means they have not assigned her—or me for that matter—to any operation. But the IRS and other government agencies have shown no such leniency. So we toil away.

"Your five minutes is up," Karen called.

That was okay by me. I stood, fished bills from my pocket, and threw then on the table.

"Hi, Jimmy," Joy called from the doorway, full makeup and all. "Hi, Karen. Sorry we're late. I'm famished. How about three pecan pancakes and a side of bacon?" she called before even getting to the table.

Lawyer Cruz came in a moment later. In answer to Karen's query, Cruz replied, "Coffee only. Please."

I hadn't even seen Cruz enter the restaurant, my view being blocked by Joy, her arms spread wide ready for a hug.

The formalities finished, the three of us sat down. The coffees were placed in front of the two women almost as soon as they were seated.

"I understand all of the charges have been dropped," I said to Cruz. "Good job."

"Nothing special from me, Jimmy. The government dropped the charges against Joy on its own. They didn't want to, or couldn't, prove chain of custody of the King's Cup."

Speculation, my speculation, has it the government was behind the stealing of the hundred million dollar art piece from Iran in the first place. The charge against Joy for possession of stolen property being dropped supported my theory and is consistent with the government knowing nothing about the money I deposited. "Is that so?" I responded, hoping my fake surprise passed muster.

Cruz winked, but Joy was clueless.

"Matter of fact, Jimmy, that's why we're here," Cruz said, her smile fading ever so slightly. "Joy, tell him your concerns."

"They are more than concerns," Joy said, her eyes revealing anger while her lips offered peace. "Frankly, I want reimbursement for the Feds stealing the King's Cup from my place. The Cup is worth over fifty million."

Actually, it's worth over a hundred million. But who's counting?

Cruz sat silently, sipping her coffee. Waiting.

"If I understand correctly, Joy," I said, trying not to add fuel to her fire, "the King's Cup I saw in your apartment was a fake. You said so yourself."

"The art piece you saw was the original!" she shot back. "The government took the original when they raided my apartment!"

I lowered my voice to a whisper. "Counselor," I said, turning to engage Cruz who had been sitting back as if she were a spectator, "you might wish to advise your client that possession of stolen property is a crime and that she is speaking to a federal agent with arrest powers."

Before Cruz could react, Joy said, "The King's Cup was not stolen property. I owned it, if you must know." She dug in her bag and produced what appeared to be a sale contract from *LaGrande International*. "Here's all the proof you require. Jimmy, you want to fight with LaGrande, have at it."

LaGrande International, I knew, specialized in Peruvian and early Persian art. The King's Cup came from Persia. Actually it pre-dated the Bronze Age, if I recall the briefing Lisa Viguet gave us. Lisa is a Homeland Security agent specializing in stolen art. According to her, the cup pre-dated Mesopotamia by more than three hundred years. And here I was, holding a sales certificate from one of the world's most trusted art houses.

"How did you...?"

"Don't look so surprised, Jimmy dear. Morris bought me a present. If you must know, he feels bad he's been away so long. You might call it a peace offering." She batted her long eyelashes. "Some men know how to take care of their women."

This was a reference to me not taking her up on her many offers to cheer her up. Morris Malcom is her husband. Well not exactly. Morris is a Mexican national whose real name is Roberto Alterez Santiago. He has a wife and several children in Mexico and is what many would call a Drug Lord. He pretended to be Joy's husband when he was in the United States. Now he's in a Mexican jail for trafficking and other naughty activities. "You were about to throw him out, if I recall right. He fed you drugs. Now that rehab's behind you, I thought..."

"That woman agent, Lisa somebody," Joy said, ignoring my diversion, "substituted a fake cup for the real thing! I want my money or I want the real one back."

Truth be told, this sounded more like Morris than Joy. She was fronting for him. But I couldn't determine if she knew it or was being duped. Another truth, unless I missed my guess, is that it wasn't Viguet in Joy's apartment during the DHS raid, but rather an imposter by the name of Sally Comings. Comings is known in the trade as Shadowy Sal. Viguet has been in the hospital recovering from, among other things, a drug overdose.

Needless to say, neither Angella, who worked directly with Lisa just prior to the overdose, nor I have been allowed to speak with her so the circumstances are a bit vague.

Joy was waiting for a response from me. "Even with that sales receipt I don't know how you're going to..."

"The money you brought out of Mexico came from selling my King's Cup. And I want it."

You'll have to get in line behind the IRS is what I wanted to say. But instead, I responded, "I can't comment on that money. But it has nothing to do with the Cup," I lied.

"Jimmy, you're no better than the rest of them. You're lying pure and simple."

Cruz put her coffee down, her face friendly but serious. "Jimmy, we'll give you a week from today. But I've been authorized to file suit on behalf of Ms. Malcom against the government for the return of the King's Cup. In addition, we will be asking for fifty million in damages for the false arrest."

"False arrest?"

"The charges were dropped because the government can't prove where that cup came from. If they can't prove where it came from then they had no reason to obtain a warrant. The whole operation was illegal. So either pay up or we'll see you in court."

"I'll pass the message along, but it won't be me you'll see in court."

"Don't bet on that. We'll be naming you personally. You have the money. And even more importantly, you're the one who took the pictures in her apartment that started this whole thing."

Actually, Cruz had a point. Since the King's Cup had been in Joy's possession and since the money I brought back from Mexico came from the sale of what appears on the surface to be her property, it logically follows that the money belongs to her—or more likely to the people she fronts for.

I pushed my chair back and Cruz said, "Mind answering a few questions?"

"Try me," I said, sitting back down. In the end, I liked Joy and really had nothing against Cruz, other than my dislike, actually distrust, of lawyers in general.

"Who does Lisa Viguet work for?"

"Homeland Security, same as I do."

"And what about that big fellow who I'm told comes down here from time to time?"

"Goes by Tiny," Joy chimed in. "But I don't know his real name."

"Kelvin Jurald," I replied, again pushing my chair back and this time standing up completely. What I didn't say is that his real name, I believe, is Emerson Sommers and that he works for the CIA on assignment for domestic cover purposes to the Secret Service.

"And he works for?" Cruz asked, not missing a beat.

"Last question, okay?"

"You got it," the lawyer replied, knowing full well I wasn't going to answer any more questions anyway.

"Secret Service." Without saying another word I left the restaurant. Karen was nowhere to be seen.

THREE

On the walk back to our condo the communicator Tiny had given me vibrated. This was the first time it had gone off so it startled me. I typed in the code I had been given, taking care to get it right the first time. It was a progressive code and each time a message came through I had to add the number of the month to the previous code. This being the first message and October, I typed in the digits "1" and "10" on the assumption the device began with zero. If I was wrong the communicator would go blank. Or, knowing the CIA, the agency Tiny worked for, maybe explode.

Actually, it did neither. VISIT LT MALONE STAT appeared on the screen for several seconds and then disappeared. I tried to retrieve the message but it was gone. I trotted the last half-block to the condo to get my car and arrived just as Angella appeared in the doorway. Apparently she had received the same message because she knew where we were going.

"What's up?" she asked, pulling her door closed. "Cryptic message."

"Beats me," I said, accelerating out of the parking area even before Angella's seat belt was snapped.

"I was just thinking this morning we haven't heard from Tiny, or for that matter, anyone, since we came back from Mexico. I was expecting to hear from Viguet once they got the drugs out of her system but…Hey, isn't that Malone over there running toward her car?"

I couldn't follow where Angella was pointing because two marked cars, their blue and red flashing lights on, came flying across the police parking lot and raced south, the second one missing me by inches. The siren in Malone's car came on even before the car began moving. I rolled down my window and waved for her to stop, but instead she accelerated onto the street and followed the other two cars.

"Shall we?" I normally leave chasing police cars and ambulances to other professionals, but because of Tiny's message I felt compelled to catch up with Malone. She worked major crimes, such as homicide, and from the looks of things she wasn't on her way for coffee.

"My God!" Angella exclaimed, "They're coming from every direction. Be careful."

Indeed, sirens and flashing lights seemed to be appearing from side streets and parking lots. A fire-rescue vehicle overtook me and I pulled into the bike lane to let it pass. Before I could regain the roadway, my rearview mirror picked up two more vehicles, their lights on and their sirens blaring, coming from the far north. I waited for them to pass. One was county and one was state.

Sirens could be heard in the far distance as well, both in front and behind us. For a small island—and even smaller community—South Padre has an abundance of police power, not to mention drug enforcement, FBI, Homeland Security, Coast Guard, Fish and Wildlife wardens and any number of constables and sheriffs.

"There's something on the bridge," Angella said, pointing off to our right. "And ahead as well. Turn right here and move over to Laguna Boulevard. Padre is blocked up ahead."

I followed Angella's instructions and managed to avoid the jam.

"Pull in here, Jimmy. We'll have to walk over to Padre, you won't get any closer than this. I think I see Malone's car in front of your bank."

By my bank Angella meant the *Marine Savings Bank* where I had deposited the forty mil.

Angella ran ahead and I struggled to keep up. Note to self: Resume your fitness training with Teran at *Island Fitness Center.* Need major gym time.

"Get in, both of you," Malone yelled to us as we approached the bank. She ran around her car and jumped in behind the wheel. "I'll explain as we go."

And go we did. Siren on, the car accelerated to what I estimated to be a hundred miles an hour. But that only lasted five blocks because from that point Malone had to navigate the stalled traffic.

"Bank was robbed. One critical back there. Armored car, must have been hijacked, but we have no reports on that aspect as of now. Might be some dead in that vehicle, just don't know."

"Where are we going?" Angella asked.

"Armored vehicle is trapped on the bridge. Port Isabel and two State Police cars managed to block the outbound lanes. Sometimes the stupidity of these people astounds me. Bank teller hit the silent alarm so we almost caught them. The first responding officer saw the armored truck pulling away but didn't pursue because he had to see what was going on in the bank. Good thing he did, he may have prevented a death. He knew the bridge would be blocked in the natural course of things. And there aren't many places on this island to hide an armored truck. Actually, the radio devices they now carry continuously broadcast their location. Not a good getaway vehicle. The only other way off this island is by fishing boat."

It didn't add up. Anyone smart enough to hijack an armored truck without triggering an alarm is certainly smart enough to know you can't rob a bank on an island with only one way off. Especially not if you plan to use the truck to haul away the loot. There's no ferry service and you can't float an armored vehicle across Laguna Madre on a fishing charter. To say that out loud is to state the obvious, so I remained silent.

The radio came alive and Malone stopped talking. It was hard to hear exactly what had been said, but Malone threw the microphone on the seat. "Shit!" she exclaimed, and accelerated through the turn onto the bridge, tires screeching. "They went over the side. Money and all! Coast Guard's been notified, but as luck would have it they're out in the Gulf investigating an illegal fishing fleet. Homeland Security is on the way, but their vessels are over in Port Isabel and it'll take fifteen minutes or so before they get on scene."

"Over the side?" I repeated. "What does that mean?"

"Tex DOT is in the process of repairing the causeway. Actually the railings are being replaced and the bridge is being painted underneath. Contractors work from below using hoists. Apparently the bad guys used a hoist to lower themselves and the money down to a waiting boat."

"What about using air to follow them?" Angella asked.

"Won't be on scene for another six minutes. Nine vessels are under visual surveillance from the bridge. Two DHS speedboats are on the way and the CG has dispatched one from the intercept task force back to the bay. Gaming and Wildlife have a boat in the vicinity, one of them is just about on scene."

This was too well planned to be foiled by visual observation from the bridge, or by some Gaming and Wildlife types. Again I held my tongue. I glanced at Angella and from the look on her face she had come to the same conclusion.

Malone slowed the car and turned off the siren. The radio again came alive and this time we could hear clearly. Two men were found inside the truck, both bound and gagged and both with heavy cloth bags tied over their heads. They were guards working for the armored truck company and from what came over the air it sounded that they added no new information.

A moment later we were walking on the bridge. Three snipers were set up using the railings to steady their high-powered rifles, their eyes pressed into their sights. What they thought they'd be shooting was unclear to me. But I wouldn't be surprised to learn that a fisherman or two disappeared this day never to be heard from again.

We listened while Malone was briefed by a uniformed State Police Sergeant. Whatever had been taken from the bank, and anything else that had been on the truck, other than the two guards, were gone. No boats had been seen speeding away. Angella and I identified ourselves as DHS agents, and I said, "Point out the boats you have under observation."

Of the nine, three were kayaks, five were flat bottomed fishing craft floating with the current, their masters standing on the bows casting their lines. The remaining boat was slightly smaller than the other five fishing boats and from the angle of the fishing line it was apparent the man holding the rod had caught a fish and was reeling it in. While one or more of the fishermen may have seen something, none of the boats were large enough below deck to hide the contraband. Aerial surveillance would be enough to ascertain if intervention was required.

"I understand DHS vessels are almost here," I said to the sergeant. "Have them take statements from the kayaks first. They're heading away. The others aren't going anywhere. They're fishing in the channel."

The response was immediate and not entirely unexpected. "You and your partner want to be here, that's fine with me, Redstone. But keep out of the way. Let us do our jobs. Those kayaks are not the problem. You can see from here there's nothing in them." He thrust his field glasses in my direction. "Wanta look?"

"Yes, sir!" I snapped, throwing a salute and taking a step backward. "Whatever you say, sir."

Angella took my arm and pulled me away before further words could be exchanged. I reluctantly followed her to where Malone was talking to one of the guards who was rubbing his hands to get the circulation moving. The lieutenant motioned for us to come over. "According to this gentleman," she said when we were close enough to hear over the noise of the traffic moving onto the island from the far lanes, "this truck is owned and operated by an outfit called *Valley Armored*. It had just been serviced and the two of them, this man and that man there, went to pick it up. That's why there was no report of a hijacking. It hadn't been returned to service when it was taken. No one spoke in their presence."

"So we don't know nationality. What about descriptions?"

"Nothing. Masks were pulled over their heads from behind and they may have been drugged as well. Tox will tell us for certain."

I turned to the guard, a guy with a big mustache curled upwards at the ends. I didn't know if his eyes were always so frightened looking but they certainly were now. I had seen him, or someone who looked like him long ago, but nothing rang a bell. "Where's the garage where the servicing occurred?"

"McAllen."

"And where was the truck when it was hijacked?"

"We stopped for gas just a block away from the garage, before getting on the highway. That's when they took the truck." A slight Mexican accent floated in the air, but that's common in the Valley, even for U. S. born citizens.

"How'd they do it?"

"Roberto pumped the gas and I went to the restroom. When I came back I didn't see Roberto. He wasn't in the driver's seat so I thought he was in the back. I opened the back door with my key and then everything went dark."

"FBI'll get his full statement, Jimmy, and follow up. You can bet on that. This is a bank robbery, so the Feds have jurisdiction. The vic back at the bank is my concern. You want a ride or would you rather tangle with Sergeant McCarthy. He and I have had our go-arounds and I can just imagine the two of you in the same vehicle—or even working the same case."

"We'll go back with you. Any report on what's missing from the bank?"

"For starters, forty-some million is gone. Some other stuff as well."

"What kind of other stuff? Papers? Investments?"

"Something in a large FedEx box. Taken from the safe-deposit area."

"FedEx box?"

"All I know at this time. Remember, the bank doesn't know what's in the packages people store in the safe deposit vault."

"Did the robbers get into the personal drawers?"

"I assume so. Where else would that box have come from? You know what I know. Now get in or walk. I'm sure McCarthy will arrange transportation if you don't like what I'm offering."

In a hearse, perhaps.

Just as I was about to get in Malone's car the hoist appeared at the side of the bridge. On a whim, I said, "I'm going to take a ride on this thing down to the water, see what I can see. Want to join me?" I said to Angella.

“I’ll go back with the Lieutenant if you don’t mind. Stay dry. Oh, and Jimmy, don’t get into it with the sergeant. This is not your investigation.”

“Good advice,” is what I thought I heard Malone say, but her actual words were drowned out by an orange-painted Coast Guard helicopter passing over the bridge from south to north.

FOUR

The ride from the bridge down to the water was uneventful. A county maintenance man was at the helm, a rope attached to several pulleys with a primitive brake mechanism. This would never pass muster for a tourist attraction, but I suppose it was okay for bridge maintenance.

"All out," the man announced when the platform was still several feet above the water. I was the only passenger and there was no boat. In answer to my unasked question, he said, "You can stand on the abutment. Not much to see down here, but people keep coming down."

"Where do they go?"

"Back up. As I said, nothing to see."

I stepped out onto the concrete slab that held the bridge supports. The top was massive, flat, and slippery. The sides, at least the side that faced the opening between the abutment I was standing on and the next one, were flat. The two abutments formed a channel where small boats could slip through under the bridge.

"How deep is the water here?" I asked the maintenance guy as he started back up toward the bridge surface.

"Beats me," he called down. "Someone said it was fifteen feet. Don't rightly know."

Fifteen feet would support a good-sized boat. I guessed the height from the water to the bridge underbelly to be in the range of thirty, maybe forty, feet.

I walked around the bridge supports and found nothing of possible interest other than seagull (or pelican, I'm certainly not an expert) droppings. They appeared to be undisturbed, except where the hoist dropped off its passengers.

I was contemplating my next move—actually trying to work a plan to get back to shore—when a small boat with two men aboard in life jackets came racing from the south. The good news is that a blue light was flashing on their bow. I flagged them down, flashed my cred pack and they slowed enough so that I could jump down onto the relatively flat deck. The notation on the side of the boat read Fish and Wildlife.

"Thought this was a bank robbery. What's Homeland Security got to do with it?" The man speaking was driving the boat and his uniform proclaimed him to be Flores. The other man was Harris and he held a large pair of binoculars.

"Same as Fish and Wildlife. Just helping out."

"We're heading over to that boat there. Harris says the boat is from Arkansas and the registration is expired."

"You can tell it's expired from here?"

"Says 09 on the decal," Harris mumbled, sounding as if he had a mouth full of marbles. "If that ain't expired nothing is."

I was flung onto my butt as the boat accelerated at full throttle in the direction of the small fishing boat. Harris made a noise that sounded like landlubber. Pick your battles I reminded myself. This is their domain and swimming to shore is not what I had in mind.

The fishing boat still had its line in the water, but it was now slack. We pulled up to the side and Flores yelled, "Game Warden. Mind if we come alongside?"

"What am I doing wrong?" the man holding the rod called back. "Just out here fishing for the day."

"For starters, your registration is expired. We'd like to see your papers."

Despite the lack of permission, Harris had a grappling hook around the bow cleat of the fishing boat. Flores maneuvered the rear of our boat toward the rear of the fishing boat.

"You have no right…"

"You have a fishing license?" Flores asked, paying no attention to the protest. "And you best get out your registration and driving license as well."

"I have no fish," the man responded. "You have no right to…"

"Have a fishing pole in your hand, line in the water, all we need."

While he was talking, Harris had tied the two bows together and was moving to secure the sterns.

"Permission to board, Captain," Flores said.

"Permission denied!" came the reply. "Get away from my boat or I'll…"

Harris had his gun out and said, "You'll do what? You threaten again I'll show you how Texas law works. Now tell us where your papers are or we'll arrest you and tow your boat in. Cost you plenty to get it back. We find contraband aboard and the government gets to keep your boat. That the way you want to play this?"

"In my wallet. In the console."

"You have a gun in there? A knife maybe?"

"Just the wallet."

"Okay, open it slowly. You're lying, you're dead."

The man produced his driver's license. According to the license his name was Jack Ross and he had no boat registration and no fishing license.

"Mind if we look around?" Flores asked for the third time.

"Seems you're going to do it anyway, so be my guest. Note that I protest."

"Take it up with the judge," Flores replied, climbing aboard. The weapon in Harris' hand never leaving Ross.

"Nothing of interest here," Flores announced a few minutes later. He handed Ross several pieces of paper and said, "Don't advise you ignoring these. We'll track you and seize the boat."

"I have a question," I called across to Ross when Flores came back aboard. "Did you happen to see anybody come down that hoist over there?"

"Who the hell are you?" he called back.

"Not your business who I am. Just answer the simple question. See anything over there?"

Ross looked to where I was pointing, thought about it a moment, then said, "May have seen some men come down from up there. Not really sure what I saw. I was busy fish…I was busy."

"Where did those men go?"

"Didn't see."

"Did they have anything with them?"

"Said I didn't see. You hear me. I didn't see what they were doing."

I didn't exactly hear what Ross called across the water as we pulled away, but it sounded like something I'd not repeat in polite company. Harris didn't pull his gun as I half expected. But he did flash a hand signal.

"You want to stay with us?" Flores asked. "We're going to talk with the other fishing boats. Got no jurisdiction over the kayaks unless they have a line in their hands. Coast Guard will have to handle that."

It was the kayaks I wanted to talk with. The folks on the fishing boats were busy fishing and I could understand them not paying a lot of attention to a bridge. But kayakers were just out paddling around enjoying the environment, seeing what they could see. There was a good chance one or more of them saw something of interest to us. "I'll stay with you if you'll drop me back on the island, say over by *Laguna Bobs,* when you're finished."

"For a beer—or two—you got your wish."

FIVE

"Let's go over this again, Redstone. Why is it that you appeared in front of Police Headquarters at the exact time of the robbery? You say you had nothing specific to discuss with me—or for that matter with anyone."

I was sitting across from Lt. Malone in her small office, having come here by invite ostensibly to watch surveillance video from the Great Bank Heist, as the robbery was now being called in the pubs around town. I couldn't very well blame it on my secret squirrel communicator without knowing why the message had been sent. I couldn't do that because Tiny had gone to ground. "Just stopping by to say hello. Nothing wrong with that now is there?"

"From anyone else I would accept that. But you're a let-sleeping-dogs-lie kinda guy and if it ain't broke you wouldn't be over here fix'n it. So I ask again, why were you here? Maybe something is broken and I just don't know about it."

"Look," I began, putting together what I could from actual checkable facts, "I was coming from a meeting with Joy Malcom and her attorney. They threatened to sue me unless I make good on the King's Cup that Joy claims was substituted during the raid on her condo."

"How's that involve me? The Feds had that one all the way."

Time to freelance. "On the off chance you had info you were willing to share. There was a murder investigation going on that overlapped."

"State took it away. Remember?"

She was still angry over her legs being cut out on that one. "Sorry, I forgot." Which was the truth.

"You're handing me bull-crap and want me to eat it like candy."

"That's my story, and…"

"You're sticking with it. Just remember, I repay in kind. Just saying."

"I wouldn't expect otherwise," I replied, knowing full well I'd come out on the wrong end of this. "So when do we get to the videos?"

"And you Angella? Your story?"

"That's my story as well," my partner replied without a trace of deception showing.

"It now takes two of you to obtain information from me?"

"He's my partner and…"

"Spare me. I wouldn't be doing this but the FBI wants to get your take, so come around here and I'll run it for you. For the life of me, why the FBI doesn't talk to you directly I'll never know."

The question hung over our heads as to why Tiny messaged us. I wanted to know the answer to that as well. There was more to this than a simple bank robbery—as if bank robberies are ever simple.

The video began peacefully and was of exceptionally high quality as it panned the lobby area of the bank. I was unfortunately very familiar with the scene, having recently spent the better part of a day sitting at a corner desk, my head bent over a ream of paper forms. The time stamp showed 13:12:05.

The little man, the Vice-President, was talking on the phone at a desk behind the desk I had sat at. Two tellers were off to the right idly chatting behind a high counter. The view through the window showed the outside drive-up area to be empty, as was the teller counter. Seemingly, the only people in the bank were the two tellers and the Vice-President.

At 13:14:12 two uniformed men came through the front door. One man stopped just inside the door, his hand resting on his holstered gun. The other man waved to the Vice-President who stood and said something. It was obvious the Vice-President had been expecting the messenger because he picked up a set of keys and motioned the uniformed man to follow him as he walked to his left across the lobby. The camera followed his movement and at 13:14:45 both men arrived in front of the massive vault door.

"I am told," Malone said, "the bank vault was pre-set to open at 1:15 PM. The armored service had coordinated the time for the pick-up with the bank the day before. The vault was also timed to alarm if the door was not relocked by 1:30. This was a tightly timed operation."

"That explains the look on that man's face when the uniformed men appeared," Angella commented.

"His name's Roberto," I replied. "My new best friend since I deposited..."

"We know all about your forty-million dollar deposit, Redstone," Malone said. "How could we not?"

"Hope to hell it's insured," I responded, mostly joking because I hadn't thought otherwise. It didn't make me feel any better when I recalled that only twenty-five million of that was mine. The IRS owned the other fifteen million.

"Not by FDIC, that much I know," Malone said, the traces of a stifled smile visible at the corners of her lips. "And beside, the FDIC limit is, I understand, a hundred grand. High rollers like you are on your own."

While we were talking, the video showed Roberto helping to load the money, which was now in sealed boxes, onto a bank cart. It took them exactly thirteen minutes. When they finished the cart was wheeled out of the vault into the lobby while Roberto dutifully closed the massive door and spun the knobs. He had a little under two minutes to spare.

On the way to the front door the cart stopped in the center of the lobby. The uniformed man by the door said something to Roberto and nodded in the direction of the safe deposit room located between where the men were now standing and the teller area.

Roberto, a perplexed look on his face, apparently refused. The guard beside him yelled something to the man at the door. Roberto took two steps away in the direction of the tellers, raised his hand and patted the top of his head. His back was now to the guard pushing the bank cart, his side exposed to the man at the door.

"Hold" I said. "Is that a signal he's giving to the tellers?"

"What does the time stamp say?" Malone asked. "Thirteen twenty-eight and forty-five seconds," she said, answering her own question. "Let me check my notes." A moment later she said, "Must have been. A silent alarm was received at approximately one-twenty nine. The first radio alert from our dispatcher went out almost immediately."

"Before you continue with the video," Angella interrupted, "I have a question. On the bridge those two hostages said the truck was out of service. But yet you also just said the bank vault timer was preset. So Roberto was expecting the truck. The trucks have GPS and are monitored. So I don't understand how a fake truck was there and the real truck was not."

"Easy to explain, but hard to pull off," Malone answered as if she had been prepared for Angella's question, which frankly I had overlooked. "Someone altered the timing by fifteen minutes in the *Valley Armored* computers. The real one, as you called it, showed up exactly on schedule, only fifteen minutes after the heist."

"Whoever planned this knew their way around," I said, mentally tipping my hat to the culprit—or culprits.

The video went alive again and at 13:30:02 Roberto crumpled to the floor between the money cart and the safe-deposit room. The guard at the door, his gun out in front of him, ran to Roberto and yanked the keys free from his seemingly lifeless hand.

The guard with the gun said something to the other guard and then pointed the weapon, a Berretta as far as I could determine, toward the tellers. He yelled something and the tellers disappeared below the counter. He then disappeared inside the safe deposit room.

"There is no surveillance inside that room," Malone commented. "Not allowed."

A third uniformed man appeared in the lobby and helped the first guard wheel the dolly out the front door. The man with the Berretta emerged from the safe-deposit room carrying a large FedEx box. He ran outside.

A second camera feed now came on, this one grainy and mostly useless. However, it did show one of the guards climbing into the passenger side of the truck and the truck driving off. A police car, its lights flashing, jerked to a stop almost immediately after the armored truck pulled away. The footage from this camera did not have a time stamp on it so it was impossible to determine if the video sequences had been compressed, but I didn't think so.

The original camera was again supplying the video and the cop who had rushed from his car can be seen approaching Roberto who doesn't appear to have moved. The growing pool of blood would be graphic evidence of time lapse even absent the time stamp, which now was at 13:33:00, three minutes after Roberto had been shot. In these situations seconds stretch forever and minutes become eternities.

The cop bent down and touched Roberto's neck. He quickly pulled back and grabbed his radio microphone, his movements animated. The cop then dropped his radio, rolled Roberto onto his right side and placed both hands, one over the other, on the left side of Roberto's chest.

The two clerks appeared from behind the counter and stood over the two men. The taller of the clerks franticly dialed her cell phone while the other covered her eyes with her hands. She appeared to be crying.

At 13:33:50 two more uniformed police came through the front door, followed at 13:34:45 by two more uniforms and at 13:35:10 by paramedics carrying large bags of emergency medical supplies. A stretcher appeared an instant later.

At 13:35:35 the first policeman on the scene released pressure from Roberto and moved out of the way. From this point Roberto's life was in the hands of the paramedics.

"How's Roberto doing?" Angella asked. "I understand he's listed as critical."

"No change," Malone said, pressing her lips tight as if Roberto was a family member.

"Any footage from the bridge?" Angella inquired. "I'd love to see what actually transpired out there. The reports are sketchy."

"We're in luck there. *South Padre Island Live* has cameras everywhere, but I don't know if they record or just play live. But I do know that Homeland Security, your employers, have cameras mounted high up on a tower down by the Coast Guard station. Ostensibly, those cameras are used for looking far out into the Gulf. But at the time in question one of them was rotated toward the bridge." She raised her eyebrows, but said nothing. "I'll bring up the footage we were given, but, and this is my opinion, this has been edited. So don't draw too much from what you see."

The video took a moment to come onto the screen. But when it did I was shocked at its clarity as well as the fact that it had been shot in full living color. It was most likely high definition, but not on Malone's screen.

The *Valley Armored* truck can clearly be seen approaching the bridge from the direction of the bank at a rate of speed that was greater than Malone had employed. But instead of accelerating as Malone had, the massive vehicle actually slowed down and turned onto the bridge at a normal rate of speed. The truck then travelled up the sloped causeway in the lane nearest the bridge railing.

The truck continued about a quarter of the way across the bridge and without stopping its back doors flew open. Several large boxes spewed out onto the roadway effectively stopping traffic behind it.

I didn't yet see any roadblock on the far side and it seemed to me the truck could have made it fully across the bay if it had so wished. But the State Police would have easily tracked the armored vehicle once it was on the land side of Laguna Madre.

The bridge is almost three miles long and about a mile further along, still on the rising part of the structure, the truck stopped. A man ran from the driver's side to the back of the vehicle and proceeded to lower the money dolly to the pavement. He then pushed it to the railing. The person riding in the passenger seat then ran to the railing and began hauling up on a rope that had been tied to the single rail. It appeared that a base portion of the railing was missing at this point.

A large scaffold appeared from below the bridge just as the cargo was ready to be loaded. The men slid the load under the rail and onto the platform. The two of them joined the money as it disappeared over the far side of the bridge and presumably into a boat waiting below.

"Any surveillance of the water down there?" I asked. "Where did they go?"

"Not that I have," Malone shrugged. "I don't guess the FBI has either. No reason not to share with us."

I could think of lots of reasons why the Feds wouldn't share info with the locals. And I was pretty certain Malone could as well. She was just being politically correct in not passing judgment.

"I was with the wardens when they interrogated the fishing boats," I volunteered. "Did the FBI get any more from them than we did?"

"It turns out the small fishing boat had been stolen and the driver's license was a phony. So it appears you did interview one of the accomplices and let him go."

"So where did the money go? It certainly wasn't on any of the boats that were interviewed."

"That's what the FBI hopes you can help them solve."

"They'd be better advised to call on Penn and Teller. I know nothing, except forty plus million disappeared on its way down to the water."

"We know that not to be true," Malone sighed, "so where…"

"Oh, my goodness! It was right in front of us all the time!" I said, mad at myself for not realizing it sooner. "The money may still be there for all I know. Get a boat to take us out there. Have a diver aboard. Angella and I are going home to change into something more appropriate for being in the water. I already ruined a pair of jeans and my dress sneakers. Where should we meet the boat?"

"Care to share?"

"Come with us if you wish."

"No, thanks. Give me thirty minutes and I'll have someone pick you up at the *Parrot Eyes* ramp. You had better know what you're talking about."

"If not it'll give your water rescue folks some practice." SPI is a water community so I knew they would be up to this task.

SIX

Emergency response teams pride themselves on always being ready and the South Padre water rescue folks are no exception. Their boat trailer was sitting in *Ted's* parking lot which was empty at this time of day. *Ted's* is next to *Parrot Eyes* with the boat ramp between them.

The rescue craft was bobbing against the bulkhead, its massive engines gently idling. A diver and a driver's helper were already aboard.

"You Redstone?" the helper called.

"You got it," I replied. "This is my partner Angella Martinez."

The diver sitting at the far back, gave a brief nod, and returned to whatever he was doing. A moment later, he said, "If you're ready, get aboard and we'll move on out."

Angella sat on the dock, eased herself forward until her feet touched down on a seat, then stepped into the boat. I followed.

"Sit, the both of you," the helper, who was now behind the console, instructed. "Need you to wear life jackets and we're off. I understand we're going over to the bridge."

"You got it." I said, pulling on a jacket and handing one to Angella.

The boat moved slowly into the channel leading out to the bay. The channel is short with houses lining each side.

The instant we cleared the last house, the driver instructed us to hold on. Almost simultaneously the big twin engines, perhaps four hundred horsepower each, roared to life. The boat's bow rose and the speed went, seemingly instantly, from five knots to what I guessed to be thirty, perhaps even forty, knots. We were literally flying.

Following the deep-water channel was about twice the distance as that of a straight line. But the straight line would take us over some very shallow water. Our captain took a modified straight line and at points the bottom was barely inches below the props. If we hit bottom the boat would stop suddenly and we'd all be pitched forward over the bow, broken necks a distinct possibility. Instead of lifejackets they should have issued helmets and neck braces.

"I understand we're heading to where they lowered the money from the bank heist," the driver yelled over the roar of the engines. It was more of a question than a statement.

"That's it."

"Dead ahead. Be there in five."

Soon the engines throttled back and the bow settled. The bridge was less than a hundred yards straight ahead. I turned to the diver who was now sitting up on the gunwale by the outboard motor mounts, a large air tank strapped to his back. "I understand you're looking for a big waterproof box."

"If it's down there," I said, "it'll be between these two bridge stanchions about a hundred, maybe two hundred yards north." I learned years ago that distances on the water are deceptive and highly dependent upon visibility levels.

"Got it boss," the diver responded. "Your wish is my command."

Everybody's a wise guy anymore. But I needed this guy so this was not the time, nor the place to make a scene.

The boat stopped almost dead center under the bridge and the diver slipped silently into the water. As clear as the water was, he soon disappeared from view leaving only a trail of bubbles to mark his position.

The assistant threw a diver-down float over the side and then began backing the boat slowly north away from the bridge.

For a long while the bubbles remained stationary near the eastern most of the two abutments and my hopes soared. Then the bubbles began circling round and round in a widening pattern under the bridge telling me the diver had not found anything worth reporting.

Then the bubbles began coming north toward where we were idling, passing beneath the boat before turning west toward Port Isabel. The diver continued parallel to the bridge structure toward Port Isabel, which was about two miles distant. Our boat moved slowly, maintaining a position roughly twenty yards north of him.

Radio silence was suddenly broken. "Mark this location and hold," the radio screeched.

The driver positioned the boat directly above the bubbles and then touched a button on the console. "Marked," he said into the radio microphone. "Your plan?"

"Tank's low. Surfacing."

The assistant went to the rear of the boat and flipped down a platform. The diver appeared off the port stern, swam the few feet to the platform, easily hauled himself up and extended his arm. The assistant grabbed the extended wrist and the diver tumbled into the boat, his mask already off.

"Nothing under the bridge in the way of a box," he reported. "But I spotted a disturbance on the bottom. Actually, it's a line made by something heavy being dragged across the shells and rock."

"Rocks?" Angella questioned. "I thought the bottom in this part of the bay is mud. Wouldn't that have filled in almost immediately?"

"There's a rock reef. Most of the rock reefs are further north, but there's one down there as well. Anyway, the reef was damaged by something. Could be a boat anchor, could be anything. The damage line runs from under the bridge to here." He pointed to where we were floating. "Actually, the reef ends here so I couldn't trace it any further. The deep water channel begins just over there." He pointed to a red buoy not twenty yards away.

"Is there anything else down there?" I asked.

"Not that I could see. When the tank's refilled I'll go back for a look. Take about twenty minutes."

While the tank was being refilled I motioned Angella forward. When we were out of everyone's hearing, I said, "That fishing boat, the one the Game Wardens first stopped, they..."

"The one that was stolen?"

"That's the one. The guy was on the stern fishing. Except he most likely wasn't fishing. I bet his fishing line was metal and the rod was some sort of a specially made heavy duty composite. My thought is that he was dragging the money from under the bridge to the deep channel."

"Is that what we're out here looking for?" Angella asked.

I nodded. "They put the stolen money cartons into a waterproof container inside the truck before they opened the doors. Bet if we go back and look at the video with that in mind we'll see it."

"So where is it?"

"Unless the container is motorized, the money is right over there. I'm thinking it's not self-propelled because that would require a submarine type vessel, probably too big for them to have managed."

"Also, they'd have to get the buoyancy just right, with no time to experiment," Angella added. "I'm with you on the container not going anywhere on its own."

"They knew they'd have to move it out from under the bridge in a way that could be accomplished even while the police were investigating. What better way than to make it appear to be a fisherman catching a fish. Blends in naturally with what's all around us. These folks are clever."

"You thinking it's still down there?"

"Either that or they came back for it last night. With a boat equipped with the proper gear it wouldn't take but a few minutes to lift the load, bring it aboard and continue on their way. The retrieving boat might not even have to stop if they had the location marked accurately enough."

"Sort of a fishing trawler type of thing, I suppose," Angella said, following up on my thoughts. "A hook hanging down catching a large eye at the top of the money crate. Perfect. Wouldn't be hard to put together, not down here anyway. This is the shrimping capital of the world. They can do anything with boats and fishing gear. FBI should be able to find out who put it together for them. If indeed they already came for it. If I were them, I'd leave it down there for at least a week, maybe two. Let things cool down."

"In their mind there's no big hurry. The money's safe in a watertight container. If we didn't know it was down there on day one, why would they think we'd stumble onto it on day two? Or even week ten. Might leave it alone for months thinking we'll never figure it out."

"You got a point there. Ye of little faith in your brothers."

"Years of observation."

SEVEN

We were back at the condo when Angella's communicator sounded. I instinctively reached for mine only to realize I had left it beside the computer when I changed for our little bay excursion.

WALK NORTH FROM WANNA WANNA the screen instructed, the message fading even as I read it.

"I suppose that means now," Angella said.

"I suppose so," I replied. "But one never knows with Tiny."

"You're assuming Tiny sent the message."

"Since it immediately disappears you'd think he'd give us a clue where the message is coming from. Nobody but us can ever read it."

"That's what spooks do. They simply can't help it. It's in their DNA." Angella said, already turning from the doorway back toward the garage for the short ride across the island.

"Let's walk," I suggested. "There's no time urgency in the message."

"If you insist."

Twelve minutes later we were walking through the *Wanna Wanna* parking lot and the all too familiar smell of fried shrimp got my stomach juices going. The locals are always debating which place has the best fried shrimp. To my mind, *WannaWan*na should be at the top of everybody's list. "When we're finished with this walk, how about lunch and a beer or two? It's been a while."

"Sounds good," Angella responded, her eyes showing real pleasure at the thought. "They're setting up for live music. Should be going strong when we get back. It'll be fun."

"How far you think we're going?" Angella asked about a quarter mile north. In late October the beach wasn't crowded, but with the temperature in the low eighties there were people playing in the surf and sunning themselves on the sand. If we were to meet Tiny here we would not exactly have privacy.

"Tiny's not easy to miss," Angella said, "and I don't see anyone up ahead who can even remotely be him. Think we should turn around?"

"Message said walk north. We're walking north. Didn't say how far."

"North pole's up north. Should have brought a heavy coat."

Five minutes later we were on a section of the beach which even in the busy season was lightly populated because there were no public access points. Today there was no one within a hundred yards of us and beyond that only a guy walking a small white dog and someone in a bright green shirt fishing in the surf.

"A car just came onto the beach," Angella announced, "up beyond that pink condo. It turned this way."

"Police and code enforcement patrol are here all the time. No other cars are allowed on the sand."

The car traveled slowly south along the top of the beach and since the tide was exceptionally far out and we were at water's edge, a distance of perhaps forty yards separated us. When the vehicle was even with us the words STATE POLICE on the front driver's door became apparent. The car continued south without stopping. We continued our trek north.

"You ever do much fishing?" Angella asked, pausing to watch the man in the green shirt reel in a fish—or seaweed—I couldn't tell which.

"With my father as a boy, but not much after that. Went out on a boat several times years ago, but didn't really enjoy myself. Frankly, I got bored."

"He caught a nice sized one," Angella said, pointing toward the fisherman. I think I might like that."

"Like what?" a voice, a female voice, a very familiar female voice, said from directly behind us. With our attention focused on the fisherman, and with the sound of the surf, neither of us had heard anyone approach. "If I had meant you two harm," the voice continued, "you'd both be floating face down in the water about now. Frankly, Cowboy, I expected better from you."

We turned to face Lucinda McNaughton. I assumed she wasn't down here on vacation. Nor was she here to give us good news. She never gave us good news. I looked around to see if I could spot Tiny, but we were alone.

"Cindy!" Angella squealed, throwing her arms around her mentor. "What are you..."

"Let's walk," McNaughton said without returning the embrace. We followed, walking a few steps behind her.

I looked at Angella and shrugged my shoulders. Clearly the former general was not in the best of moods. She stopped and turned her back to the Gulf, as if to keep long-range microphones behind her. With the noise of the surf added to the whistling wind I doubted if even the government's most powerful microphones could hear anything we said.

"As you rightly have guessed," she began, her voice barely audible, "this is not a social visit. So listen carefully the both of you. If ever asked, we never spoke. The only other person who knows I'm on this island is the driver of that car. He and I go back a long way and I trust him with my life."

"Understood," I responded, stopping short of saluting.

"For starters, the money that did not belong to you was stolen this morning."

Tell me something I didn't know, is what I would have said to anyone else. But to the general, I simply replied, "We know. Please go on."

"Because the money was not declared at the border you're now on the money laundering list of several countries."

"What the hell is..."

"Just listen! You should have left it down there. That money wasn't your business."

"It would have gone to the drug cartel. Or worse, to the uranium enrichment folks. Is that what you wanted?"

"Where it would have gone, or to whom, is not your concern!"

Really? I held my tongue.

"You prevented the uranium detonators from being enriched and leaving Mexico," McNaughton said, her voice moderating. "That was your mission and you two performed even better than expected. But the money is a separate issue, as is the King's Cup."

I took that as a partial "attaboy" and nodded.

"The money should have remained there," McNaughton continued, beginning to sound like a broken record. "Now you've presented DHS with a dilemma of the highest order."

"I brought their money home. All they have to do is claim it," I protested. "So what's the real issue here?"

"HS can't acknowledge the money, or the King's Cup for that matter, without triggering a congressional investigation. This is akin to Fast and Furious and heads will roll if the facts ever become public. It's toxic at best." She paused, lowering her voice even further before continuing. "Forty million is a nice haul. That's retirement money even for a master bank robber."

"What are you telling me?"

"I'm not telling you anything, Cowboy. Just giving you the facts of life."

"Pardon me for being blunt, madam general, but I don't believe you came all this way to tell us what you could have said on the phone or sent us by private text."

"Directly to the point, as always Redstone. As a matter of fact, I did not." Again she paused. "Forget that money. It's not yours—and never will be."

"What exactly are you saying?"

"I'll spell it out for you. You owe the IRS over fifteen million dollars. Correct?"

"That's what the IRS says. Not to say how much I might owe Joy Malcom if her lawsuit pans out."

"But you know the government can't allow you to keep the money."

"Are you telling me the government will seize the money and stick me with the IRS bill?"

"That's exactly what will happen. The IRS's relationship with the Executive branch is, as you well know, under close investigation. No one in the Executive branch will so much as make a phone call over there, let alone go on record as acknowledging that you brought government money into the country."

"They already took fifteen million."

"The money's gone, remember."

"That's the bank's problem, not mine."

"Don't be so certain. Banks are not insured for that amount. Why would they be? They never ever have that amount—in cash—in their vaults. One of the papers you signed releases them from liability should the money be stolen before they can transfer it to the Federal Reserve."

"They can't do..."

"They can. And they did."

I caught the glimmer of a smile. "So that's the bad news. What's the good news?"

"Play ball and the IRS will go away."

"What position am I playing?" I responded, knowing all too well she held all the cards.

"That package they took. I want it."

"The one in the FedEx box?" Angella asked.

"That's it."

"Don't tell me that package held the King's Cup," I said, even though I knew it couldn't be the Cup because it wasn't large enough.

"Something called the Blue Footed Golden Booby. An Aztecan piece with a long and sordid history. Worth well over a hundred million. Some say closer to two than to one."

"And you're telling us this because..."

"Because you're to find the Booby."

"What makes the Booby a Homeland Security matter?" I asked, more puzzled than ever.

"I've told you all you need to know. You'll live a healthier life that way."

"Then I'm not inter..." Angella's eyes flashed a warning note. "...certainly not going to ask any more questions."

"Good decision, Cowboy. Good decision. Now I'll take my leave, unless you have anything further to discuss."

I glanced behind me and noted the police car had returned. The driver patiently waiting by the dunes to return McNaughton to wherever she was going.

"Where do we begin the hunt?" I asked.

"You're the detective," came the reply. "Start anywhere you wish."

"Resources?"

"You and Angella."

"Reporting to?"

"Me, exclusively."

"Should we be so lucky as to find the Bird, who do we deliver it to?"

"Me. Who else?" She abruptly turned and headed across the sand to the waiting police car.

Our conversation was clearly over.

"Jimmy," Angella said when McNaughton was out of hearing, "the one thing I know about the Golden Booby won't make you happy."

"Can't be any worse than I feel now," I replied, knowing full well that things can always get worse.

"Every person who has ever touched that Bird has met an untimely demise. Most of them have had their heads severed."

That bit of news certainly did nothing to improve my disposition.

EIGHT

"Where the hell are you?" Lt. Malone demanded a few minutes later when I answered my cell. "Been trying to call for over fifteen minutes."

"On the beach, not far south of Clayton's. Taking a walk. What's up?"

"Where exactly?"

"There's a street a hundred or so yards north of our position. I see a pink condo."

"White Sands. Got it. Be there in three minutes."

"That was Malone," I said in answer to Angella's questioning look. "On her way here. I'm thinking McNaughton blocked our cell reception while she was on the beach with us."

"What's up with Malone?"

"We'll know soon enough. Here she is."

Malone's unmarked police car, its blue lights flashing, skidded as it turned in the sand and headed south to intercept us.

We wasted no time climbing in, me in back and Angella beside Malone. Even before my door was closed, sand was being thrown in all directions as she skidded the car around. We raced back to the beach access and then down White Sands to Padre Boulevard. The car then turned north. Malone flipped a switch and the siren came alive.

"Jason Smith was found dead twenty minutes ago," Malone said, her eyes concentrating on the road ahead of us. There was little traffic and most of it was coming south. But traveling at high speed is always dangerous, especially on a sand-strewn roadway.

"Jason Smith?" I asked.

"The diver, the guy you said found the drag marks below the bridge."

"Homicide?"

"Indeterminate. Appears to be an accident."

"Facts."

"He was moonlighting, checking the pilings for a water purification plant."

"I didn't know of a water..."

"Not built yet. But the pilings went in some years back. The pilings need to be recertified every five years or they have to come out. Eight pilings. Takes about fifteen minutes each."

"That's two hours," I commented, mentally doing the math. "His tank, at least the one he used earlier today, only held, what half-hour?"

"More like an hour," Angella said. "He was under the bridge a good half-hour before he came into the bay."

"Okay, an hour. So he needed two tanks. Or a refill."

"That's just it. He went down at three-ten. The manager expected him back up by four to change tanks. When he didn't appear by four-fifteen the manager called 9-1-1. Jason's the only diver we have on the payroll, so we asked the Coast Guard for help. They sent one of their rescue divers. Guy by the name of Rod. Rod cut him free of a cable wound around his ankle. Brought him to the surface at four-fifty-two."

"Dead?" I asked.

"Paramedics can't pronounce death. But they found no pulse and no breathing. Dr. Pena at the Island Clinic pronounced him dead at five-forty-five."

I checked my watch. That was exactly when my phone had rung. She had been waiting for the pronouncement.

"Cause of death?"

"Unofficial. Asphyxiation. Autopsy is tomorrow."

Malone swerved the car off the road to the left without slowing and sped down a hard-packed sand path toward the bay. "There's not much out here. Place is known as North Beach. I've already spoken with the paramedics as well as Rod. I've given you what I've got."

The real question was why had she called Angella and me? Deaths, murder investigations, were not in our job description. Actually, if I had my geography right, this death had occurred outside the limits of the city of South Padre Island and thus was not in Malone's job description either.

"So ask the question already, Redstone."

"If you insist. Why are you here? It's not your jurisdiction. I suppose my real question is, why are *we* here?"

“I could say it was because he went out with you to investigate forty million missing dollars.”

“But you won’t tell us that because…”

“Because the bank robbery is not my investigation and neither is this. This one belongs to the county, and…”

“…and you want me to call my former Texas Ranger boss, Lt. Contentus, and have you assigned.”

“He owes me one. He took that HS agent away from me a few months back”

“I’ll call him, but don’t hold your breath. I don’t hold much sway with him.” That was true enough. I long ago exhausted any favors he might have once owed me.

We stopped in the sand where several vehicles were already parked. The county coroner’s office had apparently just arrived and was unpacking their equipment. From the looks of the site there wasn’t much they could investigate because the entire scene, except for the top two feet of each piling, was underwater. The only evidence of any importance that I could see was a length of chain lying on the sand near the water. I assumed the chain had been the one wrapped around the victim’s leg.

I was about to place the call to Contentus when his name appeared as an incoming call.

“What the hell you know about a death on the island, Redstone? A drowning actually.”

“I happen to be standing at the scene as we speak Lieutenant. What a coincidence.” Contentus knows I don’t believe in coincidences.

“Happens that way sometimes. Malone with you?”

“Happens she is. Another coincidence.”

"Actually, it's not a coincidence. I called the SPI chief and he said she had stopped to retrieve you and Angella from the beach on her way to the scene. Homicide?"

"That's my guess," I answered. "There's a piece of chain…wait, I'll send you a picture." I set the phone to camera mode and took several pictures and clicked SEND. "They're on the way. I assume this piece was cut from what was wrapped around the diver's leg."

"So what makes you call it homicide? Could be an accident."

"Chain is too clean. No corrosion. No marine life. Hell, down here, you put your toe in the bay and you have to scrape off the corrosion. This chain hasn't been in the water a day. I'd say less than a few hours at most."

"So why'd Malone take you two with her?"

"Want the truth?"

"Give me anything else and you'll…"

"She wants the case assigned to her even though it belongs to the county. Asked me to facilitate."

"Play it any way you want with her, Redstone. But that's what I called the chief about. I owe her one. This has been hers for the last half-hour."

My thanks was said into a dead phone.

"Chief just called," Malone said when I walked over to her. "Case is mine. I owe you one."

"He said he owed you one. Judging from that chain, it's a homicide."

"That's what I thought, but Rod said that chain over there came out of his car when he unpacked his gear. According to him the chain that caught Jason is still attached to the piling. Rod cut out a link to free Smith. Says it's mostly rusted through."

NINE

"So our *operation* is to find the Golden Booby. And what about the forty million? Are we just supposed to let that alone?"

"Apparently she's either given up on the money or doubts you'll be able to find it," Angella replied in answer to my rhetorical questions. "Griff over at *Paragraphs on Padre* confirmed the legend about the beheadings. Joni says it's all made up to sell books. The latest tale about the Blue Footed Booby Bird is in a book called *Paragraphs: Mysteries of the Golden Booby.* It's a fun read, but I don't think it'll get us anywhere. Except..."

"I know that look. Something's triggered your curiosity."

"Coincidence mostly. And I know your view on coincidence. Look, it may be nothing, but the Golden Booby may have been smuggled into the country from Peru by a guy, a professor, from Brownsville."

"So let's go pay him a visit."

"Afraid not. Died. Most likely murdered. It's all in the book."

"So, then why tell me ab…"

"Has a granddaughter…actually a grandson as well. Seems this professor, name's Villanova, August Villanova, had more than one wife—and more than one name. He's AKA Simpson Hugo. Don't know about divorces, but probably not. Anyway, the grandson is a Federal Marshal based out of Pittsburgh. His name is Oscar Hugo."

"You've been doing some research?"

"No, just reading the book. Granddaughter's name is Anabelle Neuva. Goes by the name of Belle."

"I heard that name recently," I said. "But can't recall exactly… Oh, yes, while driving south in Mexico with that Mossad guy. He was…"

"Levi ben-Yuval," Angella filled in. "General in the Israel Defense forces."

"You seem to remember him well," I said, trying not to sound like a jealous lover.

"I was just thinking about how he faired going back to Israel with Slimy Sal."

"Shadowy Sal," but who's keeping track. Sally Comings, AKA as Shadowy Sal, is a master of disguise. She's impersonated Lisa Viguet, an HS art expert we recently worked with. She has also impersonated Angella and so well that she even fooled me. She can do men as easily as women and I have reason to believe she's impersonated me at times, but I can't prove it. And that's the problem, no one can prove who she's impersonating at any given time. Comings is not only that good, but seems to have access to information she shouldn't have. "She's probably impersonating Levi by now."

"The Mossad will shoot her if they catch her. No questions asked—or answered."

"Good riddance, I say."

"You were talking about Belle," Angella reminded me.

"In Mexico, she goes by the name of Anna. Professor Anna. Levi said she was a person of interest to the Mossad because of illegal art trafficking." I paused, trying to recall his exact words, but my memory was hazy at best. "Sorry, but I was concentrating on getting to the mine in time to stop the igniters from being shipped so I wasn't paying much mind at the time."

"Levi didn't strike me as the type to talk about stuff that is not relevant to the mission at hand. Loose lips and all that dribble."

"Hadn't thought about it that way, Angella. So just what are you saying?"

"You think it's a coincidence that you bring forty mil from Mexico and put it in the same bank where the Booby is being kept? And it's a further coincidence that the expert on the Booby just happens to be the one person a Mossad agent was talking about while you were in pursuit of that forty million? That, Jimmy, is what I'm saying."

"Message received."

"Trouble is, I don't know what message I'm delivering."

I pulled out my communicator, selected Tiny as the recipient, then typed: LWN HAS US TRACKING STOLEN BIRD. PLS EXPLAIN? I held up the device so Angella could see what I had asked of our Secret Service/CIA handler, but the message had already disappeared. I didn't know if that meant it had a short fuse or that Tiny had already opened it.

"How did you select the bank where you put the money?"

"McNaughton suggested it. I spoke with her on the trip north."

My cell buzzed and I answered it expecting to hear Tiny's voice. Instead it was Lt. Malone. "Just texted a few underwater pics showing the base of the piling where Jason Smith was found." I tapped the Messages button and studied the images a moment. "I assume that is the cut chain, those two pieces?"

"Is indeed," Malone answered. "Appears Rod is correct in that he left the chain in the bay. He only cut out one link."

"That chain looks as if it could have been in the water since the piling was put there."

"As a matter of fact, it was. The pile driver company that drove in those pilings claims the chains were used to support the pilings upright during installation. They routinely just drop the chains in place when they finish."

"How likely is it that Jason would have gotten caught in the chain without a little help?"

"Not likely. But he was down there alone. It's still classified as an accident. We'll know when the autopsy results are in. Promised later today."

"Status of Roberto?"

"Guarded. I'm told he'll survive. Blood loss not as severe as it appeared at the scene. Bullet hit nothing he can't live without."

"Lucky, I'd say."

"He should buy a lottery ticket."

"Any prints in the truck?"

"Nothing useful? Why are you asking? You have something to do with the investigation?"

"Interested bystander," I responded. Malone's nature was to keep a tight lid on her investigations. But because of my connection to Lt. Contentus I figured she'd cut me more slack than normal. If Roberto lived, she'd be cut loose from the investigation anyway. The Feds sometimes allow the locals to deal with fatalities, but they would never relinquish control of the robbery itself. "Who's handling it for the FBI?"

"Sam."

"Sam O'Rourke. You don't say!"

"Knows you I'm told."

"Haven't worked together in years."

"So I'm led to believe. See ya."

"What was that about?" Angella asked when I clicked off, her senses alert.

"I think we just caught a break," I responded, more wishful thinking than reality. "I've worked with Special Agent O'Rourke on several cases."

"I know the name. Where's he based?"

"Now McAllen. Previously, San Antonio." Better get it out sooner rather than later, I told myself. "Full name is Samantha O'Rourke."

I watched out of the corner of my eye as Angella's face went flat as she processed this information.

"Is that the Sam..."

That my marriage had broken up over. That I had planned to marry and live happily ever after with. "Yes, that Sam," I confessed, now thankful I had told Angella about my affair, except I hadn't told her everything. And I had no desire to supplement the story.

TEN

Permission had been granted for Angella and me to speak with Lisa Viguet, or so Tiny's message said. In fact, his message was late by over an hour. Earlier, Lisa had texted that she had just landed in Houston on a flight from Mexico City and planned to take much-needed R&R on SPI. She was now on a flight to Brownsville and we were on our way to pick her up.

"How do you plan to determine if she's who she says she is?" Angella asked. "Could be Shadowy Sal for all we know."

"Fingerprint scan first thing. The fact that Tiny finally acknowledged she's coming makes me feel better. I'm concerned about him being late updating us, but he did say she's genuine. They've monitored her progress across Mexico and off the plane in Houston, so if Viguet's an imposter, Sally did it back at the rehab facility."

"Wouldn't trust Houston," Angella commented, taking her eyes off the dark roadway and glancing in my direction. "That's where I was kidnapped. Don't forget."

"Different airport." I didn't add that I could never forget how, or why, the kidnapping happened. It had been the worst day of my life, at least up to that point in time.

"Same city," Angell countered. "Has Tiny ever acknowledged that we are on a case for McNaughton?"

"Claims there's no HS mission that either of us is assigned to. Denies having any knowledge of bird artifacts."

"Jimmy, I don't like this one bit."

"Not looking good," I agreed. "We'll pump Lisa for as much as she knows about the Booby, but beyond that we can't go. According to O'Rourke the armored truck yielded no prints. What's more, the two captives neither saw nor heard anything of value. Two of the three kayakers who were out on the bay that day have been interviewed and saw nothing. The third passed under the drawbridge from the bay into the Port Isabel north access channel at fifteen-twenty and hasn't been seen since. Kayak, rented from UB Captain was found tied up at a fuel dock between two fishing trawlers. Surveillance video from the bridge shows something that could be the FedEx box, but it was under a towel."

"*UB Captain?*"

"That's the place. It's just down the street from our condo. Tony, the owner, also owns the *World Flavors Coffee House,* a neat little place with great coffee. About three weeks ago I happened to be in there and he reminded me that I had *borrowed* a kayak a few years back and never returned it."

"You did?"

"Long story. But it was the time you were just talking about. When you were gone."

"Oh, I recall. My captor wanted a boat and water."

"Yak never found its way back to Tony. I'm sorry for him, but that's Homeland Security's bad, not mine." I made a note to somehow remedy the situation with Tony.

"Didn't Tony get paid up front?"

"He did, and the charges were approved, but only for the rental, not the whole boat. Stolen card. Dead end. Afraid that's the same this time. Stolen card."

"At least this time he knows where his kayak is. There's something to say for that."

"You got all that from your friend Sam?" Angella said, her tone curious—and cautious. It was clear she was giving me space—or as some would say, plenty of rope.

"Listen, Angella. I've told you about our affair. But what I haven't told you is that we worked several bank robbery cases together back when I was a Ranger. Solved them all. We work well together."

"Bet you do."

"What's that mean?"

"Nothing."

But it wasn't *nothing* and we both knew it. "She wants my—our—collaboration on this one. Forty mil makes it high profile. Good for her career."

"Bet it's good for a lot of things," Angella sniped.

"She's married, two kids. Husband's..." Angella gripped the wheel with both hands, something she only does when she's upset. "Want me to decline her offer to assist?"

"What, and piss off Mommy Longlegs? Not on your life."

"McNaughton's got nothing to do with the money. She's focused on the art."

"You don't know what the general is focused on. Without access to the bank investigation we'll have nothing to go on."

We pulled into the Brownsville airport a few minutes early expecting to see other cars coming to retrieve arriving passengers. There were none. The cabstand was empty as if the airport was closed.

"Place looks deserted. But we know Lisa's plane is due to land in five minutes." I checked the text from Lisa to be certain I read the time right. I held the phone up so she could see for herself.

A black SUV pulled into the parking spot on my right. The window rolled down just far enough so I could identify the driver. It was Tiny with his finger across his lips making the 'be quite' sign. Before the window went back up he nodded for me to get into the SUV.

"Come," I said to Angella, repeating the quiet sign for her, "you can wait for me in there."

A moment later the SUV backed out of the parking spot and we left the airport. Tiny drove several blocks before he said, "I suppose you guessed by now I'm not trusting the equipment. Even the new communicators are suspect."

"Who do you believe…"

"Not relevant at this point. What is relevant is your assignment by the General. It's off the books. No one knows of it—and I mean no one. I called in a few favors and had the FBI assign the heist file to Sam. Your problem, Redstone, is you burned too many bridges with the FBI and she's the only one who will play nice."

"You sent me—and Angella—over to the bank before the alarm was turned in. Mind telling us how..."

"Chatter on the airwaves. What's important is that they—and I don't yet know who the they are, maybe I'll never know—set the heist up to make it appear as though you stole your own money. I wanted you with the police, let's just say for alibi proposes."

"How were they..."

"Ballistics. The Berretta in your holster is not yours. It's been changed. The guy at the bank was shot with your weapon. For all I know the weapon's been returned to you already."

"You got all this from chatter?"

"Perhaps a few favors tossed in. Watch what you say in your car and in your apartment. I'll have both electronically cleaned once a day, but even then, go talk on the beach."

"What do you know about the missing Booby?"

"It's worth well over a hundred million. Viguet is the expert."

"Why has McNaughton sent us after it?"

"That one you'll have to answer for yourself. Scuttlebutt, and it's just that, scuttlebutt, talk, mind you, has it she's involved in some major off the books operation. My advice to you both, pay attention or you'll find eternal rest. Kapish?"

Tiny dropped us back at the airport exactly twenty minutes after he had picked us up. Viguet's plane had just landed and, as expected, the airport was busy. Now three cabs were in the cab-stand and a line of cars waited by the front door for arriving passengers. "How did you change the landing time on Viguet's text?"

I asked the big guy knowing he'd never give a straight answer, but wanting to hear his nimble mind at work.

"Magic of modern communications," he immediately answered, apparently without much thought. "Don't believe everything you read. Kapish?"

It took another ten minutes before Lisa Viguet appeared. Angella ran to her the moment she came through the door and threw her arms around the woman who had been captured and drugged by Shadowy Sal atop a mountain range in western Mexico.

From me Viguet received a polite handshake and an invitation to place her thumb on the screen of my phone. "I'm sure you understand my concern for your true identity," I explained, effectively blocking her entrance to Angella's car.

"Do what you must, Jimmy, everyone else has. I've been printed and videoed more times today than I can count."

Within thirty seconds the screen went green. "Welcome to South Texas," I said, ushering her into the front seat. I put her bag into the trunk, climbed in behind her, and we were off. Viguet had already begun relating to Angella the narrative of what had transpired when she had gone missing. I picked up the story at the point where she had just been removed from the train.

While she was talking, messages began coming in on my cell. As Tiny had warned me earlier, ballistics traced the bullet to the Berretta assigned to me. Compounding the situation, fingerprints found on the abandoned fishing boat were also mine. Those were easy to explain, or so I thought. But what troubled me was a shirt stuffed into a fish tackle box, the shirt having Roberto's blood on the sleeve. The shirt was mine, traced to me through a dry cleaning tag.

"I'll need your written statement," Lt. Malone had politely typed into her text, "at your earliest convenience."

My initial response began with the word "Go." I quickly replaced those letters with, "How about ten AM?"

"How about now?" came the reply.

"At Brownsville Airport. How about an hour?"

"Make it thirty minutes. Want a police escort?"

"No thanks."

"See you in thirty. Sharp."

I broke into Lisa's story to tell Angella about me getting to Malone in thirty minutes. She promised to fill me in.

"Do you own a fish tackle box?" came another text message.

"Don't fish. No box," I typed back.

Malone responded, "The one in the fishing boat appears to be yours."

"Appearances can be deceiving. Don't own a tackle box."

"Even the one with your fishing license inside?"

"Have no fishing license."

"State of Texas says otherwise."

I read the exchange of texts to Angella and Viguet. Angella replied, "We won't make it in thirty minutes."

"And just why not," I asked, not in any mood for games.

"Because I have to stop for a toothbrush and fresh underwear for you."

"I'm not laughing," I said.

"Sounds like a classic frame up," Lisa said. "Any reason why..."

"How much do you know about the bank heist?" I shot back at Viguet.

"Nothing more than a piece of art, something called The Golden Booby, was believed to have been stolen from a bank vault."

"And why would you know that?"

"Because before I was assigned to assist you two with the King's Cup, I had been tracking the Booby. That's why I was down here in the first place. The Booby had been in Mexico after a murder that occurred right here. In Port Isabel to be exact. I lost the Booby's trail when it was smuggled back to the States."

"Last chance to pick up toothpaste—or anything else you might require," Angella called as we approached the island *CVS*.

The police station was just two minutes ahead on the left, and toothpaste was the furthest thing from my mind.

ELEVEN

Time slows down when you're not having fun. I painfully learned this fact of life during the many nights I sat doing surveillance, the empty coffee cups and candy bar wrappers piling up on the floor around me. Usually that floor was inside my car, which necessitated frequent trips to the full-service car wash in a futile attempt to remove the stale odors.

I stepped from Angella's car in front of police headquarters. "I'll drop Lisa at the *Riviera,*"she said, blowing a two-fingered kiss. "Call or text when you're finished."

"According to you, I'll be spending the night here so don't wait up."

"I hope that's not so."

"From your lips..."

Somewhere on the steps up to Malone's office time began to slow, coming to almost a complete stop the moment I passed through her threshold and into the ambush.

"Hello, Jimmy," Sam said, standing and extending her hand. Hugs were out of the question. "You're looking fit."

"As are you." I turned to Malone. "You didn't tell me..."

"No reason to burden you. Do please sit."

O'Rourke leaned forward in her chair. "When I asked for your assistance I didn't know you were...shall we say, compromised."

"I prefer the term, framed, if you don't mind. You both know I didn't..."

"In truth, Jimmy, we really don't know anything other than your prints were on the getaway boat and the victim's blood was found on a shirt in your tackle box. The shirt, it appears, belongs to you."

I didn't like this game. "Where's the statement you want me to sign? I told you I touched the boat when I was with the Game Wardens. I also told you I don't fish, don't have a fishing kit, and certainly don't have a fishing license."

"Let's work backward," Malone said, pushing a paper across the desk. "Here's a copy of the license. Trust me, it's authentic. The information matches your driver's license."

"Where was it issued? And when?"

"In Brownsville a week ago. Store owner remembers seeing you in the store."

"Wasn't me."

"Video camera caught you in the parking lot. Looks like you."

"Imposter," I said, not knowing how much I could tell Malone about Sally Comings. But in truth it could not have been her. She was on her way to the Middle East with the Mossad agent Levi.

"In fairness, Jimmy," Sam injected, "the surveillance video is poor quality, poor light, time lapsed, the whole bit. In short, I'm not believing it's you. Malone may have her own ideas, but that video alone won't be enough to go on."

I'm not certain, but Malone may have tossed a look at O'Rourke before she said, "Hand me your weapon."

I protested.

O'Rourke, taking the role of mediator, said, "Look, Jimmy, we know Roberto was shot with a weapon registered to you. If this has been on your body since the shooting and if it has not been fired then we know for certain you're being framed."

"Who's performing the ballistics?"

"FBI field office in Corpus. That okay with you?"

"I suppose it has to be. But I want a certified chain of custody for this weapon. I also want it marked with my signature. I'm certain this wonderful police force has a metal marking tool."

Malone glared at me and said nothing.

Sam said, "Reasonable request."

"Might take a while to locate the tool this time of night," Malone finally said and stepped out of the office.

"You know this complicates everything," Sam said when the door closed. "On every level this case is compromised, so why should I have expected this to be otherwise?"

The door opened and Malone was back in the room before I could ask Sam about the compromise.

"Be a while, Redstone. Okay, let's get started on the statement." She fished a small recorder from her top drawer, checked the battery level, and when satisfied, she said, "Okay, from the beginning. Let's start with why you just happened to be at police headquarters when the alarm from the bank came in."

The recorder clicked on. And time moved even slower.

While Malone droned on and on walking me through every minute of my day beginning with my conversation with Joy Malcom, O'Rourke studied a file. "Jimmy, let me see your driver's license again," she said, slipping a marker into the file before flipping it closed.

The license was sitting on Malone's desk and she pushed it toward the FBI agent without missing a question.

"Look at this," she said. Then remembering I was being taped she motioned to Malone to turn the recorder off. Satisfied we were no longer on the record, Sam continued, "The Texas Parks and Wildlife database shows the expiration date of Jimmy's license to be this year. Actually a month from now. But…and this is telling, the actual license, I mean the one you just handed us, expires seven years from now."

"That's because I renewed it last month."

"What did you do with the old one?"

"Threw it in my drawer."

"When did you last see it?" Malone asked.

"When I threw it in the drawer."

"Is anybody home you can call to see if it's still there?"

"We can try Angella."

Malone, rather than allow me to speak with Angella, picked up her cell and speed dialed. To my surprise Angella answered immediately. Malone relayed the information from me as to which drawer to look in for the license. After a short pause Malone thanked Angella and hung up. Turning toward me, she said, "It's not there."

"Draw your own conclusions, Lieutenant," I said, breathing a lot easier now, "but if this were my case I'd conclude the license had been stolen and used for the fishing license."

"I could just as easily conclude you are smart enough to have renewed your license early and gotten the fishing license with the old one. It all depends upon whether you're predisposed to find a person innocent or guilty. Sometimes the evidence appears the same."

"If I was that smart then give me credit for not leaving the license in a stolen boat."

"He does have a point," O'Rourke said, enjoying Malone's interrogation. I'm certain that hours ago they both had known I hadn't been involved in the heist. O'Rourke leaned closer. "I understand you're living with someone. I assume she had access to your old driver's license and your weap..."

"That *someone* is my partner!"

"Why so defensive, Agent Redstone?" O'Rourke asked. "I'm certain if the roles were reversed you'd have my live-in booked and fingerprinted long before now."

I smiled my calmest smile, but it was all I could do to remain in my chair. "I won't dignify your comment with a response."

"My, my, Jimmy. I hit a nerve. Sorry."

"How much longer, Lieutenant? I believe I've answered your questions and filled in the entire time line—twice."

"You're free to leave anytime. But, like I tell all persons of interest, don't leave the state without my permission. Is that understood?"

I stood. Malone stood. O'Rourke remained seated. She had lit the fuse and now had a front row to the fireworks display. I wasn't under arrest and Malone had no authority to restrict me in any manner. But she could make my life miserable. So I simply responded, "Anything you say, Lieutenant. I'm at your service twenty-four-seven." I threw what I considered a snappy salute and marched out of her office and down the hall.

There is no telling what I might have done had I still had possession of the Beretta. Perhaps that's why they had taken it from me to begin with.

TWELVE

"Redstone, I have good news for you and bad news. Take your pick." It was O'Rourke, but the number had come up unknown.

"How about the bad news? The good news is never as exciting."

"You have a point there. The gun you handed us last night tested positive for a bank shooting in Pittsburgh. Teller at a Third Seventh Bank took one in the gut. The perp pleaded guilty and at some point the gun went missing from the evidence locker at the Federal Court House."

"You finished with the bad news, or is there more, Special Agent?"

"My, aren't you the testy one this morning. What's the matter, not getting enough sleep?"

"Tell me what you're going to tell me and get the hell off the phone." I wasn't in the mood for good news/bad news games, especially from her.

"I thought we were going to be partners on this one. My bad."

"You kidding me? After last..."

"I was going along with Malone. Playing to the audience so to speak. Seems the Lieutenant has a love hate relationship with you."

"And you?"

"Neither. I'm married with kids. The past is gone. I promise."

"So what's the good news?"

"The weapon you handed us wasn't the weapon registered to you. You should be more careful with your things. Perhaps who you allow in your condo."

"Are you referring to my partner?"

"As a matter of fact, if Malone hadn't vouched so strongly for her, I'd say yes. Personally, no one with access to your place is ruled out."

I could see her point. It would be relatively easy to break in and take the old license. But I have never allowed my weapon to be lying around in a drawer. It's either locked up or on my body. "That it?" I asked, trying to sound neutral.

"For now. If you're up for working with me I'd be happy to have you on the team. As you know, there's more than just the forty million. There's a piece of ancient Peruvian art. Makes the money sound like chump change."

"Invitation extend to Angella?"

"She's your partner. She's in." O'Rourke didn't say it, but I heard her add, *That way I'll be able to keep an eye on her.*

I can't imagine how information exchange between a current lover and a former lover will inure to my benefit, but going this alone without Angella was a formula for certain disaster—on many fronts. "What's the next step?" I asked, not wanting to get into my theories just yet.

"Join us here at the *Riviera*. Viguet and I are having breakfast in fifteen. She'll fill us in on the elusive Booby."

"I suppose the *Riviera* is the new hot digs on the island," I commented as Angella and I made our way down island to the hotel which was positioned almost directly opposite the base of the causeway. "Before yesterday I had not heard of it. Now both Viguet and O'Rourke are staying there. What gives?"

"According to what I'm seeing on Facebook, their rates are fantastic and the food is good. Rumor has it the hotel's for sale. A guy by the name of Philip DePierio owns it. He got himself into big time gambling trouble. Deal closes in a few days. He's desperate."

"I suppose that ties in with the good rates. Drives occupancy up. May not improve the overall financial picture, but it looks good." October is a notoriously slow month on the island and if the overflowing parking lot was any indication, the *Riviera* was doing exceedingly well.

When we finally made it to the dinning room, Viguet and O'Rourke were deep in conversation, their food hardly touched. "Didn't know if you two were going to make it," O'Rourke said, standing. She thrust her hand in Angella's direction. "I'm Special

Agent Samantha O'Rourke. Call me Sam. And you know Lisa. She was just telling me about your adventures in Mexico. You're both lucky to be alive from what I understand." Sam then turned in my direction. "Glad to see you survived your little ordeal last night. Sorry about that, but Malone insisted on touching all the bases. Come sit, order breakfast. Lisa has also briefed me on the King's Cup, as well as the money you…shall we say…brought to the states for…safe keeping."

Nodding to Viguet, I took my seat and said, "Angella filled me in on your adventures with Shadowy Sal out in the Sierra Madre. We know Sally has no hesitation slitting people's throats, so why do you suppose she allowed you—and Angella—to live?"

"For what it's worth, I'd say confusion. She can impersonate me and Angella easily, so by allowing us to live she has more opportunity for infiltration into HS."

"That's what I believe as well. So I understand you're to brief us on…"

The waitress, a tall skinny woman, skinny to the point of appearing malnourished, no older than twenty, appeared beside Angella. "Coffee?" she asked, the glass pot shaking in her hand. Her badge read Marge.

Both Angella and I said yes, and in response to her question about our orders, we both ordered eggs, mine over light with a side of bacon and hers scrambled with tomatoes and cheddar cheese, no meat.

No sooner had the skeleton moved away but another person appeared. This one was well proportioned and looked as if he had worked out all morning in Teran's gym. Bowing deeply, he introduced himself as Philip DePierio. He sported a small David Niven mustache, but the smile was forced.

"Are you enjoying your stay here?" DePierio asked. Not waiting for an answer, he continued, "Three beautiful women. My, aren't you the lucky guy. I hope your stay is as wonderful as these ladies are."

"I'm just here for breakfast," I said, instantly uncomfortable.

"These two," he replied, the phony smile not backing down, "I know, are guests. Please enjoy the facilities and our great cooking. If I can be of service please do not hesitate to call upon me." He again bowed deeply and mercifully moved on to another table.

When he was out of hearing range, Sam said, "DePierio is well-known to us. Seems he loves the women, but he loves the cards even more. Lost close to fifteen million one weekend in Atlantic City and borrowed against this hotel and another one he owns. His plan was to make the money back by, you guessed it, cards. Outcome; he again lost. FBI has reason to believe he's engaged with the drug cartels in Mexico and ATF tried to turn him. Problem is, the drug lords got wind of it and everything, pardon the pun, went south. He now has less than a week to close on this place or..." Sam made a slash across her throat. "The good news for him is that he has a contract for the sale. Fire sale, but it'll be enough to buy him time. Sorry, Lisa, go ahead."

Viguet said, "I've been asked to brief you three on the Golden Booby." Without waiting for a reply, she launched into her lecture.

"From what I've pieced together, a professor from the Valley, a guy by the name of August Villanova found—or stole—the

Bird from a cave in the mountains of Peru on one of his many expeditions."

"Exactly where in the Valley did this Villanova live?" I asked, trying to visualize the story as best I could.

"He lived and taught in Brownsville. And just to confuse the story a bit, Villanova also went by the name of Simpson Hugo."

"The Bird is solid gold, weighs sixty pounds, more or less, and was crafted on the island of Aurora, now called Maewo, in what is now known as the Republic of Vanuatu in the South Pacific. From what I gather, the Vanuatu were adventuresome and sailed east, eventually landing and exploring coastal Peru. Apparently, the explorers found fish to eat by following the boobies. Once back home the Golden Booby was crafted in tribute to their good fortune, using gold and jewels they found in Peru. How the Booby got back to Peru is anybody's guess, but most likely it was stolen from them by pirates operating in the South Pacific.

"The Golden Booby, it seems, is the missing treasure in any number of fantasies going around. You know, a ship is wrecked and gold coins are washed ashore type of stories. Usually, the tale has a pirate burying his treasure somewhere along the Gulf coast and the treasure somehow gets lost. Hurricanes play a role here as well. Over the years, just enough coins and valuables have been found—or claimed to have been found—along this coast to fuel interest in treasure hunts."

"How's that all play into the Golden Booby?" Angella inquired, her body language indicating boredom with the shipwreck aspect of the story.

"Only that there have been numerous Bird sightings over the years, but always the Bird disappears soon thereafter. To those in the know the Golden Booby is the Holy Grail of art. The current value of that artifact is well over two-hundred million."

"So who owns it now?" Angella asked.

"I'll tell you who think they own it. That would be the two grandchildren, Annabelle Neuva and Oscar Hugo. Annabelle, or Belle as she likes to be called, disappeared shortly after the Booby was stolen from the Port Isabel Museum when the curator, a woman by the name of Carol Flores, was killed."

"So who does own it?" I asked, not following the logic of this.

"I'd say nobody. There are no title papers. There can't be because it's been smuggled everywhere it's been. Some professor from Pitt claims the old man owned it, but there's no way to prove, or disprove, that assertion."

"So it's finder's keepers." I was thinking back to my schoolyard days.

"Pretty much," Viguet answered. "Pretty much."

Angella frowned. "So if the curator, that woman Carol, was killed when the Bird was stolen then whoever is found with the Bird could be the murderer."

Sam leaned forward. "Lisa omitted one critical fact in her otherwise excellent narration."

I glanced over at Viguet who didn't telegraph whether or not she knew what was coming.

Sam continued. "You should know that the Bird on display when the curator was killed was a fake. It broke when she was hit with it. Solid gold would not have broken. Assuming it was real at some point, which we all believe it was, it went missing sometime before the murder."

"My takeaway from all this," I said when Sam finished, "is that whoever gets possession of the Booby Bird dies shortly thereafter."

"More or less," Viguet responded. "But, and here's an interesting fact, it's at the times when possession changes when the deaths occur. From my research, each possession change results in exactly three deaths."

"How many have died on this particular possession change?" Angella asked, glancing in my direction.

"To my knowledge, one," Sam answered. "But possibly two."

"Then we have at least one more to go," I quipped.

"Not funny, Jimmy," Angella responded. "Not funny at all."

THIRTEEN

"Jimmy, to say that was uncomfortable, is an understatement. The way Sam looked at me, actually studied me, was unsettling."

I was driving back to the condo and Angella sat fidgeting with her blouse sleeves. I had never seen her do that. "Sam didn't say or do anything that I noticed," I responded, foolishly trying to defuse the situation.

"That's just it. Except for the bit about the hotel owner, she let Viguet do all the talking. We don't know what she's thinking or what she knows. She paid more attention to me than she did to the Booby story. She makes me uncomfortable."

"To the point of not wanting to work with her?"

"You can't get me off the case that easy, my friend. Beside, someone needs your back."

"You're saying..."

"I'm saying I don't trust that woman."

"There's nothing between us. It's all behind us."

"Maybe for you, Jimmy. Maybe for you. But let me tell you one thing, and I'll say this just once. It's not romantic notions that concern me. I agree that's behind her. But I don't believe she'd shed a tear if…well, let me put it this way, if you were to turn up in a body bag I'd run her gun through ballistics. 'Nuff said."

Angella was being a bit extreme, but her point was well taken. "Again I ask, are you suggesting that we decline to work with her?"

"As I said the last time you asked, we have the order, or whatever the hell it is, from McNaughton to retrieve the Booby. I think that means, at least for now, we have to work with O'Rourke."

"Unless you think we should blow off the General as well."

"That would be certain suicide. Both our careers, such as they are, would be gone. No law enforcement operation in the world will touch either of us if we get on the wrong side of Mommy Longlegs." Focusing on the elephant in the room, Angella asked, "How do you think they exchanged your gun? And when?"

"The money questions. If we knew the answer then we'd also have a time frame for the planning of the heist. It would be helpful to know what came first, the money or the bird."

"The Bird," Angella answered. "The money is a bonus."

"Some bonus! Forty million worth."

"You keep saying there was forty million in the vault. Didn't the IRS take fifteen?"

"That they did. But it was a paper transaction with the money to be delivered by the bank, like a ball player, at a later date."

"Concentrate on the gun. As far as I can recall, it's only been on your person or in the safe. You're too careful for anything else."

"That's my memory as well," I confirmed. "But at some point it was..."

"Jimmy! We went to the firing range! The one over in Brownsville, out by Boca Chica. Week from yesterday. Did you...?"

"That must be it! Guy came in, said he was thinking of buying a Berretta and wanted to feel the balance. I handed him mine and..."

"And he put it in his belt under his coat jacket and then pulled it out as if he was firing at someone fleeing."

The tires screeched in the U-turn as I turned back toward the causeway.

"Can't we just call?" Angella asked, adjusting her seat belt. "Save us racing around."

"Nothing like seeing their eyes. I had the impression the guy was a regular, possibly military. Won't get anything on the phone. Lucky to get anything in person. But you're right, that's where it was substituted. Had to be."

The normally forty-five minute drive took us just over thirty minutes. Several trucks and two cars were parked outside the building when we skidded to a stop in the sandy lot. "Recognize any of them?" I asked Angella as I studied the vehicles.

"Those two trucks, the white one and the purple one were here. I don't know about the cars."

The only person in the store was the same man who was behind the sales counter the last time, only now he was in front of the counter unpacking ammunition crates. "You the owner?" I called, trying not to sound official.

"For twelve years. Why?"

"That your truck outside?"

"Don't see as that's your business. Unless you want to buy it, that is." His tone was upbeat, but in charge.

"White one or the purple?"

"You a buyer?"

"Just looking."

"Red. White one belongs to Mainer. He's out back."

"And your name is?"

"Call me Krispy. Given name's Bill. Bill Kreem." He bent to pull out two boxes of Hornady 338 Marlin Express rifle cartridges. Placing them on the counter, he continued, "This is not a used car lot. You didn't drive all the way out here to buy a truck." He studied me a long moment, looked Angella up and down a few times, then said, "Didn't I see you, and the lady, in here not long ago? Never forget a shooter."

"You did."

"The lady shot lights out if I recall right. Perfect score. You didn't do as well."

"The lady's name is Angella and she's my partner." I flashed my Homeland Security badge. "Do you recall a man coming up to me and..."

"Didn't make you for the law. My bad. Guy asked for your weapon, put it in his belt and then drew a few times. Said he wanted to get the feel, I think he said balance, of the piece. I was worried he was here for...for something other than using the range."

"That's him. Do you know who he is?"

"I don't. Not seen him before or since."

"What about your shooting log? We had to sign in."

"He handed the Beretta back and walked out. Never went into the range and didn't buy anything."

"Mind if I look at the security tapes?"

"See'n as though you're Homeland Security and all I don't reckon I have all that much choice. Now do I?"

"I reckon not."

"Come over here. Can bring it all up on the computer. Not like the old days where it took forever and it was erased on a forty-eight hour rolling schedule. Now it's all there for as long as I want to keep it. You recall the day?"

Angella checked her phone calendar and held it up so Krispy could see it. "Call it one PM. May have been a few minutes later, but not much."

A moment later video began to play showing Krispy dusting the counter top. No one was in the front of the store, but muffled sounds came from off in the distance. I took the sounds to be target practice from the range.

Then Angella appeared from off camera. I glanced away from the computer screen to the actual room and noted the positioning of the security camera. Translating that back to the video, the front door would be off to Angella's left. I appeared, coming from the same direction. We both walked over to the counter and the video caught me speaking to Krispy, asking about the shooting range.

"Sign your names in that log and show me your driver's license and carry permits," Krispy had said.

He then ran our documents through a scanner and said, "Be a few minutes and I'll have a range open. Have some coffee. TV's over there."

The camera caught Angella and I moving back toward the front door when a man intercepted us. Now that I could study his motion it was clear he had the familiar stance of a lawman, or a professional gunman, ready for action. I kicked myself for not noting that at the time. Dialog took place, but the video only caught mumbles and isolated words. I handed him my weapon and he pulled his jacket back and slipped it behind his belt just as I had recalled.

He spun and drew the gun. I remember thinking at the time he was practicing being a cowboy drawing on an hombre in an old-time western movie. He repeated the draw several times and then handed my weapon back. Some words were exchanged and he appeared to be walking toward the gun counter. Our names were called at that point and we moved toward the range.

"Play that segment over, please."

This time I focused on which side he had placed my gun. It was on his left and he drew across his body with his right. Not unusual, but not common either. But that was not what I was looking at. I wanted to know from which side he produced the gun he gave back to me.

While spinning completely around after the last draw he slipped the gun under his belt again on the left side. The camera caught it perfectly, but my vision had been blocked. When he came around to face me the Berretta he produced clearly came from his right side. The guy had practiced that move. He was flawless.

We now knew how the gun was substituted, and we almost knew by whom. What we yet didn't know was why.

"I assume you have video of the parking area as well," I said to Krispy.

"That was a neat gun switch," Krispy noted, "I didn't notice at the time. I assume you didn't either. Your agency requires videos be maintained in a safe place for two years. Got them of the parking area, this lobby and the range. They're downloaded automatically to a server every hour. Here's the lot at the same time."

A blue Toyota Tundra can be seen rolling to a stop about a minute after Angella and me. The man who switched my gun stepped out. He glanced quickly at my car and then walked briskly into the building.

"That's him," Angella said, taking a note of the truck and its license plate number. "I'll run the plate."

We thanked Krispy for his help and walked out to my car. Angella said, "It's registered to AVIS, based at Brownsville. Be a minute or two before we'll know who it was leased to at that time."

"Most likely a cut-out," I said. "A dead end."

"Never know, do we? Hey, here it is. Name's Oscar Lowell. Driver's license is Pennsylvania. I'll run it through the DHS database."

Angella was concentrating on her cell and we were halfway back to the Island when she said, "I've checked all the data bases available to us and can't find a single hit. Oscar Lowell doesn't seem to exist."

"We've heard that name recently. Not feeling good about this."

The text message tone sounded on Angella's cell. Her screen read: OSCAR LOWELL. DATA BLOCKED. ACCESS LEVEL A.

"Level A requires director's approval and is reserved for undercover agents and witness protection." I thought of the implications of that statement and added, "Now why in the world would some low-life require director's approval?"

"Because this is not a low-life operation, Jimmy. Not low-life in the least."

FOURTEEN

"Tiny says he's blocked as well getting into the Lowell file," Angella said, as she briefed me following her phone conversation with our handler—perhaps former handler.

"Tiny's never blocked!" I replied, frustrated by not being able to obtain this simple bit of information. In Texas at one time you could be hanged for stealing a man's horse. In my mind, the gun is the new horse. I wanted this man's picture posted in post offices everywhere. "They should bring back the rope. We can practice on this one."

"What are you babbling about?"

"Never mind! Call Sam and have her run the name."

Angella did as I suggested, but the result was the same. Only Sam followed up with a statement to get our collective butts over to her war room at the *Riviera*. Butts might not have been the actual word Sam used, but Angella was going easy on my sensibilities.

There were four chairs in the small meeting room and I assumed the fourth was for Viguet. "So tell me what's the story on Oscar Lowell? Level A only makes sense if..."

"Enough of Oscar Lowell!" Sam barked, giving me evidence that this was not the woman I remembered. "Focus on the heist and not on who took your weapon."

"Oscar Lowell took my weapon for the sole purpose of framing me for the heist. He's our best and right now, only, lead. If we haul his butt in, we might get something useful." I marched to the white board Sam had set up in the corner and wrote the name Oscar Lowell under a heading I labeled, POI, short for Person of Interest.

"The diver, Jason Smith, is now a homicide rigged to appear an accident. His neck was badly traumatized consistent with hands clamped around his windpipe. Large strong hands. Smith's foot was positioned behind the chain after he stopped breathing."

"How do they know the sequence?" Angella asked.

"No leg or foot trauma. If this had been an accident he would have kicked and tugged his foot. There would be evidence of a struggle. Some skin trace was found under his nails."

"DNA?" I asked.

"Possibly, but the locals think not."

"And from what I recall," I injected, "the foreman didn't see anybody else out there."

"Yes," Sam answered, "but remember the foreman was in his truck nearly a quarter mile away. Jason had driven across the dunes to the piers alone. The foreman didn't go out there until Jason didn't return on time."

"And he didn't use a helper, or an assistant? He certainly had one when we went out."

"He was operating under the City's rules when he took you out to the bridge. Rules require a second person. Doesn't have to be a certified diver, but must know how to operate the boat and the equipment. Anyway, Smith's Malone's case, not ours. We need to concentrate on our own plate." Sam was refocusing us and if the roles were reversed I would have done the same.

While we were discussing Smith, Viguet slipped into the room. "What about Oscar Lowell?" she asked when Sam looked up. "The guy who worked the substitution on Redstone."

"Enough with this Lowell character," Sam snapped. "We're running him. Nothing yet."

"You'll never find him under Lowell," Viguet volunteered. "For some reason the record was blocked a few years back. The man who blocked it is now dead so it'll take an act of Congress to unblock the file."

"And you know this why?" Sam asked.

I knew the answer even before Viguet said anything. Aging memories are never good, but when you are chasing bad guys they can be deadly.

"Changed his name," Viguet answered. "Oscar Lowell is August Villanova's grandson. He now goes by Oscar Hugo."

I opened my cell, found the picture I wanted and shoved it across to Viguet. It was a picture I had taken from Krispy's video. "This him?"

"That's him, alright. Federal Marshal Oscar Hugo."

"Add gun thief to the end of that. If I get my hands on him you can make that *dead* gun thief."

"Hugo's already on our list of people to speak with. Trouble is, he dropped out of sight. As did his cousin, Belle Neuva."

I went to the board, drew a line through Lowell and added Hugo. Under Hugo's name I wrote the name Belle Neuva on the board. I recalled my conversation with Levi ben-Yuval. He had spoke of an Anna being involved with a booby bird in Mexico. I added Levi's name to the list and next to it I wrote, Mossad.

"Please erase that last notation." O'Rourke commanded the instant my body unblocked what I had written. "No need to create an international incident."

"This is private work. Not for publication," I said in defense.

"Not a secure facility. I'm uncomfortable with the names being up there, but for now it'll be okay. But get that agency off the board."

I dutifully erased the word Mossad, noting to myself that Sam couldn't even bring herself to say the name out loud. Bad blood runs deep.

"Belle has a condo here on the island. We know Oscar met her here several times. Then they both disappeared."

"Before or after they put the Golden Booby on display?" Angella asked.

"Sometime after. Belle took a leave of absence from her teaching in Mexico and Oscar did the same from the marshal service."

"Maybe they went off on a holiday together."

"If so, it's most likely not romantic", O'Rourke said. "They're cousins, they share a common grandparent. Once or twice removed, but cousins nonetheless."

"Happens," I said. "No law's stopping them from sleeping together."

Angella shot me a warning glance.

"Just say'n," I added.

"Maybe in your family, Redstone," Sam shot back, "but not..."

"Fight nice, you two," Viguet said, her voice raised an octave. "I happen to agree with Jimmy. That Bird's worth a lot of money and what better way to keep an eye on each other than to play together?"

Viguet broke the awkward moment by adding, "It's not a coincidence Oscar Hugo works out of Pittsburgh. He asked for that assignment. There is reason to believe, strong reason to believe, Peruvian antiquities are coming into the country labeled as junk. Junk, by the way, is my term. We have reason to believe Belle is working with Professor Winston Demont who, until recently headed up Pitt's Department of Antiquities. We've not been able to actually gather enough evidence to prove anything."

"Where is this Demont?" I asked.

"Now he's at his home in Pittsburgh."

"And before today?" Angella asked after studying Viguet.

"He was here on the island. Actually had a room here at the hotel for several weeks."

"And...?" Angella asked, sensing there was more to the story.

"And he had an account, as well as a safe deposit box, at the *Marine Savings Bank.*"

FIFTEEN

"Mind dropping in for a visit, Redstone?" the voice on my cell asked. "Have something for you." The voice belonged to Captain Ernest Boyle, head guy at the local South Padre Island Coast Guard Station.

"Mind telling me what this is about?" I replied.

"Of course I mind," he barked. "You can bring your partner, but not those other three. I expect you in ten minutes."

I relayed the brief conversation to Angella and asked, "What three? Viguet, O'Rourke and...?"

"Malone," Angella said without missing a beat. "That was his way of telling you this is about the bank robbery."

"It was one of his men who recovered Jason. Could be about that."

"Maybe he's inviting you to be the Veterans Day speaker for Coast Guard Station South Padre Island."

"More likely to be the piñata."

"You're former military, that counts."

"Army Ranger, not Coast Guard."

"But you were Special Ops. Jumping, diving. Same job, different uniform is all."

We turned onto the CG property and rolled to a stop in the mostly empty parking area. The sentry snapped to attention when we approached the front door. As we passed, he said, "Captain is waiting for you. Second door to your left."

I threw a smart, at least for me, salute and proceeded to the already familiar conference room. Boyle was sitting in a chair near the front of the room, a table separating him from us. A young petty officer stood at attention off to the side, back ramrod straight, eyes facing the wall behind his captain, face impassionate. I strained to read his nameplate but the angle was wrong. I had seen this man somewhere, but could not immediately recall where.

"Glad you could make it Redstone," Boyle said. "And you as well, Ms. Martinez. Petty Officer Telson has something you might be interested in. At ease, Petty Officer."

"Sir," the young officer began and when he turned to face us I instantly recalled that Telson had been the CG diver who had gone down for Jason Smith, "if you recall, I am the diver who recovered Jason, Jason Smith, from Laguna Madre."

"I certainly do recall, Petty Officer. And I thank you for coming on scene so quickly." For the benefit of his commander, I added, "You were most professional."

"I've done a lot of thinking and playing the scene over and over in my mind, sir."

"And..."

"And...and something's not right. That chain was wrapped tightly around the piling, sir. It was difficult to position the cutters between his leg and the concrete. Jason was a former SEAL and would never force his foot behind something that tight."

"Good observation, son," I responded. "Medical Examiner has just confirmed that Jason was dead before his foot was forced behind that chain."

"That's good to hear, sir. I mean, it's not good Jason was killed, but I feel better knowing he didn't die because I got there too late to save him."

"There was nothing more you could do."

"But..." Telson glanced at Boyle, who nodded his consent. "But...I believe Jason dropped something."

"What makes you think he dropped something?" I asked, wondering why Boyle brought this to my attention and not to the SPI police.

"Jason and I are...were...condo mates. We shared a condo in town." He glanced over at Boyle, who gave no indication of what he was thinking. "One thing I know is that Jason never dove without his camera. Never ever. I've looked, sir, and I can't find his camera anywhere."

"So you think he dropped it on his last dive?"

"That's what I think, sir. I have been searching my mind, but I don't recall seeing the camera when I was down there. But in truth I was concentrating on cutting him free. The bottom at that location is mud with heavy vegetation. Objects tend to filter to the bottom out of sight because of the vegetation."

Boyle turned to face me. "Bottom line, Redstone, you're a diver. Petty Officer Telson would like to go back down there and look for the camera. He has my permission to go down tonight."

"Why at night? Why not..."

"Redstone, you don't understand. Coast Guard's job is to patrol the waters. Murder investigations are nothing we need get involved with. Petty Officer Telson is the only diver I have and he's critical to our mission. If he gets tangled up in an investigation on the hard I'll pay the price. This is his idea of closure. We have no idea where that camera is, but if he wants to spend his off-duty time diving I won't stop him."

"If he finds anything it'll have to be turned over to the locals. He'll get involved..."

"That's why you're going down with him. That's why it's at night. Do I have to spell it all out for you?"

I started to protest, to tell Boyle I wasn't certified. But that wasn't true. I had recently been recertified for diving from the sky as well as from boats. I was good to go and Boyle knew it. I couldn't think of a valid reason why I couldn't go down with Telson.

"It's off the books anyway," Boyle added. Can I count on you being there with him? Say at eight?"

"Aye, aye, Captain," I said. Angella caught my eye before I threw an ill-advised fake salute. "I'll be there with bells on."

"Skip the bells, Redstone. Dive gear, however, will be most appropriate. Give Telson your size and preferences and he'll bring what you need. That'll be all."

Petty Officer Telson, brought his shoes together, saluted, did a full one-eighty turn and marched across the room and out into the hallway.

We had been dismissed. The only problem being that I didn't work for this man. I addressed Boyle. "If indeed we do find something down there what am I to tell Malone about what I found and why I was out diving at night by myself at the scene of a murder?"

"From what I understand, Redstone, you're pretty good at concocting stories. Showing up with misbegotten treasure is not entirely a new concept for you."

Before I could get into trouble, Angella had me by the arm and we followed the young Coast Guardsman out of the room without another word being said. I did, however, renew my vow to deck the good captain when the opportunity presented itself.

Outside, Angella said, "I'm proud of you for not making a fool of yourself back there."

"In what way?"

"Not throwing a punch. He's baiting you. If you're going to deck him, and I'm sure the thought is fresh in your mind, do it when he's not on his own turf and not in uniform. Better yet, don't do it at all."

My vow to deck Boyle and Angella's comment about not doing it made me think about my conditioning. Actually, the lack thereof. That caused me to think of Teran at the gym. That, in turn, led me to the hotel owner Philip DePierio. When I had met the man something was off, but I didn't know what it was. I still couldn't place what was bothering me. But the man did appear to be in top physical condition, hence my connection between him and Teran.

"Mind if we stop at the gym for a moment," I asked Angella as we drove up Padre Boulevard.

"You planning on bench pressing? Boyle certainly gets you worked up, never fails."

"As a matter of fact, I want to find out if Teran knows that guy DePierio."

"The hotel owner? You think maybe he works out at the gym? Bet the hotel has its own fitness center."

"Probably does. But that guy works out. Teran knows everybody."

"I'll wait in the car. Don't take too long."

I pulled to a stop in the shopping center lot below the gym and got out. As luck would have it Teran was coming down the steps and heading for his truck. I called him over.

"Jimmy," he said, "it's been a while since you…Hey, if you want a session now I'm afraid I'm on my way out. But you're always free to use the equipment."

"Actually that's a good idea—for several reasons." *Island Fitness* has a punching bag and I could tune up, blow some of the rust off. "But I stopped by to ask you about a guy I met today. Guy that owns the *Riviera* hotel."

"Hotel's for sale. Owned by a group. Philip's the front man. Guy's a piece of work."

"You know him then?"

"When he first came to the island a few years back, before he got in with that consortium, or whatever they call themselves, he came in here every morning by six-thirty, seven the latest."

"He looks like he stays fit, that's why I thought of…"

"In shape—and strong. To warm up he'd do fifteen pull ups using a wide grip. He'd rest a few seconds and then repeat the set twice, sometimes four times. Guy can easily do two close grip two-twenty-five pound sets of twelve. He always ends by skipping rope for ten minutes. Man's a master at it."

"Sounds to me like he knows his way around gyms."

"Should. He's Special Forces."

"Still active?"

"Don't know, but wouldn't be surprised if he was."

"Anything else about him I should know?"

"People say he has a gambling problem. I don't know about that. That's rumor and this island runs on rumors. Most of them are baloney. Hey, got to run. Come in tomorrow and we can continue."

Back in the car I filled Angella in. When I finished, she said, "The name DePierio seems out of place. That name could be Italian, but even so, his accent is not Italian."

Angella had put her finger on what had been troubling me. The name. His dark hair placed him, in my mind, in the Middle East. Egyptian, perhaps. "You're right. I'd make him for Semitic."

"That narrows it down to only about twenty countries. Bet it turns out he's from Minnesota. Or Wisconsin."

"Hair's too dark."

"As you wish. Now let's get home. I have laundry to do."

That was Angella speak for this discussion's going nowhere. Similar to arranging the sock drawer.

SIXTEEN

Angella was indeed doing laundry. But instead of working on my socks, I called O'Rourke. "I assume someone interviewed those two guards who were found in the back of the truck."

"We did."

"You have their names?"

"Of course."

"Mind sharing?"

"Do partners share? Is that how it works?"

Trick question. "Depends," I answered, "on what the information pertains to."

"Stop with your cat and mouse bull crap, Redstone! You got the name of Oscar Lowell from Krispy! You should have told me immediately. Not only the name, but where you got it."

"To set the record straight, I didn't get the name of Oscar Hugo from Krispy. I got the name of Oscar Lowell from Avis."

"I said, cut the crap! As you pointed out earlier, that gun was used in a bank robbery, the very same bank robbery that you and I are partnering on. If for no other reason you had an absolute obligation to give me Lowell the minute you got it together with all the details."

"I ran the name, it was blocked. Angella called you. I was pissed about him stealing my weapon." I was digging the hole deeper and although I knew better, I was helpless to stop.

"A federal marshal steals your weapon; the weapon used in a bank robbery and all you can think of is 'he stole my weapon!' You sure have a warped sense of partnership. You do that with Angella?"

"I found out from Viguet he's a Federal Marshal the same time you did." Now I recall why it hadn't worked with us before, she brings out the worst in me. This was going from bad to worse. Get a grip, I told myself. "Sorry. Won't happen again."

"I'll take that as an apology and it's accepted. Just to show you I play nice, the names are Roberto Vega and Billy Jaspers."

"Which one has the mustache?"

"Jaspers. Why?"

"I've seen him before. Or his picture. No mustache, but same build. Thanks."

"Don't mention it. Just..."

"What?"

"Remember to share."

"I will. You also."

My next call was to Malone.

"Mind if I come down and view the video again? The bank robbery part."

"Suit yourself. But I thought you were working with O'Rourke. She has the video file and possibly even more of it."

"You're closer."

"Five blocks. What's the matter, have a falling out already?"

"Not exactly."

"I won't ask. See ya."

***

A few things jumped out from the video. While there were three guards caught on camera at the bank, only two of them had climbed out of the truck and gone over the side of the bridge. The third guard at the heist was none other than Billy Jaspers and he was in the back of the truck with a forth man. The mask covered Jasper's mustache in the video, but nothing could mask his build and smooth way of walking.

I thanked Malone and turned to leave.

"Are you planning to share your findings with O'Rourke?"

"And just how did you determine I had *findings?*"

"It's written on your face."

That caught me by surprise. I have never been transparent, except perhaps to Angella. I must be losing it big time.

"Just ringing your bell, Redstone. You replayed that third guard walking in and out of the bank enough times that even I realized he was the same man we spoke to on the bridge. When we found him he was tied up and we bought his story that he worked for *Valley Armored*. But that's not right is it?"

"Actually, he does work for them. He's the inside guy who arranged for the timing to be changed. He probably also had the FedEx package stowed away on the truck when we got there."

"Doubt that. The truck is still in FBI custody."

Against my own DNA, I followed Malone's advice and called O'Rourke. After telling her my theory on Jaspers being the third guard at the heist, I asked if the FBI had, by chance X-rayed the truck.

"No reason to," O'Rourke replied, her answer tenuous. "Should we have?"

"If you want to find the missing package you should."

"We still have the truck. Get back to you."

"How about bringing Jaspers in for questioning. If you want, I'll join you at his place."

"Back at you." She was gone.

Nap time. Actually not nap time, but rather think time, but with my eyes closed, legs up. Something else I had seen in the video had caught my interest and I wanted to dwell on it.

Fifteen minutes later I was up and on the phone to O'Rourke. "Angella, come join me," I called while the call went through. "Hi, Sam. I got Ange..."

"Redstone! You're about a half day late. The truck was released two hours before you called. Billy Jaspers picked it up from the Brownsville lot."

"Go get it back," I instinctively said, as though I was in charge of the FBI investigation.

"Field agent went out as soon as I called."

The tone of her voice told me all that I needed to know. But I had to follow up. "And?"

"And it's gone. Never arrived back at *Valley Armored*."

"What about Jasper?"

"Gone as well."

"What aren't you telling me?

"I ran Jasper's prints, and...and got a hit. In the DHS database. On a file you worked as a Ranger."

"I don't recall a Billy Jaspers."

"How about Paco Santino?"

"I know that name!" Angella exclaimed. "Drug runner. He's the guy who tried to kill us out on the beach! When we first met."

That's why I didn't remember him. We were in the tent doing surveillance and he tried to knife us in the middle of the night. They showed me an old picture of him the next day.

"I thought he died of radiation poisoning," Angella continued. "From that dirty A-bomb he brought ashore."

"It's hard to kill some rats," I reminded Angella. "He's a transporter. The best in the business moving people, product, anything, across the border."

"We have a bulletin out on him. Pictures, prints, the whole nine yards," O'Rourke said.

"Truck will show up in an hour or two, but they'll not catch him anytime soon," I said after pressing the END button. There was no need shaking all the wind from her sails.

"So Paco's back," Angella said, after making certain the connection was dead. "What's your take on that?"

"Try this out. What if the bank robbery was, in fact two operations."

"Not following."

"The money and the package are separate heists. The first guard acted surprised when the second guard, Paco, demanded that Roberto open the safe-deposit vault. That's because the first guy knew nothing of the package. His job had been to pick up the money. An easy task because the bank was eager to hand it over. The first guard and the driver went over the side of the bridge with the forty million. There was a false compartment inside the truck where Paco hid the package."

"If your time table's right, we don't have long to wait until the truck turns up."

Now I knew where to start and the exact sequence of events that would follow. Find the truck. Find Paco. Find the Bird. Get McNaughton off my case. Easier thought than done. By everyone's assessment, Paco was the best transporter ever to work the border, more phantom than substance.

My real nap was interrupted by a dog bark emanating from my cell. That was the sound I had assigned to O'Rourke. "Found the truck in the parking lot of something called the Sunshine Mall. Jaspers, or should I say Santino, made it easy on us. Parked it directly in front of the Best Buy security camera. He opened the back door so we could get a good look at where he had hid the box. Guy's got class. Not certain we would have caught it had we X-rayed. The spare tire's been replaced by a hollow metal crate formed to appear on an X-ray as the tire. Package in question was inside the metal crate. This guy's good."

"What's the status of our little talk with him?"

"On hold. The address we have for him turns out to be a pizza joint. Nobody at the pizza place knows him or has ever seen him."

"Warrant out?"

"In progress. And Border Patrol has been notified."

Border patrol? That assumes he plans to go across one of the many bridges linking the two countries. I doubt if Paco has ever gone through a border access point in his life. "Let me know how that works out," I said, failing to mask my disbelief at her naivety.

SEVENTEEN

Petty Officer Telson was waiting out front of the Coast Guard Station, a pile of equipment at his feet. The air tanks alone filled the trunk of my car and he loaded the masks, regulators, wet suits, and several baskets of other stuff in the back seat. I offered to help, but he shook his head, saying, "It's easier if I do this myself. It'll be dark out there and I'll know where everything is."

On our way north, I said, "You must be pretty certain there's something down there to go to all this trouble."

"I saw something, that much I know. Might have been a cell phone now that I think of it. I felt I had to report it to the Captain. This dive is his idea. He wanted it at night so it's not picked up by the surveillance cameras."

"There are no cameras out there."

"Drones. Boyle has drones all over the bay. Daylight he uses high altitude satellites. At night he uses drones. He can't control the satellites, but those drones are operated from the station."

Telson went on to talk about other operations the CG was running and while he didn't give anything away that I hadn't already known or guessed out, it was clear he was disturbed over the extent of surveillance going on. It was also clear he didn't much care for his commanding officer.

"I suppose you've heard about my...my friction with your Captain?" I said at one point.

"Talk of the station. We have a pool going on about who's going to throw the first punch and when."

We turned onto the hard-packed sand and across the dunes to the site of the piers. I said to Telson, "You didn't bring a boat. Planning to wade in?"

"That's the easiest way."

"You have enough tanks for a whole team to go out. You expecting company?"

"Just thought I'd bring them along. When you go underwater you never know what to expect. Got plenty of light and power." He reached into a box and pulled out a long thin bladed knife. "This knife blade is special. Cut through anything. Just be careful, bone to it is the same as flesh."

It took twenty minutes before we were ready to step into the water. Telson patiently explained how the regulator worked and how to change tanks under water. This equipment has come a long way since I last dove officially for the military and I was happy for the refresher course.

The bay at this point is shallow with very little drop-off. Except that the area near the pilings had been dredged to forty feet and I could only assume someone had plans to dock large vessels here if and when the desalinization plant, or whatever was going to be built, ever became a reality. The forty-foot depth came very close to shore and I found that out when suddenly there was no bottom below me.

I trailed behind Telson and noticed that while large quantities of bubbles were rising above me there was only an occasional bubble above Telson.

The water was fairly clear and ahead I could see rows of what appeared to be concrete pilings extending from far below to just above the surface. Telson saying the bottom was heavy vegetation made no sense.

Instead of going straight out along the near pier line he angled diagonally toward the middle pier on the far side. As we moved through the water, the lighting began to change. What a moment earlier had been nothing but darkness beneath us began to reflect light. With each forward stroke the reflection increased until just before we reached the far piling I could see fingers of waving grass.

Then the fingers came together and filled in around the piling. Telson had his light focused on a chain that was wrapped around the piling several times. I moved in close to get a good look. Hanging down from the looped chain were two chain ends. I reached down and brought them both up assuming they would form another loop around the piling, but there was a two, possibly three, inch gap between the ends. I guessed the missing link was the one Telson had cut. He was certainly right when he said no rescue diver would ever get his/her foot caught in such a tight loop. However, that was not now an issue because the medical examiner had ruled the cause of death came earlier than that. But confirmation, consistency, is always a good thing.

Telson pointed downward, I nodded, and he started down. I followed, making note that my bubbles, while still far in excess of Telson's, were now much lower than they had been when I first went under. My old Ranger training was coming back. Slowly, but coming back it was.

It soon became apparent that whatever Telson had seen was no longer hanging in the sea grasses—if it ever had been. He carefully parted the grass and made his way lower and lower. I remained above the bulk of the grass and shined my light down to add additional illumination. The few bubbles he emitted floated slowly upward without a discernable pattern.

My tank was running low. I had been expending oxygen at a rate even faster than I had anticipated. Telson's tank was most likely still three-quarters full, but I had to change mine. I swan directly back to shore and came out of the water perhaps a hundred feet north of where we had gone into the water. I started down the beach toward my car when a figure, who had been bent over my trunk, suddenly stood up and ran off toward the road. I don't know if he—or she—had seen me or was finished doing whatever they had come to do.

Nothing seemed to be out of place within the trunk. I checked the back seat and all was in order there as well. I slipped a new air tank from the trunk, placed the expended one in its place, closed the trunk and ran back to the water.

I was about to go under when Telson emerged. "Got it," he called, holding what appeared to be an electronic instrument above his head. "I knew I had seen something."

There was one important problem with what he had found. Actually, not with the what, but with the where. I hadn't seen

Telson find it and thus there could be no chain of evidence. For all I knew, Telson had the item all the time and me going into the water with him was an elaborate hoax. My tank may not have been completely filled. I hadn't checked. Shame on me. "What did you find?" I called, my signal that I had heard him.

"His camera, like I thought." He handed it to me. "If you're lucky he took a picture of his attacker before he dropped it."

Judging from the willowy nature of the grass beneath where the body had been found I doubted if something this heavy could have been on top where Telson said he had first seen it. "So where did you find it?"

"Almost didn't see it. Mostly buried in the mud and silt directly below where the body was found. About a foot from the piling. Case is gone. Couldn't find it."

"Good work, son," I said. "Anything else out there worth me seeing, or are we finished for the night?"

"I'm finished. You want to dive you can. Have plenty of air."

"No thanks," I said, slipping off the fins and wet suit. "I'm anxious to see what's on the camera."

We packed up in relative silence and a half-hour later I dropped Telson at the Coast Guard station. I hadn't bothered to tell him about our visitor out there on the dunes. After all, as Captain Boyle had clearly stated, it wasn't the Coast Guard's business what occurred on the hard. Not that the sand was all that hard, but to the hull of a boat it's the same.

As he walked across the lot I wondered what, if anything, he would tell his command about his findings. Of even more importance to me, I wondered what, if anything, I would tell Lt. Malone.

EIGHTEEN

"Now that you've seen the photos twice, what's your take?"

"I think we can rule out the pics of the beach bonfire," I said in answer to Angella's question. "And the kite-boarding ones as well."

"I vote for eliminating all the ones of him and Telson and the dog," Angella volunteered.

"What we have left are underwater pics of dives he made in the last five weeks."

"But they're all of tourists exploring some old off-shore wreck."

"Not all. Some of these are of underwater structures. It's too dark to see much and they appear distorted." I looked over his camera and didn't immediately notice anything amiss. The lens was screwed on tightly and the water seals seemed intact. "Camera appears okay, but I'm no expert."

My cell buzzed. O'Rourke's name came up and because it was almost midnight this couldn't be good news. "What ever happened to nine to five?" I asked as pleasant as I could.

"What ever happened to the promise you made about partners being in the loop?" Sam countered.

"Don't know what..."

"I'll tell you what, Redstone! I'll tell you what! That little swim you took off the north beach tonight. Just a little recreation I suppose."

Busted. "I wanted to see the crime scene for myself."

"Ten tanks worth of air? Sophisticated dive equipment. You and several of your best friends!"

"Just being prepared is all." Again, the more I talked, the deeper the hole became.

"At night. I suppose next you'll tell me you were alone down there."

Time for the offensive. "Listen, Sam," I began, forcing indignity into my tone, "what I do on my own time is no concern of yours or the FBI's for that matter. I want to dive at night, I'll dive at night."

"Not at a crime scene," she replied, but her ire had lessened. "We're supposed to be partners. Remember?"

"That is not an FBI crime scene," I reminded O'Rourke. "Smith was a City employee working on a private job. If I am not mistaken the scene belongs to Malone at the request of the Texas Rangers. Nothing to do with the heist."

"You went out there for a reason," O'Rourke replied, now my new best friend. "So what's the reason?"

"Curiosity. Wanted to see for myself just how he got his foot caught." I was again digging the hole.

"I call BS on that, Redstone. You were told it wasn't an accident. You forget I know you too well to fall for your fast talking."

"What's that supposed to mean?"

"It means you're off the case. Partners share, and that's simply not your nature. I tried, but once a lone wolf, always a lone wolf. I catch you meddling in the bank robbery, I'll bust you big time!"

"That your final word? You want to think about it, call me in the morning?"

"Can't if I even wanted to. Washington has taken this out of my hands. Your gun being involved disqualifies you."

"But, you said yourself it wasn't my weapon."

"It was your weapon alright, Redstone. That much is certain. Granted, the one you handed me was not the one used at the bank. But even you are smart enough to have switched weapons. Better be thinking of hiring a good defense lawyer because as Washington sees it your weapon was used in an armed bank robbery and attempted murder."

O'Rourke didn't have any of the videos showing the substitution by Federal Marshal Hugo. The originals are with that Krispy character. Not good. I made a note to get copies. "You know full well it wasn't..."

"It doesn't matter to Washington what I know. You and I have...let's just say...history. I wouldn't be surprised if I'm yanked from the case as well. In any event, tell your lovely partner good luck."

"I'll do just that," I replied to a dead line.

I relayed Sam's side of the conversation to Angella who had easily guessed most of what O'Rourke had been saying. "Did she really call me 'your lovely partner'?"

"Her exact words."

"Sexist, bit..."

"More like she's jealous, I'd say."

"You wish!" Angella snapped. I didn't know if she was angry with me or with Sam. Probably both.

"Hey, we're off the case," I said, trying to calm Angella. "Neither of us has to work with her. Isn't that what you wanted?"

"Would have been better if we—you—had done it on your own. Having the FBI fire us is not a good move."

"Quitting on the FBI is not a good move either. If I had told anyone about the dive, I would have told Malone, not O'Rourke. Jason's death is not the FBI's investigation."

"Keep telling yourself that, Jimmy. Keep telling yourself that."

Angella walked off and I turned back to the camera images I had downloaded onto my computer to see if I could make out what, if anything, was there.

Angella retuned, her mood mellowed somewhat. She leaned over my shoulder. "What about the time stamp?" she said, more in the way of a suggestion than a question.

"I'm not sure how to...there it is. The first one that we're interested in is dated October fourteenth at two-fifteen."

"Isn't that the time when he dove under the bridge?"

"More or less. We don't know how accurate his camera is, but I'm willing to assume he took those while he was down there searching."

There were eleven images in this last group and Angella said, "Hey, we can use the metadata to find the exact location where each of these pictures was taken."

"Will it work, I mean the location, under water?"

"I don't know how it's done, and I understand it's not perfectly accurate, but the bottom line is yes."

"The first five images have the same numbers," I said. "They are 26.0867 and -97.184."

Angella entered the numbers in her log file. These are not GPS, Jimmy. They're latitude and longitude."

"That works for me. The numbers on the next two are slightly different. They are 26.0889 and -97.19."

"I'll plug those into Google Maps, see what we get."

While Angella fiddled with her computer, I studied the first set of images. I could just make out some sort of solid structure with what appeared to be metal beams or something coming out from the top. But the image was dark and grainy and I wasn't certain that I was right. There seemed to be something in the background.

"Jimmy," Angella called, "those first numbers are on the causeway. Come look, I have it up."

The image on Angella's screen showed South Padre Island on the right and Port Isabel on the left connected by the causeway bridge, which curved toward the south almost midway across Laguna Madre. A red exclamation point was positioned on the bridge a short distance before the bend and exactly where I remembered the armored truck being located. "Plot the second set of numbers," I said to Angella.

She entered the new numbers and another exclamation point appeared on the screen. This one was out in the water near where we had stopped the fishing boat. "Distances on the water are deceiving," I said, "but near as I can tell we were not that far from the bridge. And not that far west."

I went back to my computer and brought up the two images in question. It took some jiggling with the focus and zoom controls, but suddenly it became abundantly clear that we were looking at a waterproof box just large enough to hold the missing money. The box was resting on the bottom of the bay just west of what appeared to be a dark wall.

"One thing we now know for certain," I commented to Angella, "is that Jason Smith was not a saint."

"Most likely in on the heist as well. Forty million can fill a lot of wallets."

"And buy a lot of assassins," I added, thinking about the person I had seen running from my car. A bullet through my head would have been a simple thing for any hired sniper. So I must not have been the target.

NINETEEN

"We know the money's at the bottom of the shipping channel," I said to Angella, again recapping what we knew. It was past two in the morning and I was not sleepy. "More accurately, that's where it was hours after the robbery. We know that Jason either put it there or found it there. We know that he most probably lied to us about not seeing that box lying on the bottom."

Angella apparently wasn't ready for sleep either because neither of us had made a move toward the bedroom.

Then I remembered that we hadn't examined the last four camera images. I pulled them up and these were much clearer than the others. They showed what I took to be the bottoms of four concrete pilings. Each of the pilings disappeared into mud with sea grass growing thickly around them.

"Look at the date, Jimmy. These last four images were taken a day after the others."

"So they were," I said while typing the lat, long numbers into a neat converter my search engine had found. "What the dickens?" I said, when the location came up as some forest in northern Myanmar. "Where's Myanmar?"

"Used to be called Burma. Why?"

"'Cause that's where these were taken."

"You're tired. Bet you forgot the negative on the longitude number."

I quickly added the minus sign in front of the 97.198 that I had typed and sure enough the location popped up as being in the Laguna Madre. The only physical location the screen showed was the convention center and the red arrow was positioned north of there. "These last four images," I announced, "are of the pilings Smith had gone down to inspect. Seems he only did four before...before he was killed."

"Let's be certain there aren't any more on the camera, Jimmy."

"You thinking he may have shot his assailant?"

"Possible," Angella replied. "Certainly possible."

I checked the camera and then passed it to Angella to double check. We both agreed there were no more images on the device.

When I returned to the living room Angella wore a confused look. She started to say something then stopped.

"Out with it. At this time of the morning everything seems a bit confusing. What's troubling you?"

"Only that...that Smith is the one who told us about the skid marks beneath the bridge. We wouldn't even know the money box had been down there had he not told us about those marks."

"Maybe he changed his mind. Maybe after he saw what his camera had captured he put two and two together and figured where there's forty million there's room for negotiations."

"How'd he know the right person to negotiate with?"

I could count on Angella being practical. "Maybe he didn't. Maybe that's why he's dead?"

"Maybe your theory is, pardon the pun, under water. Come, I'm ready for sleep. Tomorrow's another...Who are you calling this time of night?"

"Texting. I'm texting Malone a message." NEED TO TALK. SEE YOU AT TEN.

MAKE IT EIGHT! came the immediate reply.

"What the hell's she doing up at this hour?" I exclaimed.

"What the hell are you doing up at this hour?"

NINE, I replied.

DON'T BE LATE.

***

"Confession time," I said, simultaneously placing a box of *Captain Donut's* freshly baked donuts on her desk. Angella was carrying the coffee and slid a tall cup under her nose.

"You must have really stepped in it this time Redstone. Just what the hell did you do now? Don't tell me you shot someone and left his body out there on the north flats?"

She already knew about my dive. Maybe that's why she was up so late last night. "No dead bodies that I know of," I began, "but I wanted you to know I dove on the site where Smith's body was found."

"And?"

Now I was really off-guard. "And...and I wanted you to know. After all it's your crime scene."

"Nice of you to think of me—after the fact. Would have been proper protocol to have given me a heads up *before* you went out there."

"Had an itch and had to scratch it," I answered.

"At night?"

"Less prying eyes after dark is all." Malone was capable of exploding, but nothing came. Something was wrong. *Keep talking or shut up? If in doubt, shut up.*

"An underwater crime scene is hardly secure, so any number of eyes could have been out there."

Malone was trying to tell me something. "Meaning?"

"You weren't the only one prowling around it seems. What time was your little visit?"

"Don't know when we began but we finished a little after nine-fifteen."

"We?"

"Oh, Angella and I."

"I didn't know you dove, Agent Martinez."

"His...his spotter if you will."

"At eleven-nineteen we received a call from the Coast Guard saying one of their surveillance cameras detected human activity in the area of the pilings."

"Who was it?" I asked, trying to process this data point and failing miserably.

"Don't know. I was hoping you could help us out with that. Maybe a diving buddy of yours."

"I have no diving buddies." I thought about the guy I saw running from my car. That guy had moved like Paco, but he appeared to be much larger.

"A Game Warden apprehended a man coming out of the water at the pilings. The perp refused to provide identification, claimed it was not illegal to swim—or dive—in the bay regardless of the time. He was unarmed and had no identification." Malone held up a picture obviously taken with a cell phone, the flash bouncing off the target's face like a reflection in a mirror. "Ever see this man before?"

Actually, I had seen him once—or possibly twice. The second time might have been as he ran away last night. Before that I had spoken to him at the *Riviera* hotel. He was none other than fitness buff Philip DePierio, he of the David Niven mustache. I gave Malone his name.

"Owner of the *Riviera* hotel?"

"One in the same."

"What the hell was he doing out there?" Malone asked. She made a note on a pad and looked up.

I filled her in on my conversation with Teran. Malone reached for her cell and texted a note to someone. She ate her second donut and drained her coffee without saying a word. I sensed she was waiting for something, so I sat back quiet for once.

Her phone sounded. She read the message and turned to Angella and me. "Two facts for you to digest. First, Mr. Philip DePierio is listed as the managing partner of a limited partnership that owns the proposed water treatment facility and the land it will sit on. Second, there is no file on him with any of our

Special Operations forces and not even with any branch of the military. Your friend Teran has that part wrong, I'm afraid."

I stood to leave, my mission accomplished and my hide intact. Why Malone was playing nice I didn't know, but I wasn't about to look a gift horse…"Oh," I said halfway to the door, "mind if we go view the body? Maybe something will pop out at us?"

"Knock yourself out, Redstone. We're not partners so there's no need to worry about non-cooperation."

Again she surprised me. "So you heard about the FBI?"

"Don't look so surprised. Nothing happens in this town I don't know about. Nothing."

I continued across the office and just as I started through the doorway, Malone called, "May I assume you didn't find anything on your dive belonging to the investigation?"

"You may," I replied, being careful not to move any faster than I had already been moving. Committing felonies is not in my job description and I had just committed a big one.

"What's with the morgue?" Angella asked once we were back in the car.

"It's not so much the morgue, but I want to see the pictures."

"So why not just ask? Oh, I'm a bit slow this morning. You didn't want to explain why you're interested in just the pictures. That will focus Malone. "I'll call and get it set up. We going now?"

"Before Malone changes her mind."

Angella called the Coroner's office and from her side of the conversation it wasn't going well. We were already on Route 48 heading to Brownsville when Angella turned to me and said, "Proverbial bad news-good news situation. Coroner's office refused to release the pictures without Malone's specific consent. Good news is the body's been removed to the *Treviño* funeral home."

"That's where…You okay going back?"

"At least we know our way around the place. By the way, you haven't told me what we're looking for."

"I don't know. I mean I don't know how it'll manifest itself. But I'm thinking Smith didn't drop the camera while he was alive. First off, it was located near the piling where his body was found. But he was killed away from the piling."

"How do you know where he was killed?"

"The killer had to get his arms around his neck. That would have been difficult if they were close to the concrete."

"Current could have moved it. I assume we're not speaking of great distances. Few feet maybe."

"You're right, the current may have moved it. But…but I doubt if Smith dropped it."

"His friend…roommate…Petty Officer Telson told us he saw something caught in the vegetation."

"So either Telson is lying or we need to find another explanation," I said.

"When it comes to water related mysteries, your buddy, Captain Boyle, comes to mind. Forty million can turn a lot of heads, Jimmy, as you well know."

"Being over here reminds me. Call Krispy at the gun range. Tell him to make a copy of the video showing Lowell switching guns. The one we looked at the other day."

Angella placed the call, told Krispy what she wanted. When he began to respond she switched the call to speaker mode.

"...all wiped clean, I'm afraid."

"What's wiped clean?" I asked. "This is Redstone. I didn't hear the beginning of what you said."

"Computer. Someone broke in here last night and wiped the hard drive clean. Lost everything on there."

"Backups?"

"Of some stuff, yea. But not the videos. Takes up too much storage to pay for it. Sorry."

"Lowell—Hugo?" Angella asked when the call was clear.

"Or the FBI for all I know."

"Don't rule out Sam."

"I'm not ruling out anybody."

TWENTY

The visit to the funeral home started off rocky and went down hill from there. If I never hear the phrase, *rights of privacy,* again I'll be a happy man. That phrase was thrown around first by the undertaker on duty, then by her boss and ultimately by the owner. This despite the fact we continued to hold our Homeland Security credentials in their respective faces.

It wasn't until I suggested that if we walked out empty handed the next visit they would receive would be Border Patrol, followed by the IRS. Suddenly the owner remembered that dead folks don't much care about their privacy.

Now instead of relying on the official coroner's photos we had our own to work from. But images don't tell the full story, so I leaned in a little, well more than a little, and got from the boss that the fingers on his right hand had been broken.

The actual statement was, "The number two proximal and middle phalanges, and the numbers three and four middle phalanges, showed severe trauma."

"In layman's terms," I had demanded.

"His right hand was busted up."

"Give me your speculation as to what caused the trauma."

"Seen it many times. He was holding something someone wanted. Rigor hadn't set in yet, so he must have still been alive when someone forced his right hand open."

On the way back to the island I said to Angella, "You're being quiet. Your thoughts?"

"Are all over the place. But on the broken hand piece, my take is Smith tried to take a picture just before he died. Maybe he took the picture, maybe not. If he did, he, or someone, trashed it. The camera was wrestled away after he died but dropped near the piling so the killer could come back later and find it."

"I'm buying all that, except then how did Telson see the camera when he went down looking for Smith? Wouldn't it have immediately sunk to the bottom where it was eventually found?"

"Didn't Telson say it had some flotation?"

"When Telson handed it to me there was no cover, just the camera."

"Maybe the cover came off? Maybe a fish ate it?" Angella suggested.

We were making progress in all the wrong areas. I wasn't on the murder investigation team and now I wasn't even on the bank heist investigation team. To make matters even worse, the proof that my weapon had been stolen was now gone.

Our only assignment, and to call it an assignment is to do violence to that term, is to find the Golden Booby. In effect, we were working off the books, with no official cover and no official mandate. Using our HS credentials to gain information for the Booby investigation was wrong. It was doubly wrong, if there can be such a concept, to use the creds for a murder investigation we were not commissioned to pursue. Malone, O'Rourke, Contentus, any number of law enforcement folks, could arrest us and the likelihood of getting out of jail quickly would be *nada*. The vision of Guantanamo loomed large. I hope they move fast and close that place before I find myself on a plane south.

We were on the causeway when Angella said, "I was just thinking about the guy you saw on the beach. The one who ran away."

"DePierio."

"That's who we saw in the picture, but we don't know for certain if he's the same guy you saw running from your car."

"Good point. But I believe they are one and the same."

"Lot's of men are tall, well-proportioned. Let's keep an open mind here."

"Noted. We'll see. My money's on DePierio."

***

A familiar scene in the movies, and now on TV thrillers, is for a person to walk into his or her own house and find some antagonist, almost always a male, sitting peacefully in a chair facing the door, a large weapon lying across his lap.

So I suppose I shouldn't have been overly surprised to find that exact situation, minus a visible weapon, waiting for us when we got back to the condo.

"You should add a few locks, my friend, you make it all too easy to get into your place."

"Would several locks have stopped you?"

"Hell, no. Would have taken a bit longer, maybe cause some damage, but no, I'd still be sitting here."

"There's your answer," I said, making a note to actually make it harder, a lot harder, to get in and out of our place. The revolving door must stop.

It took Angella a few seconds before she realized who our visitor was. When she did, she calmly said, "Levi, I don't know how you folks do it in Israel, but in this country it is customary to ask permission before entering a person's place of residence."

A big smile formed on his broad face. "That's not what I hear about your place. Scuttlebutt has people coming and going with some regularity. How about offering a thirsty friend something to drink?"

"If you wanted a dinner party you could have at least set the table?" I said, walking over to shake his hand.

"A beer will do, my friend. You both look like you're in need, so please join me."

"Don't mind if I do," I said.

Angella nodded and I dutifully trotted off to the kitchen leaving her to entertain Mossad agent Levi ben-Yuval. Levi had just worked with us in Mexico and when I last saw him he was on his way back to Israel in the company of the impersonation artist, Shadowy Sal.

"Here we are," I said, handing Levi a bottle. I placed Angella's on the side table next to where she was now sitting. "Snacks anyone?"

Hearing no answer, I rejoined them anxious to learn the reason for his unorthodox visit. Levi turned to me, "I understand you are again working with Agent Viguet, this time looking for the illusive Booby Bird."

"I'm not at liberty to..."

"She's already confirmed it, thank you."

"Don't tell us you're treasure hunting as well," I remarked. "Didn't know Mossad agents did that sort of thing."

"You'd be surprised what we do, but perhaps not for the same reasons as you do."

I didn't know if he meant me personally or our government. Before I could have him clarify, he continued, "You ran some names."

"Guy by the name of Hugo."

"Him as well. Federal Marshal."

"Why in the world would you know about a U. S. Federal Marshal?"

"Person of interest is all. You ran Philip DePierio as well."

"Local hotel owner. What could you possibly want with him?"

"The question of the moment is what you want with him."

Classic standoff. The general rule is whoever speaks first loses. But in this case I didn't see anything I had to lose. Levi could make up any story he wanted and we'd be no wiser. If we were to gain any information at all we'd only get it by cooperating. Ben-Yuval knew as much, so he sat quietly drinking his beer and waiting.

"We met DePierio a day or so ago. As I said, he owns a hotel here on the island that's for sale. I understand he's lost a lot of money at the gaming tables and the hotel must be sold to bail him out. Closing is scheduled very soon. The local gym guy claims he was some sort of Special Ops. So I ran his name."

"Find anything?"

"Nothing important anyway," I answered. "I confirmed he's only a part owner of the hotel though."

"And part owner of a lot of other properties, including the property where the diver Jason Smith was found dead."

Mr. Mossad agent is giving back, but he didn't come all this way to tell us about property ownership. "So why exactly are you here?" I asked, ending the dance routine.

"That, my friend, will require another beer. And perhaps some of those snacks you offered."

When I returned with a bowl of pretzels and another bottle, he took a long swallow, put the bottle down and leaned forward. "Your Mr. Philip DePierio is the front man for what used to be called the Mafia. Now let's just call it the Mob. Drugs, prostitution, you name it. The *Riviera* is primarily used to launder money."

"If you know that then so does our Government. So why not bring it down?"

"Government is protecting DePierio. We believe because he's providing information on the drug operations in Mexico. Possibly more."

"Are the gambling debts real?" Angella asked, "Or is that another cover for the property sale?"

"They're real, and they've caused major disruptions. His *partners* have tried to fix the debts, but there are too many eyes. The *Riveira* must be sold within days or our friend DePierio will be found floating in the Gulf half eaten by sharks."

"Surely the Mossad can't care about DePierio's health and well being," Angella said.

"Most astute, Agent Martinez, most astute. Would it surprise you to learn that those of us who follow such things believe a guy by the name of Oscar Hugo is the brains behind the heist of the Booby Bird?"

"So, in your mind, who possessed the Bird before the heist? Who put it in the safety deposit box?"

"The sixty-four million dollar question. If I were a betting man I'd say Professor Anna Neuva."

"Belle," Angella said. "Doesn't she own it already?"

"Ownership of these things is tenuous. At one point, yes, she and Hugo, Oscar Hugo and her are cousins, found it and put it on display in Port Isabel. I assume you know that much."

"Go on," I said. "We do."

"There was a substitution made that was only uncovered because the fake Bird broke during the robbery. My intelligence believes Anna, Belle as you call her, Belle was the one who made the substitution. She's the one who put it in the safe deposit box. But truth is, Hugo took a box in that vault as did DePierio. Actually, so did Lucinda McNaughton."

I could understand the other three, but not McNaughton. "Do you know where she is?" I asked. "I mean Belle. I'd love to speak with her."

"Best guess," Levi answered, draining his second beer, "swimming with the sharks."

"At the hands of?" Angella inquired.

"As I see it, her cousin. Belle always believed the Golden Booby was hers. She never even knew she had a cousin. Hugo comes out of nowhere and suddenly she's half owner of something she had dreamed of her entire life."

"Certainly, two hundred million, even one hundred million, is enough to share and be happy," Angella said.

"Belle is an antiquities professor. Her love for art goes deeper than money. She wanted that Bird to possess, to look at in private, to cherish for its self, not to sell. That's what true art collectors do. The money is how they get what they want and that's why certain items are priced where they are. You wouldn't sell your child. Belle won't sell her precious artifact."

"I gather then that Marshal Hugo wanted the cash," I commented, the story starting to make sense.

"Not only did he want the money, but it had become an obsession with him long before they even found the Bird, actually even before he knew anything about Belle. He even changed his name from Lowell to Hugo to get closer to his grandfather. He was assigned to Pittsburgh at his own request because he had traced the Bird to Pitt. I think he was on the wrong trail, but that's all he knew—until very recently."

"Unless you—or your government—is after the Bird, which I doubt, then what's your great interest in all this?"

Ben-Yuval sat back in his seat. He was clearly going to tell us something, but he seemed to be debating exactly how to say it. I thought about offering another beer, but this guy was highly trained and it would be unlikely the looseness of his lips depended on his blood alcohol level.

"Your Philip DePierio is known to us as Moshe Abrams. He was a highly trained Mossad Special Ops agent before going rogue. He now sells himself to foreign governments, primarily in the Middle-East and he's becoming a major liability to...to us."

"So why not just go in and take him out—or whatever your orders are?"

"He would have had a bullet through his head long ago if your government wasn't protecting him."

"The U.S. is protecting him?"

"Very much so. That's why McNaughton's down here. She's his primary protector. Runs Washington cover for him."

"You're telling us this because?"

"Because your government is fickle and I sense an opening, however small it might be. If DePierio manages to get tied to the heist, or to the murder of the diver Smith, he'll be abandoned faster than...faster than you can draw your weapon."

I studied ben-Yuval a long moment before I offered, "He'll use his connections with the drug cartel to disappear in Mexico—or Columbia. He'll be gone before you can move."

Ben-Yuval leaned even further forward, his voice barley audible. "Believe me, Jimmy, the instant he's out of protection he's a dead man. And that, my friend, is a promise."

TWENTY-ONE

"Got a lead for you," ben-Yuval said when I answered the phone. "The location of Marshal Hugo."

"Cost to us?"

"Can't a guy do a favor for a friend?"

I didn't know people in our line of work had friends. But I suppose the old adage, 'the enemy of my enemy is my friend', was at play here. The trouble was, I didn't know who the enemies were or who the friends were. "I surrender. Where is he?"

"Pittsburgh."

"That's where he's based, but he's not been seen for a while."

"Trust me on this. He's there."

"Thanks. It's a big city. Need more."

"Tell you on the way."

"What's that mean exactly?"

"I happen to be aware of a private jet going east, leaves from Brownsville in an hour. Room for the three of us. You in?"

"Just a minute."

I relayed the conversation to Angella who took it all in before she shook her head in agreement.

Ben-Yuval said he'd pick us up in fifteen minutes. "Timing's tight, so be ready you two."

I threw two day's worth of clothes in a bag and while I waited for Angella I typed: CAN LEVI BE TRUSTED? I hit Tiny's name and the message was gone.

Within thirty seconds, as if he had been waiting for the question, my cell buzzed.

"Depends on many factors," Tiny began without preamble.

"Such as?"

"Such as to do what?"

I briefly explained ben-Yuval's offer of a ride to Pittsburgh to meet Hugo.

"Hold." The phone went quiet as if he had hung up. I waited several minutes before he came back on the line. "Flight plan shows Mexico City."

"Mexico City?"

"That's where Professor Neuva's based," Tiny replied.

"Hugo's cousin?"

"Only she's not in Mexico. She's in Brownsville."

"Levi's taking us to find Hugo not Belle," I responded, confused and now concerned.

"Suggest you stay where you are. Let Hugo come to you."

"What makes you think he'll do that?"

"A carrot."

"You're not making sense."

"Let's just say Hugo's not in Pittsburgh. He's not in Mexico City either. But he's searching for the same thing you are. He'll be redirected."

"If ben-Yuval knew Hugo was not in Pittsburgh why did he offer to take us there?"

"Would you have climbed into a private jet headed for Mexico?"

It wasn't meant as a question, so I didn't answer.

"Remember," Tiny said, "your objectives and Levi's are not the same. You're okay until they diverge. Kapish?"

"Kapish," I answered, fully expecting the phone to have gone dead as it does when Tiny's finished talking. But he was still on the line.

"FYI," he said, "Paco's on your tiny island."

Now the phone was dead.

"You ready?" Angella called from the bedroom. "Levi should be out front any minute now."

I briefed her on my exchange with Tiny and said, "When we first met Levi in Brownsville before our last trip to Mexico he had a partner. Mean looking little guy. Probably also Mossad. Cover me when I go down to meet our friend. Don't hesitate to shoot. As we now know, he might not be our best friend."

"You're not going with him are you?" Angella's question sounded as if she thought I would.

"Not voluntarily I'm not. It's your job to see that I don't go involuntarily. But we need closure. Stay close and out of sight."

Angella positioned herself behind a pillar near the front of our building and I walked out to the curb to await ben-Yuval.

Until we appeared it would be in keeping with his training for him to wait on Laguna Boulevard instead of on our side street. In his world—and more and more in ours—getaway planning is critical to survival.

A moment after I set my bag down at the curb a car turned the corner and rolled to a stop in front of where I stood. Ben-Yuval was driving and appeared to be alone. Instead of getting in I walked around to the driver's side and motioned for him to roll down the window. I was vulnerable to being shot by him, but I didn't think that likely. Kidnapping was my concern, but with my knee firmly against his door he couldn't open it fast enough to catch me by surprise.

The window came down and Levi, properly interpreting the situation, maintained his hands on the steering wheel where I could see them. That precluded him from calling in reinforcements, if, in fact, he even had reinforcements.

"So," I began, "tell me again where we're going and why?"

"The why is easy my friend. I'm delivering you to Oscar Hugo."

"What about the where?"

"Change of plans. He's no longer in Pittsburgh. My latest intelligence puts him in Mexico City."

"So if I understand you right you plan to fly me to Mexico City?"

"That is most correct."

"When were you going to tell me?"

"You didn't actually give me a chance. On the way over to the plane."

"I have no passport with me. I'd be a sitting duck down there."

"Papers have been arranged, my friend," he said without apparent thought. "No worries."

I had long ago realized that top agents, such as Levi and Tiny, always had several stories ready. They were prepared for all contingencies. I have not yet mastered that art, but am working on it. "Thanks," I replied. "But no thanks." Ben-Yuval's facial expression conveyed genuine concern, but I guessed that was an act. I wondered if there was such a thing as Academy Awards for spies.

"Is there something wrong, my friend? I thought you wished to locate Hugo. I am mistaken? Yes?"

"You are not mistaken. It is only...only that going to Mexico at this point is out of the question."

"I'm sorry you don't trust me. But I understand. I will cancel the flight." He laughed. "My accounting manager will be pleased."

"It's not lack of trust. It's..."

"I will await your success in finding the dirty bird. Now please step back from the car. I get nervous on small dead end streets."

Now it was my turn to laugh. "Stay safe."

"That is certainly my plan." The window started to close, then stopped. "Your partner would be well advised to practice keeping out of sight. You both would now be dead had the situation called for it. Just saying."

The car tires spun full-bore looking for purchase on the sandy roadway as General Levi ben-Yuval accelerated in reverse. He fishtailed onto Laguna Boulevard and headed south toward the causeway followed closely by a black van that I hadn't noticed a moment earlier.

TWENTY-TWO

We used the reprieve from chasing Hugo to do research on Paco, turning up essentially nothing. While Paco certainly wasn't an imposter in the same way Shadowy Sal was, he used disguises to move around Texas and back and forth across the border with ease. That knowledge brought us no closer to finding rocks we could look under.

His file contained several images of his various makeovers, including the one we had seen in the armored truck. I was ill at ease with him being on the island, but knew we wouldn't find him by us walking the streets, or by having drinks at likely bars, although I have to admit that did sound tempting. If the intelligence was correct, finding him, or even locating possible safe houses—or whatever the facilitator trade called their hiding holes—would go a long way toward retrieving the Booby Bird.

But finding him was highly problematic. It was more likely he would find us.

Directing my attention to Belle's cousin, I said to Angella, "If Hugo's in Mexico City then it'll take a day or so for him to show up here, assuming that's what he wants."

"That depends upon who arranges his travel plans," Angella reminded me.

"You have something in mind?"

"Levi seemed anxious to have us find Hugo, so if he can't deliver us to the marshal then perhaps he's delivering the marshal to us."

"McNaughton could be orchestrating this as well. We just don't know."

"She certainly has access to government assets."

"A possibility," I said. "A good possibility. Then we do nothing. My preference would be for us to find him first. That way we establish the ground rules."

"If ben-Yuval wanted us in charge of the ground rules, Jimmy, then Mexico City would not have been on his agenda. We have no standing—and no weapons—down there. That argues for the marshal to have the high ground when we meet. Forewarned is..."

"Timing is everything. Timing trumps preparations. Offense is easier than defense, usually. We need to change the odds."

"Advice?"

"Get a good night's sleep."

We knew Hugo was coming, but neither of us thought it would be three-thirty in the morning when four men, two in uniform, came forcefully through the front door of our condo and into our bedroom.

The uniforms identified themselves as South Padre Island police officers. They held weapons, one pointed at Angella and the other at me. One of the street-clothed men held up a folded piece of paper and in a voice louder than necessary announced his name as Detective Cruz. He also announced that the paper was a search warrant. The fourth man was Federal Marshal Oscar Hugo.

Angella and I held sheets up against our bodies, but said nothing. So much for planning. Hugo held the high ground.

"Either of you have weapons on you or in this room?" Cruz asked.

"Mine is in this drawer," Angella answered, pointing to the side table that held her reading lamp.

"I have none," I said, conveniently overlooking the back-up Ruger in the closet inside my boot.

"Okay," Cruz said. "Get dressed and come into the living room. You come armed, you get shot. Simple as that."

So much for setting our own terms and being prepared.

I came out first and Cruz searched me. He was quick, but efficient. When Angella appeared, he did the same to her. Finding nothing, he turned to the uniforms, "Find it?" he asked.

One of them held up a plastic bag.

Cruz nodded. "Put it in my car and wait down there. "I'll be finished here in a moment."

I couldn't see what was in the bag, but it wasn't much.

"Show me the warrant?" I demanded, not so much because I doubted its authenticity, but I wanted to ascertain the target of the search.

He holstered his weapon. "I understand you're expecting Marshal Hugo," he said, crumpling the paper and throwing it in the corner. "I'll leave you three to your business." Cruz turned and left the condo.

"So we meet," Hugo said. "I understand you wanted to see me."

Oscar Hugo was taller than I remembered, standing roughly six three. His slender frame made him appear even taller. There was no doubt that he kept himself fit. I wanted to take command. "You didn't have to break down our door, scare the hell out of us to drop by. Maybe just a phone call, a knock on the door."

"Lot's of people, it seems, are looking for me. Some of them with criminal intent. Besides, the warrant was not my idea. Saw it in the system and asked to tag along. You got a door issue, take it up with the landlord."

"My take is that the search was staged. Those three are actors and not on the force."

"You'd be wrong, Redstone. Dead wrong."

"I'm not seeing it that way."

"Believe what you wish. So why am I here?"

"For starters, I understand you're interested in the Golden Booby."

"What's it your business?" The sudden anger—or fear—in his eyes told it all. I had hit a raw nerve. His legs set, his knees flexed. His hands remained in front of him, at least for now.

I knew not to pick a fight with an armed man, at least not when I wasn't armed myself. But this guy was like a death-star inside my shoe. There was no going forward without excising it.

"Both of you," Angella commanded, "stand down. Nothing good'll come of this if you don't. Oscar, you sit in that seat over there and stay put. Jimmy and I are stepping into the kitchen to make coffee. We'll be back after a proper cooling-off period for you both. You take yours how?"

"Black. A little sugar," Hugo answered, standing his ground.

I reluctantly followed my partner to the kitchen where she promptly said, "Aren't you the one who always says don't pick fights with armed folks? So what're you doing?"

"He had no call to bust in here. Guy stole my weapon. I should..."

"Drop it, Jimmy! He's here now. I know those cops. They're good guys doing what someone higher up told them to do. So let's get what you want from Hugo without all the testosterone. He's keyed to the Bird. Work that angle."

"But..."

"But nothing. Settle down before you get yourself—and me—shot. Or arrested."

"Arrested?"

"Just because they didn't show us the warrant doesn't mean it wasn't issued. We're both on the crap list as it is. He'll claim he was covered by the warrant, he found something, you resisted, and you'll go down hard. Nobody will protest against a federal marshal shooting a white guy in the line of duty. Might even get himself a promotion."

"Your point's made. I'll behave."

"What did they take? What was in the bag?"

"We left the camera on your desk near my computer. That's where the officers were standing. I'm thinking the camera."

"That's actually good. The withholding evidence charge can now be dropped. Fetch the sugar. Coffee's almost ready. But don't go out there without me."

"You think I'll start something?"

"I'm certain you will. Now fetch the sugar and a tray and we'll do this together."

I did as I was instructed. When we returned to the living room Marshal Hugo was pacing the room examining everything in sight. Instead of going off on him, I placed the coffee tray next to his assigned chair.

Angella said, "If you'd like something to eat with your coffee just let me know. This isn't *Ted's so* don't expect much." She stood facing him, her hands wrapped around her hot mug, much as one might do in the northern climes after a brisk walk.

"No, thanks. Coffee's fine."

I had seen her do this on many occasions and I've come to learn that it disarms her adversaries who see this gesture as one of being relaxed, easy going, when, in fact, she was actually coiled, ready to pounce.

I fell into the chair across from his, sipped my steaming coffee, and waited. Angella sat on the corner of the sofa doing the same.

Hugo moved over to the large window and stood with his back to us, his eyes focused somewhere out in the bay, or perhaps on the few lights visible from Port Isabel.

I can only measure how long he took to speak by the coffee level in my cup. There was perhaps a large gulp remaining when he finally slipped into his assigned chair, spooned a small amount of sugar into his coffee cup, took a long swallow of the now lukewarm liquid, and said, "My cousin and I own the artifact called the Golden Booby. You knew that or you wouldn't be looking for me. It was in a safe deposit box at the *Marine Savings Bank* here in town. As you also know, the bank was robbed of over forty million in cash. The robbers took the Booby as well. I'm looking for it and I assume you two are as well."

"So you actually know why we wanted to talk to you." I said.

Angella flashed me one of her, *now is not the time to get in his face looks*.

Hugo went on as if I hadn't spoken. "But what I can't determine is why you're on its trail. Homeland Security has no open case on the Booby and your involvement with the FBI, before it was terminated, extended only to the money. To my knowledge the FBI is not tracking the Booby because the bank's insurance company hasn't as of yet asked them to. You doing this on the side? Working for a private insurance company or something?"

That actually was a good question, and one that had skipped my mind. There actually was a good chance some insurance company had an interest in the Golden Booby. "Mind if we start at the beginning?" I said. "That way we'll all be on the same page."

"Artifacts such as the Booby really have no discernable beginning," Hugo responded, settling back in his chair for the first time. "But for the sake of the story, let's place the start point to where the Booby enters the States."

"From?" Angella asked. "Peru?"

"Actually from Mexico. Well, that's not entirely accurate. My grandfather, August Villanova, Professor August Villanova, found the artifact in his travels. For one reason or another he brought it back to Mexico. From Mexico he presented the Booby to the world's expert on Peruvian art, Professor Winston Demont III, who at the time was on the faculty of Pitt. Anyway, Demont proclaimed the Booby as essentially worthless. That determination allowed the Bird to be imported. Actually, technically it allowed the Bird to be exported from Mexico. When grandfather died the booby came into our possession. My cousin's and mine. We put it on loan to the Port Isabel Museum from which it was stolen. Whoever stole it put it in the bank for safe keeping."

"And you know nothing more?" I asked, skeptical mainly because he told us nothing more than what was readily available.

"And that's where my trail ends."

"So why are you on the island?"

"Because I understand you may have information."

"Your understanding is faulty." Give nothing, get nothing. And Mr. Federal Marshal gave nothing.

"So it's a standoff," Hugo commented, now back at the window.

"Seems that way," I said.

"Need to give to get," Angella said. "You know as well as anyone, information flow is bi-directional."

"I told you what I have."

"You told us what you knew we knew," Angella answered, not backing away. "You want, you give. Simple as that."

"You asked why I'm here. Okay. I have reason to believe a woman by the name of Joy Malcom is key to all this."

"Malcom?"

"I take it you two know her?"

"We do."

I filled Hugo in on Joy's background, leaving out her involvement with the King's Cup.

When I finished, he said, "My sources tell me she maintains an extensive art collection, both public and private. You know anything about that?"

"Your sources are right about the pubic portion. Public to the extent she allows friends up to her condo to see the collection. By private, I assume you mean held in a vault somewhere."

"Or displayed only to extremely trusted friends."

"The private part we don't know about."

"I'm led to believe she hired a man by the name of Paco to get the bird out of the bank and hide it for her. She was acting under the direction of the guy who masqueraded as her husband before he was put in a Mexican jail for smuggling."

"You know way more than we do," I said. "I wouldn't think Malcom has any involvement with the Bird." I said this in a weak attempt to keep her alive.

"You leveling with me?"

"We are," Angella said. "No reason not to."

Hugo turned from the window and headed for the door. "Sorry about the door damage," he said. "I'm staying at the *Holiday Inn Express* in case you remember something I'd be interested in."

"I'll keep that in mind. Where should I send the bill?"

"My advice would be to store the receipt in a dark personal location."

Angella was off the sofa and standing directly in front of me before my second leg came out of the chair. "We just got the best lead of the day," she whispered, "so don't blow it."

Angella, thinking better than to try and physically stop me, quickly stepped aside; she knew I wasn't finished with Marshal Hugo. I came through the door into the common hallway expecting Hugo to have disappeared down the steps.

But he was standing less than two feet away, braced for an assault. "So the book on you is true," he said. "Hair trigger, I'm told. Good thing you don't have a weapon or you'd be dead my friend."

"Jimmy," Angella called from behind me. "This is not the time or the place. Settle up later, if you must."

"You win this round," I said to Hugo, my jaw clenched to avoid waking the neighbors. "But I won't always be unarmed."

"That a threat?"

"Take it any way you want. You come into my place again uninvited and you're going out feet first."

"I suggest you read the warrant. Then you'll know what to do with the repair bill."

Angella had uncrinkled the warrant and was studying it by the time I had secured the front door. I made a mental note to call Steve Hathcock over at *Almost Always Available* Locksmith. I wanted the door fixed and more secure locks put in place. He could build a doorframe out of steel if he had to, but I wanted this place secure.

"How do you figure we got a good lead?" I asked Angella when I joined her in the kitchen. Her tight movements signaled how pissed she was. I was the likely object of that emotion.

"Jimmy," she said, not responding to my question, "the warrant is very specific. That indeed was the camera in the bag. It was all they were authorized to search for."

"Who signed the affidavit behind the warrant?"

"Lieutenant Malone."

TWENTY-THREE

"So why haven't I been arrested?"

"There's no mention of the camera images. Maybe they don't know there's anything on the camera." Angella responded to my rhetorical question.

"But Malone knows about the camera and she knows I withheld evidence. Not good. Okay, can't do anything about that now. What were you saying about a good lead?"

"My friend Billy Wharow works..."

"That the guy goes by Wahoo?"

"One in the same. Anyway, Billy is the bartender at Louie's Backyard and he knows from times past that we're interested in Joy. I bumped into him at the *Blue Marlin* this morning and it seems that Joy's been back there several nights in a row now."

"High?"

"He didn't say, but I hope not. He senses she's waiting for something—or somebody. Comes in about seven, leaves at nine.

Sits by herself and drinks orange juice. Tips as though she had been drinking scotch."

"Have him call you when that someone shows up."

"Ahead of you on this one."

"By chance do you recall the name of that guy down at UT Pan Am Coastal Studies Lab? The one who told us about the macrolides a few years back.

"It's funny Jimmy. You remember macrolides and not his name. Unusually bright fellow. A bit off center. Name's Hildigo Francese. Why? Hey, put your phone down. It's barely five o'clock in the morning. Even a dedicated scientist is not in his office this early."

Of course, Angella was right. I responded to the offer of leaving a message by reminding Hildigo of who I was and asking him to call my cell. His office hours started at six-thirty AM, Monday through Friday according to the announcement. Apparently marine biologists wake up with the birds. In his case it would be the marine life. Same difference.

"So, fill me in," Angella said when she slipped a plate of eggs scrambled with cheddar cheese in front of me. I was already on my third cup of coffee and fourth piece of toast. My theory being the toast slowed down the caffeine absorption. Angella sat opposite, drinking orange juice, a slice of toast sitting uneaten in front of her. "You didn't suddenly become interested in marine life. So what gives?"

"The images taken under the bridge show something down there around the bridge structure. Francese deals with underwater stuff. He might shed some light, so to speak."

"He's a marine biologist not a...a...I don't even know who looks at underwater structures."

"An underwater structural engineer I suppose. But since I don't happen to know one of those, a marine biologist will do for now."

"Good luck."

***

We were sitting outside Pan Am's laboratory in Isla Blanca Park at five-forty-five. Two other vehicles were parked in the small lot. A ten year old, mostly rusted, mini-van was near the side entrance. I assumed that vehicle belonged to the young scientist, Francese.

We knew exactly who the Mercedes SUV belonged to. *Space X* was emblazoned on the door panel.

"*Space X*,"Angella remarked. "Not exactly who I expected to see here."

"Probably making certain their launches are environmentally safe. Those rockets pack a lot of energy and there's concern about the chemicals they plan to use."

"But they passed all the environmental impact studies with flying colors," Angella reminded me. "Can't imagine that's their concern at this point in time."

As we spoke, a tall slender woman wearing jeans and a jacket covering what appeared to be a white, or light blue blouse, came out through the side door and walked briskly toward the Mercedes. She glanced in our direction and paused for an instant as if in recognition.

She quickly ducked into the SUV, started the engine and fishtailed out of the lot, her back wheels spinning when she accelerated onto the roadway. Sand and gravel flew as the car raced north out of the park past several parked RVs.

Angella shrugged her shoulders. "What's her hurry? It's not as if we can't identify the car."

"I read it as she's pissed because she was seen at a place where she would have preferred not to have been seen and at a time of day that invites questions."

"Pitching a tantrum certainly didn't do anything to reduce our curiosity."

We proceeded inside and found Dr. Francese sitting in his office studying the door the woman had exited through. He didn't appear happy.

I re-introduced myself and Angella. Before I could say another word he thanked us for protecting the bay from destruction. Obviously we were not strangers to him.

While the good-fellowship mood still prevailed, I asked, "That woman who just left. What's her name?" I held my credential case where he could easily see it.

"She's a private client. Do I have to answer?"

"I'm certain I could get your records and find out myself."

"Okay, then. Just don't tell anyone I gave you the name. I suppose you saw her car outside. The client is *Space X* and she's their chief geologist. Name's Dr. Mollie Mayfield. Goes by MM."

"Geologist? I thought you were interested in marine life, not geology. Aren't those the folks who locate oil deposits?"

"Among other things," Francese replied. His toe tapping gave away his nervousness.

"What other things?" I asked.

"Rather not say. It's confidential."

I toyed with the idea of leaning on him, but what he did for *Space X* was outside my sphere of relevancy. "Have it as you like it. Mind looking at a few photos for us?"

"Marine life?"

"Sort of," I replied.

"Okay. But I have work to do. Can't spend much time."

Angella held up her cell phone. "Do these mean anything to you?" she asked

The instantaneous fear in his eyes was a dead giveaway. He not only knew what he was looking at, but he knew the image was trouble. A true professional would never have allowed even an eye blink. An apprentice would have recovered within a second. This man had no experience with subterfuge, and try as he might, he couldn't remove the fear from his face.

Finally, he stammered, "No,…these…these mean nothing… nothing to me."

"Let me give you a good piece of advice, Dr. Francese. Free. No charge. Don't ever, and I mean ever, play poker. You'll not even have gas money to get home."

"I…I…"

"Son, you can do this the easy way. Or you can make it difficult. But I promise you we'll get the truth, the full truth and nothing but the truth. You understand me?"

"Ye…yes. But…but…"

"The full truth. No buts."

"But…this involves my client, they're… pay…they're counting on me."

Angella stepped between us. "Hildigo, listen to me." Her voice was soft, seductive even, as she spoke to the young scientist. "You give us what you know and give it to us straight and we'll keep this conversation between us."

He looked from her to me and back to her. "Promise?" His fear had advanced to terror. "I've been thinking of calling you two, but… Oh, this is bad."

"We promise," I answered, taking Angella off the hook. The truth is that we can never make such promises. Anything of importance will have to be passed on to one agency or another.

"Those pictures are of the bridge. Actually, of one of the causeway abutments. If I'm not mistaken, about twelve hundred meters east from the highpoint."

"So far, so good," I encouraged. "Go on."

"See this line? That line shows the abutment has shifted east beyond the calculated displacement distance."

"What does that mean exactly?" Angella asked.

While Francese thought about what and how to explain it to us, I watched as relief slowly settled in. This man, who spent his entire life caring about, and for, marine life in all of its forms, had been harboring a secret that had been eating at him. He now willingly convinced himself that he had no choice but to make a data dump to what he considered the authorities. All we had to do was passively receive what he had to tell us. This actually happens more times than a layperson would suspect.

Angella noted his demeanor change and said to him, "Would you be more comfortable talking out in our car? That way we won't be interrupted."

"It would be best if we weren't seen together. How would it be if I met you down at Dolphin Cove by the point? Say by the Boy Scout campgrounds. Shouldn't be many people about."

"Are you thinking right now?"

"Best to get this over with. Do it now. You drive over and I'll meet you there."

I nodded and started for our car. Angella held back and said something to him I couldn't hear.

We drove out of the lot and turned south. Dolphin Point was less than a quarter mile away, but out of sight behind the RV parking area.

"So what did you say to him?"

"I reminded him the deal's off if he didn't show up."

When we were out of sight of the Pam Am building I turned down one of the RV lanes and doubled back so we could observe Francese. My assessment was that he wanted to speak with us as much as we wanted to hear what he had to say. But it's not my nature to leave anything to chance. After all, this investigation already had too many moving parts. We didn't need another dead body.

Francese didn't immediately come out of the lab and Angella asked, "Should I go back for him?"

"Give him a few. He might be gathering information. While we're waiting I'll message Tiny about Dr. Mayfield."

Tiny's response came back almost immediately. MOLLIE MAYFIELD PHD, GEOLOGICAL PLATE FORMATION SPECIALTY. SHE JUST RAN YOUR LICENSE PLATE NUMBER.

TWENTY-FOUR

Ten minutes later we were still waiting for Dr. Francese to make an appearance. No one had come or gone from the lab in the time we had been observing. But he had ample time to call in reinforcements if that was what he wanted.

"Let's give it another two minutes and then we'll go in," I said.

"This is one time you have more patience than I do," Angella answered. "I'm concerned."

"No one else is in there with him."

"Not that you know, anyway."

A car sped into the park and headed directly for the Pan Am building. We both immediately slipped out of our vehicle and dropped to our knees. Our car was our only shield and we were sitting ducks for professionals with automatic weapons.

The car, a green Honda with Michigan plates, continued directly toward us. Angella had her weapon out and I motioned for her to come around to my side which was further from the roadway. The car sped past the end of the RV lane we were on and without slowing turned toward the beach. A moment later the Honda slid to a stop and a young couple jumped out and ran across the sand to the water's edge, cameras in hand. They had missed the glorious sunrise by a good hour, but that didn't appear to diminish their pleasure.

"Not every speeding car presents a threat, Jimmy." Angella reminded me as we ungracefully rolled out from underneath our car and brushed the gravel from our clothes.

"Watching too many shoot-um up TV shows," I answered. "It's never that way in real life."

"Tell me about it."

Just then the side door opened and the good doctor stepped out. He glanced around as if expecting someone. Not seeing anything disturbing, he got in the ancient van, cranked the engine several seconds until the thing finally decided to come to life. Francese drove slowly north toward the park exit instead of south to where he had agreed to meet us.

By the time we were back in our car and backing out of the RV lane we had been parked in he was close enough to the exit so that no mater how fast I drove we wouldn't be able to catch him before he was out of the park.

"He's bolting," Angella proclaimed. "Wonder where he's going?"

Instead of giving chase I slowed and went into tail mode.

Francese passed through the exit gates, but instead of speeding up he moved to the left lane. About two hundred feet up the road he turned into the empty parking lot of *Dirty Al's* fish restaurant. I couldn't be certain if he was turning around or trying to see if anyone was following him.

We continued past him and made a U-turn in front of the *Sea Ranch*. He was stopped in the lot so we stopped where we were.

"What's he doing?"

"Guy's afraid of his own shadow," I answered. "I think he's trying to make up his mind whether or not to meet us or run."

He waited less than a minute before coming back out onto the roadway and turning south back into the park. We followed, keeping far enough behind so that we wouldn't further frighten the kid.

Francese continued all the way south and drove into the parking area of Dolphin Cove. We pulled along side, and Angella motioned for him to get into our car.

"Where are you taking me?" he asked before getting in the car.

"This lot is a bit too public," I said. "We can talk in the RV Park away from prying eyes."

He looked around as if he was contemplating bolting, but there was no place to hide. Terrified, he opened the back door and got in, slouching as low as he could go.

It didn't take two minutes until I was satisfied we hadn't been followed and no one would find us tucked in between two large and well-used RVs, their bikes, fishing boats and spare cars spread out around them.

"What took you so long?" Angella asked. "And what's with going out of the park?"

"Gathered some papers for you. But also Dr. Mayfield called. She wanted to know your names."

"Did you tell her?"

"I had to. She said she had already looked up the car registration, but just wanted to confirm. But I didn't tell her you were Homeland Security."

"Leaving the park?" Angella pressed. "What was that?"

"Wanted to make sure no one was following me. Just being sure is all."

"You did good, son," I said, trying to calm him. "Now let's just start at the beginning and tell us what's going on. Don't hold anything back. Okay."

"Okay. I'm actually relieved to get this off my back. I'm not a geologist, and frankly I'm not interested in how plates shift and landmasses move. The water is my life."

"We know that. Now what's troubling you?"

"Those pictures you showed me. They demonstrate that the bridge abutments have shifted eastward."

"Meaning?" I asked.

"As I said, I'm not a geologist, but I do believe there's major controversy over exactly what is happening. It appears a fault line has emerged due to the transform zone where the Caribbean Plate subducts the North American Plate."

"Meaning?" This time it was Angella who asked for a translation.

"Meaning there is evidence that the Padre Island chain, including South Padre Island, is moving away from Port Isabel. We know SPI is a relatively young island, about forty-five hundred years give or take a year or two," he smiled at the humor only a scientist would think funny. "Actually the Gulf side is in its erosion phase while the bay side is accreting."

"Hildigo!" I scolded, talk English.

"The island structure, primarily the sand, is moving west."

"But you just said the island is moving east."

"That's what the problem is. The natural forces on the surface are moving the island west while the continental tectonics is shifting everything east."

"I won't ask you to repeat what you just said, but what's your take? What has you so worried? And tell us in plain English as if you are writing a chapter in Geology for Dummies."

"Short version. The island is a fault zone and buildings will crumble."

"You got all that from the image I showed you?" Angella asked. "All I see are pieces of what appears to be concrete."

"No not just from your pictures. From lots of other data. But it's all confusing and very hush hush."

"If you are right that the plate, is that what you called it, the plate, is shifting, how soon?"

"Well, left unattended, the bridge will collapse sooner rather than later."

"Days, weeks, months, years?"

"A year maybe, based on your picture."

"To prevent that?"

"I would think all new abutments would have to be built for the bridge. But I'm not qualified in that area. Really I'm not."

"And what about the existing buildings on the island?" Angella asked. "Are they coming down as well?"

"The single family houses might be okay, but the multi-floor buildings, like the hotels, will be uninhabitable within, I would think, ten years."

"So how does this affect *Space X*?"

"Only they can answer that. They are not technically on South Padre Island, but the site is only six miles south and Brazos Island is part of the same geology. I imagine they don't dare build a rocket launch site on a fault line."

"Is that Dr. Mayfield's opinion as well?"

"Dr. Mayfield, it appears, does not agree with the theories espoused. She believes all the photo evidence see's seen has been doctored, Photoshopped. I don't believe she is right, but who am I?"

"Photoshopped? Why?"

"By environmentalists who oppose the rocket launches. The folks who think *Space X's* chemicals will hurt the marine life."

"So where are you in that regard?"

"Remember I have a major grant from *Space X* to track toxic activity along the western Gulf coastal areas, so I profess a bias. But I firmly believe their launches will not impact the environment."

"About the plates slipping?" Angella said, reminding him of the question.

"I don't know what to believe."

"If the images turn out to be accurate, I mean not Photoshopped, then what does Dr. Mayfield say?"

"She won't address that possibility. She's convinced all the evidence she's seen so far is a fraud. She's dived on the site herself and her pictures show no fissures. The environmentalists claim her pictures are doctored. But, if the images you showed me are true, then Dr. Mayfield would be forced to agree the island is moving."

"If that were the case, what would it do to *Space X's* plans?"

"Delay them for several years while new studies are conducted. If the subduction lithospheres are actually moving I'm afraid nothing will be built, either on SPI or on Brazos."

"In plain English."

"Crap will hit the fan! The state won't rebuild a bridge to a barrier island that is shifting around. The cost to rebuild the infrastructure on the island will be greater than the economic upside."

"What's your thought on which images are correct? Mayfield's or the ones we showed you?"

"I want to say, Dr. Mayfield's. But I've seen other marine evidence that could, and I emphasize could, be explained by a credible fault-line theory."

"Angella, any further questions for Dr. Francese?"

"I don't know where to begin, so until I digest what we've heard I'll pass for now."

"I have one question," I said, "and it's this. Why not send down people from both sides and take joint pictures in a manner that they can't be doctored?"

"Actually, that will happen next week. We've been waiting for a dive platform to arrive which it did a few days ago. Holds four or five people and is state of the art. We'll be able to travel the entire coast taking as many pictures as is necessary."

"Thanks for your time, Dr. Francese. Hope it all works out for you."

"If you folks don't mind, I'll get myself back to my car. I have nothing further to add to what I've already told you."

Angella nodded her approval. I cautioned him to call me if anything more occurred to him. He promised he would and leaped from the car and sprinted across the RV lots in the direction of his car. He was moving as fast as I had ever seen anyone his age run.

It was as if he was running from the fault line itself.

TWENTY-FIVE

We were not out of the park and my cell sounded.

"Get your butts over here the both of you before I send a car to pick you up." The line was dead before I could acknowledge that I heard and would obey the command.

"Malone has requested that we visit her at her office."

"That sounded like more than a request."

"Whatever."

"You have your…thoughtful…face on. Are we going directly or do you have something else in mind?"

"If the plate slipping theory is correct there would be plenty of motive to suppress the images at any cost."

"*Space X* has a lot riding on it," Angella noted. "But so does anyone with a property interest on the island."

"Precisely, and didn't we hear that the *Riveira* hotel guy, DePierio, was in financial trouble to the mob?"

"You thinking he killed the diver Smith to prevent the pictures going public and the buyer walking?"

"Don't yet know what to think. But that's certainly the direction my thoughts are taking."

"That look on your face tells me we're going to pay DePierio a visit."

I glanced in my rear view mirror before responding. "Well, you'd be wrong about the DePierio visit."

"Oh?"

"Take a look behind us." An SPI marked unit was directly behind us. Officer Cruz was in the passenger seat.

"I suppose Malone is serious—and a bit upset," Angella quipped.

"More than a bit I'd say."

"Any thoughts as to what you plan to tell her about withholding the camera?"

"There's still five or so minutes before I need an answer. I'll work on it."

"While you're working that out, mind if I call Dr. Mayfield and set up an appointment? It'll save her the trouble of finding us."

"Good plan."

"And while you're working things out, Jimmy, factor in that our friend Philip DePierio is most likely a Mossad special ops guy named Moshe Abrams being protected by our government."

"Stop talking. I only have four minutes remaining to build a story."

"I have every confidence in you. You're the best at ..."

Blue and red flashing lights lit up our car. The police car directly behind me had speeded up and was now in front and moving into my lane. My choice was to hit it or pull into the parking area in front of *K's Jewelry & Beads*.

I chose *K's*, not because I was planning on making a necklace, but because I was already in enough trouble. Besides, running from the locals is never a good idea and an even worse idea when you are on an island.

My wheels hadn't completely stopped when the passenger door of the police car in front of me flew open and Cruz came out weapon in hand. Not a good police move if I was dangerous because he was fully exposed.

Another car had followed us into the parking area blocking me from behind. Cruz approached on Angella's side and motioned for the window to be rolled down. When he was close enough for us to hear, he yelled, "Both of you get out."

When we complied, he said, "Get in that car." He pointed to the one behind us. "Angella in the back seat. Redstone you up front."

The dark tint on the side windows prevented me from seeing the driver's face, but I knew exactly who it had to be. "Good morning, Lieutenant Malone." I said, before I actually saw her face. "We were just on our..."

"Save it!" snapped a brusque male voice with a slight hint of a Spanish accent.

Angella was quicker than I, possibly because she had worked with this man before she joined me at Homeland Security. "Chief Garcia! I didn't..."

"I said, save it. I'm the chauffer."

We sped north, passing the convention center, the flats where Smith was found dead, and eventually the Island Equestrian Center. Lieutenant Jose Garcia, who has been the acting Chief for several years now since the former Chief had been murdered, was driving without siren or flashing lights. But he certainly wasn't obeying the speed limit.

It seemed to me the police were using the north end of the paved highway, which is about five miles from their headquarters, as their office. Possibly because they thought headquarters was not safe from prying ears. Most likely the Feds' prying ears if I was to guess.

If South Padre Island had a firing squad this would be the perfect place to handle their business. There's hardly ever anyone up here—other than them. Climbing out of the car at road's end I half expected to see four or five uniformed officers neatly lined up.

Instead, I was greeted by a fly-over of pelicans in formation heading south. Mexico immediately came to mind, and with that thought came the image of Paco Santino, AKA Billy Jaspers, the Golden Booby held high over his head.

Which in turn focused my attention on Marine General Lucinda Westminster McNaughton, now retired, but very much at the center of things. I again asked myself whether her involvement with the missing bird artifact was for her own account or was she fronting for someone. That led me to think about her long time lover, retired four star General Maxwell Jamison. And that brought me full circle to the firing squad. Most likely they were waiting just over the large dune to our left.

"Both of you," Garcia barked, "over that dune." He indicated the dunes on the bay side of the road which were significantly higher, maybe forty feet high, than the ones on the Gulf side. "I'm just the delivery boy on this one. Not privy to your business. Have fun." With that, he spun the car around and raced off, a sand cloud gusting behind him.

"What's this about, Jimmy? It's a long walk back to town."

"Someone wants to talk to us in private."

"We're in the book, for goodness sakes. Everybody and his cat has found their way into our condo, mostly uninvited. Let your fingers do the walking—or talking—or whatever the saying is. Didn't have to have the police chief kidnap us."

"Whoever it is wants us to know this is official business and we have nowhere to hide."

"Local or Feds?"

"Can't be local, the chief is as high as it gets."

We were halfway down the far side of the dune before I spotted a Jeep mostly obscured by sand and seemingly long abandoned. I motioned toward the vehicle and a moment later Angella whispered, "There's a body next to that Jeep. Maybe two. The sun angle makes it hard to see clearly."

We moved as silently as we could and soon it became apparent that at least one body was, indeed, sitting in the sand propped against the far door. There was no sign of anyone else. I looked around for a weapon, perhaps an old board, a piece of flotsam or jetsam, anything. No such luck. A handful of sand in the eyes was our only defense. I bent and filled each hand with the finest grained sand I had ever felt. Talcum powder has more substance.

Angella shrugged, but followed suit. She motioned for me to come around from the left while she took the right. Just as my head reached the front of the jeep the apparent corpse said, "You planning on doing something stupid with that sand?"

My focus wasn't on the hulk in front of me who was rising to his feet, but rather on the vision of Angella standing wide-eyed behind Tiny, sand slowly slipping through her fingers. I only hoped my expression wasn't so comical.

Tiny raised his hand, his index finger crossing his lips in the universal sign to remain quiet. I wasn't certain Angella had seen the signal so I relayed it her, causing Tiny to spin on his heels. For a man who stood just shy of seven feet I have often remarked on how agile he was. This was no exception. Not only had he turned completely around, but he had deftly moved out from between us. Had Angella fired a weapon, or physically attacked Tiny, I would have been the recipient of her aggression.

Without another word he moved across the sand and into a marshy area. My first thought was of quicksand, but Tiny out weighed me at least a hundred pounds. If he didn't sink, Angella and I were relatively safe.

Then my thought turned to snakes. Local lore claimed there were twenty-five varieties, including Western Diamond -back rattlers, lying in wait for unsuspecting visitors. I noted Tiny wore boots. I noted also that Angella was wearing low-cut moccasins and I had on sneakers. Not exactly the footwear for trekking through snake territory. I mentally ran through my Ranger jungle survival training and quickly realized I didn't even have a basic knife to cut the required X marks.

Thankfully, the marsh was shallow and less than a hundred yards wide. The bay was still a distance off when Tiny stopped. Turning to us, he said, "Obviously, I'm not supposed to be here; called in a favor Garcia owed me."

I assumed that his new encrypted, immediately disappearing message system was itself not even secure since he didn't use it to set up this meeting. I also assumed we were out here to avoid our conversation being monitored. Obviously, Tiny had concerns being seen with us.

"We have less than fifteen minutes, so let's not waste time," Tiny continued. "Next drone surveillance is at zero nine twelve. They have your heat signatures and the cameras will instantly lock on. Where the cameras go, the microphones follow."

What Tiny didn't say was that whether or not they had access to his heat signature, his size would be a dead giveaway.

"All hell'll break lose if I'm seen with you two."

"I assume the feds."

"Time for that later. Jimmy, you screwed up."

"Seems I've done that a lot lately. Be more specific."

"The camera. You're facing jail time. Automatic expulsion from DHS. When we're done here get your butt down to Malone's office and fess up. Withholding...well, you know the drill. Boyle set you up to find it, so...so beware."

"They took it last night. Had a warrant, knew it was in our condo."

"Go fess up anyway. That's a ticking bomb for you."

"Is Boyle involved?" Angella asked.

Tiny lowered his voice even further, glancing over my shoulder in the process. "That's why I'm here. As a friend, mind you.

Someone in the military, or with excellent military or law enforcement connections, orchestrated the heist. Boyle comes to mind. As do others."

"If you're talking about how precise everything worked out, I remind you the military doesn't have a lock on precision operations."

"The fact that a hundred million dollar artifact just happened to be in the bank at that exact time is curious. Factor in that a Federal Marshal, a Mossad agent, and a couple of retired Marine Generals are interested in the missing Bird with the fact you got a tip about the camera from a guy who normally wouldn't buy you a glass of water, and I'd say the military is involved."

"CIA have anything? Does this operation extend outside the country?"

"No need to know. Sorry."

"You thinking Jamison's involved?" That would tie in with Cindy McNaughton putting us on the Bird's trail. Two generals, a powerful combination. While Jamison is retired, he enjoys full command status because of his being the President's go-to guy in times of crises.

As if reading my thoughts, Tiny said, "Rumor has it the President has, or soon will, cut Jamison lose. I've asked Chief Garcia to keep his ear to the ground for possible sightings."

"He's on the island?"

"If he's involved he'll show up down here, assuming he's not already here."

"McNaughton certainly was here." Angella injected.

"Is," Tiny corrected. "Is."

"What do you know about tectonic plate movement?" I asked, taking a chance I wasn't giving away more than I would ever get in return.

"Only that the Texas coast is said to be free of plate movements. I know that because it's a main factor in *Space X* locating on Brazos Beach. If the rock formations below this sand were even thought to be unstable, a lot of people would be most unhappy. A lot of people, including Jamison and McNaughton."

"Why them?"

"Jamison is heavily invested, way over his head invested, in *Space X*."

"I thought Elon Musk owned the company."

Tiny checked his watch. "Love to remain and chat. We have less than a minute before the satellite comes into range. I suggest you two dig holes and bury yourselves deep enough to mess up the signatures. Bye."

"You can't just leave us hanging about Jamison?" I called to Tiny. I again noted how fast he moved for a big man.

He turned back toward us and yelled across the sand. "Follow the money is your motto, Redstone?" He said something more but the wind blew his words into oblivion.

TWENTY-SIX

I hadn't noticed the last time I was here, but the *Riveira* hotel is one of those places that is all hat and very little substance. Not that it doesn't have the obligatory pool and outdoor eating area. It does, but they are both undersized for the property and in need of extensive tender loving care, most likely involving a bulldozer and a construction crew. A hurricane, and the resulting insurance payout, would be a blessing. Maybe that's what DePierio has been waiting for.

The indoor bar and the accompanying restaurant was, however, first class. So was the penthouse suite where Philip DePierio was now standing as the private elevator door opened. Behind him the Gulf of Mexico formed a perfect panorama as seen through floor to ceiling windows. "So welcome to my home, Ms. Martinez, Mr. Redstone. Do come in. I've fresh coffee and the kitchen is bringing up freshly baked cinnamon rolls. Be here in a moment. Anything else I can get for you? A drink perhaps?"

DePierio was dressed casually in slacks and a tailored sport shirt and appeared to have just stepped off the cover of Men's Fitness, the European edition. For this island where shorts and a T-shirt are standard issue, he was far over-dressed. The suite was magnificently furnished and looked to have been recently refurbished. My eye immediately went to the artwork hanging on the walls, and then to the glass pieces displayed on pedestals. "No thanks," I said, thinking of the promised pastry and simultaneously comparing my stomach to his. Mine could easily pass for the ice chest to carry his six-pack abs.

Memo to self again: Call Teran and get back in the gym.

The elevator opened and the space filled with the unmistakable aroma of hot cinnamon and sugar. The server placed a large plate on the table directly in front of us and ceremoniously removed the silver cover. The fragrance intensified and my resolve to abstain vanished.

My first, and hopefully my last, bun was even tastier than the aroma promised. Warm and moist. I was hooked.

"They're excellent, aren't they?" DePierio said, reaching for one himself. "Go ahead, Ms. Martinez. Less than 100 calories each. With your figure you have no reason to count."

Our host's cultivated old world charm was disarming and came across as genuine. But then again, a con artist can't be successful if he or she appears to be anything but genuine.

"These rolls, we call them *bulle* in honor of their Swedish heritage, are a house specialty. My great grandfather was a baker in Sweden. I know, I know, I don't look Swedish. But that was a long time ago. Secret recipe and all. I won't divulge the source, but the real secret lies with the raisins. Even the chef doesn't know their age or point of origin."

"I can't imagine keeping the source of raisins secret from the staff. Shouldn't be all that hard to trace an invoice—or a bill of lading."

"I assure you, Mr. Redstone, it is a secret. Such as it is with many things in life, everything is not always straightforward. Surely you know that."

"Not everything is as straight-forward as it appears, I must agree."

"Take for example this visit. You and Ms. Martinez announced yourselves to my staff as being interested in being introduced to me for the purpose of selling me an investment opportunity."

"Indeed we did," I said, leaning toward him in preparation for the spiel I had worked out. "We'd like..."

"Your reason for being here is not entirely accurate. If I were to cut to the chase, as they say, I dare say I'd label your reason for being here a total fabrication. Am I accurate Mr. Redstone?"

"You indeed are," I confessed. Charade over. We were here and that was our first objective.

"If I were to guess, and mind you, I do a fair share of guessing in my line of work, I'd say you are more interested in the art artifact stolen in the recent bank robbery than you are in what I plan to do with the money from the sale of this property. Is that a fair assessment?"

"Fair enough," I replied. "What do you know about the Bird?" He wanted to play straight, so straight it was going to be.

"What do I know? Or what am I prepared to tell you I know?"

"I would hope what you know," Angella injected, "and what you are prepared to tell us is one in the same."

"Only a fool tells all that he knows, Ms. Martinez. I trust you don't take me for a fool. Please don't answer and spoil our morning."

"What are you prepared to tell us?" I pressed, fighting the urge to inhale another house specialty *bulle*.

"As you can see around you, I am a person who loves fine art. I would welcome the Golden Booby into my collection. But, alas, it is not to be."

"Any idea where the Bird is now?"

"Everyone has an idea as to who has that cursed artifact and where it is currently hidden. I dare say they are all wrong."

"And what do you base that assessment on?" Angella asked, a hint of the skeptic sneaking in.

"Naivety doesn't become either of you two."

"Meaning?" Angella asked.

"Meaning just that. If I had a clue where it was I'd be on it. So would a whole host of other people. Some official, some not. You can't think for one moment a prize worth well over a hundred million dollars would be allowed to sit anywhere for any length of time."

"It's somewhere," I said stating the obvious.

DePierio got up, walked to the side table and refilled his cup. Without looking up, he said, "It's no secret I'd love to get my hands on the Bird. Solve a lot of problems for me. But so would some very nasty people. I'm certain you're aware that art is one of the prime currencies used these days to finance terror operations. A hundred million buys a lot of weapons. If the Bird is your mission then I wish you good luck. Actually, let me revise my statement. If the Bird is your goal then I wish you continued good health and a long life."

I waited for him to look up before I responded, saying, "I take it you don't believe finding the Bird and living a long life are compatible."

"Recent events have shown the two to be incompatible, Mr. Redstone. That I can say with a high degree of certainty."

"I appreciate your candor, Mr. DePierio. Mind telling me if we have ever met before? I seem to remember…"

"If we had, I would certainly remember it. Now would you answer a question for me?"

"I'll try."

"You two Homeland Security or CIA?"

"What makes you think we are either?"

"I thought we were beyond playing each other for fools. CIA or HS?"

"What if I said neither?"

"Answering a question with a question is too basic for either of us. Now which is it?"

"HS."

"Both of you?"

"Both."

"Then please tell Tiny hello from Moshe. From what I've been told, he hasn't lost a step. He's the best the CIA has ever had. Man has more connections than a Facebook server."

***

"Talk about smooth," Angella said once we were outside. "That guy's the real thing."

"Meaning?"

"Meaning, he could look you in the eye, smile, and shove a knife through your heart all in the same motion—and with no emotional involvement. A psychopath if I've ever seen one."

"Worse. Psychopaths operate out of a combination of low self-control and just plain meanness. Put that together with lack of empathy and dislike for other humans and you have your typical sociopath. They usually act out of impulse with a lack of planning and that makes them relatively easy to catch. DePierio's highly trained and extremely disciplined. In my estimation he's one of the most dangerous animals roaming the earth today."

"So what do you plan to do about it?"

"For starters, not meet him in a dark alley—actually not in any alley. The guy doesn't need dark."

"From what you say, he doesn't even need an alley."

"Good point."

"Do you really recognize him or were you testing him somehow?"

"I've seen him before. I just don't know in what context. Possibly he was in the background of some image we've seen. But...but there's something different about him as well. Very different. So I'm probably mistaken."

"Visiting DePierio," a female voice behind me said. "Or someone else?"

I spun around and came face to face with Detective Malone. I searched for a trace of friendly and found nothing.

"You tailing us?"

"Just answer the question, Redstone."

"DePierio."

"Subject?"

"You want to know what we told him to get in or what we wanted?"

"I know what ruse you used to get in. Frankly, no rational human would buy an investment from you."

"Wanted to get to know who he is and…and what he knew about the Golden Booby."

"Tell you anything?"

"Only that a lot of folks are out there looking, but no one knows where to look."

"He looking as well?"

"Most likely."

"He know you're one of the ones looking?"

"Wished me a healthy life."

"In other words, the closer you get to the Bird the shorter your life expectancy."

"Seems to be his sentiment exactly."

"It's mine as well for what my opinion is worth."

"That's not reassuring."

"I'm not the South Padre hospitality person. But I am debating increasing your health prognosis if you really want to know."

"And just how…"

"By throwing your sorry butt in jail and losing the key."

"For?"

"Don't play stupid, Redstone. The camera. Withholding crime scene evidence. And that's just for starters. Take a ream of paper to print it all out."

My options were to fess up and plead for mercy or think of a good excuse. I could claim the camera was planted in my condo.

Or I found it while walking along the bay. Or I found it when I dove down but didn't connect it with the dead diver.

Or I could take every lawyer's advice and say nothing.

I said nothing.

"I take it by your silence and lack of protest you know you did wrong and are pleading the fifth?"

"The fifth sounds good—assuming the Constitution applies to me." If she had wanted to arrest me my hands would already be behind my back. "Did you know DePierio is—or was—Mossad?" I asked, giving her something of value while also changing the subject. "I believe his name is Moshe Abrams."

Malone's eyes widened for an instant. "That explains it," she mumbled, obviously fitting a piece of some puzzle she was working.

"Explains what?" Angella asked. The two women were friends. When Angella first joined the SPI police she had worked several months for Malone.

"We executed a search warrant on his place early this morning. Same time as on yours actually."

"Mind telling us the subject of the search?"

"Not at all. His diving gear."

"Diving gear?" Angella said. "Lots of folks down here dive. I would think..."

"Not with highly sophisticated diving tanks they don't."

TWENTY-SEVEN

"I agree with you, Angella, this is most likely a wasted trip."

We were at Houston's Hobby airport waiting on our now one-hour delayed flight to Pittsburgh. Weather conditions, or some such thing, was the given reason for the delay. But my cell phone showed no sign of bad weather anywhere our plane could be coming from or going to.

"At least Pittsburgh weather promises to be a pleasant relief from the sun. From ninety to seventy-five. Can't say as I mind the break. It'll give us some time to think this through."

"If all else fails, do something different. And frankly, all else is failing. Keeping a low profile with Malone is more than prudent and possibly Dr. Demont can get us focused."

"You're putting a lot of faith in Demont."

"The man is the world's expert on pre-Inca and Peruvian artifacts. He's the guy who certified the Bird to be a minor piece."

"We now know that certification was not entirely accurate. Fraudulent even. So what makes you think he'll..."

"Beside the Bird, I want to know who this Belle character is. To know Belle we need to understand her grandfather, professor August Villanova—and her cousin, the good Marshal. Demont knew Villanova well and I'm betting he knows Belle just as well."

"Port Isabel police report shows Villanova was found dead behind a shopping center. It's all recorded in the book *Paragraphs: The Mysteries of the Golden Booby*. The island has a Mystery Week in January every year and the missing Golden Booby was the topic that year. I followed up with Detective Vega who investigated Villanova's death and off the record he believes the professor's death was a homicide. But that's not how it's carried on the books."

"I'm thinking nothing about the Golden Booby is on the books as it really is. Perhaps Professor Demont can shed some real light on the subject."

"Mind telling me how you got Demont's address? He retired from Pitt a while back and I can't find anything on Facebook or any other social media for that matter."

"Tiny obtained the address from the Pitt records and he claims it's the latest they have. The good news is there is no record of him leaving the country."

"Is this stealth mode or are we using the locals."

"There's nothing to notify them about. This is background, he's not a suspect. And quite frankly, I'd prefer if Hugo didn't know what we are doing."

"I suppose the good Marshal's well connected in Pittsburgh."

"According to Tiny," I replied, "he's one of the best they have. You don't get that reputation without being well connected. Hey, they're boarding, let's get on. I can use a few hours of down time."

***

"I need to set the record straight," Angella said the instant we came out of the Fort Pitt tunnel and on the bridge to downtown Pittsburgh. That's Heinz Field there off to the left. Steelers play there as does Pitt. Pirates are over at PNC Park up that way."

"So why are telling me all this?" I answered, concentrating on moving to the right to catch I376 East to Oakland. "Last time we were here you pointed it all out."

"Last time we were here I called the ball park Three Rivers Stadium. That's been gone for fifteen or so years. Had an old guide."

"Not the most important fact. Now or then."

"All facts are important. Especially in what we do. Get them wrong and..."

"Just help me navigate and don't sweat the small stuff, as we used to say. We're looking for Forbes. Oh, here it is. That came up fast." A moment later we were stopped at a traffic light. "We're looking for McKee Place."

"Here it is," Angella said, pointing to a map displayed on her iPad. "Three blocks ahead."

It was almost nine o'clock and the mid-week traffic was light. We passed several small office complexes nestled in among what appeared to be century old apartment buildings. A moment later Angella called, “Okay, next right.” When I made the turn, we drove a half a block and she said, “Park anywhere you can find a spot. He lives in one of these old apartment houses.”

At one time these structures may have been single-family dwellings, but now they clearly housed multiple unrelated folks. From the look of things, these old buildings were destined to fall at the practiced hands of demolition crews, all in the name of progress.

I’d say Professor Winston Demont III, former chair of the Department of Antiquities at the University of Pittsburgh, lived a frugal life. This judgment was highly influenced by the fact he lived on the fourth floor of an ancient building in desperate need of repair. Unless he had combined apartments, he lived in less than a thousand square feet of space. This was a classic walk-up.

Of course, this could have been his on-campus pad and he could be maintaining a home somewhere else, but there was no record of any such place.

“What the hell you banging on my door this late at night for?” an old man said, his eyes half-closed. He wore a good weeks worth of whiskers along with a formerly white T, now mostly gray and decorated by remnants of meals past. His shorts were even dirtier than his top and his feet were filthy. On a table behind him was an open bottle of what appeared to be Jim Beam.

“We’re looking for…”

“He ain’t here! I told the last guy the same thing.”

“Who’s not here?”

“Man you look’n for. People want to know where he is. I didn’t tell them and not tell’n you. Now go away from my door before I call the cops!" He tried to pull the door closed but it caught on my outstretched foot. The man staggered backward and without the door to steady him, had trouble maintaining his balance and collapsed to the ground. "I'm call'n the cops on yinz."

"Not a good idea," I said, following the man into the apartment. "We're looking for Professor Demont. This his place?"

"My place now!" the man shouted, using the doorknob to pull himself up. You're invading my place. Now go away. You hear, go away!"

Over the years I've heard lots of drunks shout, but this guy beat them all in volume. He took a wobbly step forward and pulled back his arm to throw a punch. A quick jab to his over extended jaw and this guy would be out for the count.

Instead of laying him out, I stepped aside and watched as he propelled himself forward, his thrust missing me by a foot, the momentum causing him to stagger through the door into the hallway. He landed heavily against the old wooden railing and it looked for a moment that it would give way and he'd fall onto the steps. I ran to catch him before he broke his neck—or worse.

The old adage about God looking out for babies and drunks was at work because he bounced off the banister and landed on his butt with a thud. His breathing was shallow, but steady. He hadn't even hit his head.

The man's most immediate problem was not the trauma, but rather the drinking. I didn't expect to have much influence on the latter.

"What happened?" A female voice from behind me called.

I turned to find a very thin, overly thin, woman standing in the doorway of the apartment next to Demont's. She had an ancient bathrobe pulled around her and I saw no hint that she was wearing anything else. I guessed her age at eighty, but I could easily have been off by fifteen years either way. "He fell," Angella said. "He's okay. We'll help him back into his apartment."

"Man goes on binges. Sometimes they last a week. Sometimes a month. His daughters tried to dry him out, but he don't stay at those homes, or wherever they take him. He's a decent man when he's not drinking. Brings me my mail. Goes to the drugstore for me. He can't shake his problem. Be the death of him."

"What's he do when he's not drinking?" I asked.

"Teaches at the University you know. He's a good man."

"What's his name?"

"To tell the truth, I only know him as Professor. That's what he told me to call him, Professor."

"Professor of what?"

"Don't rightly know. Literature…oh, I remember now. Art. Old art."

Angella, in her *talk to grandma* voice, asked, "By any chance could his name be Winston? Winston Demont?"

"Gracious no, dearie! Professor Demont moved several years back. He," she said pointing to the man on the floor, "worked with Dr. Demont. What a nice man. At Pitt. He's his tenant."

"Does Demont still own this place?"

"No one owns here? We all rent. Dr. Demont rented his to the Professor. Poor man spent all his money on his sick wife. She died last year. You see the results."

"Do you happen to know where Demont moved?"

"I most certainly do."

"Would you mind telling us?"

“Why should I do that? You a friend?”

Without missing a beat, Angella replied, “His great uncle died and left him an insurance annuity. It is important to find him so we can give him his money.”

“Well, that is important isn’t it? I suppose there’s no harm in telling you. He lives downtown in a fancy apartment building. Near the Point. Right by the river.”

Using her best get-what-you-want tone, Angella asked, “By chance do you know the name of the building?”

“I remember him calling it Gateway. I thought, what a nice name for a building looking out over the Ohio River. You know that river starts right here and is the gateway to the west. Or at least it was when the country was young. Wait, he gave me a card.” The door closed and didn’t open for a long while.

The man at my feet moaned and grabbed my leg. It took me a few beats to realize he wasn’t fighting, but was making a poor job of trying to stand. I bent to lift him and he fell backward, his head hitting the wooden railing.

I bent over his prone body.

“Is the Professor going to be okay?” the old woman called. Her door was now open only a crack, I suppose to prevent us from barging in. At first I thought she was referring to Demont, but her focus was on the man at my feet. His eyes were open, unfocused, and he looked as if he was about to let it all go.

“Nothing a little sleep—and staying away from the bottle—can’t cure,” I said. “Come, Angella, help me get the professor into his bed.”

From the slit in her doorway the neighbor lady watched our every move.

When we emerged from the professor's apartment she opened the door a bit further and held out a card. "Here take it. I don't suppose I'll ever need it. Can't get out much these days. Please say hello to Professor Demont for me. Tell him Alice Barninsky from 4C said hello. Tell him I said I hope he enjoys his money."

TWENTY-EIGHT

Downtown Pittsburgh is bounded by the Allegheny and Monongahela rivers as they merge to form the Ohio River. The confluence is referred to by Pittsburghers as the Golden Triangle and is highlighted by a massive fountain throwing water a couple of hundred feet in the air. I pointed to the fountain as we passed the Wyndham Hotel.

My gesture prompted Angella, who had been studying her iPad to comment, "Listen to this. That fountain is designed to stay down and not rise with the pressure from the rivers. Apparently that's a big problem. I mean keeping it down. Usually structures are designed to not sink, but this one is designed not to rise."

"That's more information than..."

"There's more! The water that feeds the fountain comes from an underground river fifty-four feet below the surface. That river runs all the way from the Great Lakes."

"Sorry to burst your bubble here, but we're looking for the Gateway. It's not more than a..."

"It's the building right over there. I thought you'd be interested in a bit of...culture."

"Guided tours can wait. Get me to Gateway."

"Aye, aye, my captain. Turn right at the stop sign and pull into the first driveway on the right. It's not that difficult."

"If you have an iPad on your lap." Gateway Towers is a neat old building overlooking the Allegheny. I passed under the portico and headed toward a small parking area that most likely was reserved for tenants dropping off groceries. Ahead of us, walking a small white cottony looking dog was a slender woman I had seen before but couldn't place her at the moment. A beach image appeared and vanished. The dog was different.

"Jimmy," Angella called, "the doorman is motioning for you to move on. I don't think this is..."

"All doormen motion you to move on," I snapped. "That's what they do. That woman there, you ever see her before?"

Angella studied the woman before replying, "Can't say as I have. Maybe at the beach. I don't know."

"Okay, let's go pay the good professor a visit."

"Apartment 3M"

"Not very high up."

"Not surprising based on the place we just visited. I can't believe he'd spring for anything in this building. This is some prime location."

The doorman motioned for me to roll down my window.

When I complied, he said, "Can't park here."

"I'm going to see a resident."

"Okay. Park over there. No more than an hour. Okay?"

"So be it," I replied, moving the car to the parking area he had pointed out.

I stepped from the car and a familiar voice said, "So we meet again, Redstone. You too, Angella. Welcome to Pittsburgh my friends."

I mentally kicked myself for letting my guard down. We had approached a work site as tourists, paying more attention to underground rivers than to what was happening on the surface. I was trained to see what others didn't want seen, but Marshal Hugo had positioned himself well. He had won this round and, of course, I was pissed.

"You folks don't look happy to see me," Hugo called. "Keep your hands where I can see them and come this way."

"What are you doing here?" I asked, as if he'd give us any valuable information.

"Same as you are. Come, let's grab a bite to eat."

"Only have an hour parking."

"We'll only be gone half of that. Hope you're hungry cause we're going over to *Primanti Bros*."

"That the outfit puts French fries on the sandwich?" Angella said, obviously having studied the local literature.

"That's the place. Two blocks from here. Walk will do you good. And on the way you can tell me what brought you to Pittsburgh."

If he had followed us from the airport, which I didn't think he had, then he wouldn't necessarily know we were here to see Demont. If he had been standing watch on the Professor's condo, then he would already know why we were here. The story I told him depended on what he already knew. "You first, Marshal. You're the guy hiding in the weeds."

"Wasn't exactly hiding."

"Wasn't exactly out in the open."

"Matter of fact, I was visiting an old friend. Catching up on life."

"That's what we're doing, visiting a friend."

"I call BS on that Redstone. First off, far as I can tell you don't have many friends. And second, you're two thousand miles from home and no one travels that far to visit a friend without advance coordination."

"How do you know we didn't plan this trip weeks ago?"

"Cause you booked it on the way to the airport. Stop playing with me and let's hear your story."

We were walking through a park area, tall buildings all around. A circular fountain lay straight ahead. We'd pass within a few feet of it. My plan was to maneuver him as close as possible and dump him over the ledge. Angella read my eyes and slowly moved herself to his other side and began crowding him toward me. We had him perfectly sandwiched and moving on a trajectory that would take us within inches of the fountain.

When we were ten steps away from the water I started the mental countdown. I held my hand out, my fingers spread wide conveying to Angella that we'd dump him in five steps. Her almost imperceptible nod told me she was ready.

Four.

Three.

Two.

Hugo stopped dead in his tracks, turned to face me and said, "Nice try, Redstone. True to form you are. I half expected you to come out of your car firing away. You must be working on self-control. Good for you. Homeland Security is doing wonders. Angella, if you want my advice, I'd say don't go along with him. He'll ruin your career. What will dumping me in the water accomplish? Nothing. Then you'd never know why I'm here and what I know—and don't know."

"So why are you here?" I asked, knowing he was right. Ego was the only reason I had for dumping him over the ledge. And as he pointed out, ego wasn't going to solve anything.

But it certainly would feel good.

"I actually told you that back on the island. I'm looking for the Golden Booby."

"So?"

"So Professor Demont, my Grandfather's longtime colleague and the man who knows more about the Booby than any other living person, lives in that building." He nodded across the park to the Gateway Towers.

"Is that who you were visiting?" Angella asked.

"He wouldn't authorize me to go up. Sure, I could have flashed my badge and forced the issue, but…but that would make it official. The last thing I want is the government in the middle of this."

"Middle of what exactly?" I asked, pressing for as much information as he was willing to impart.

"The missing Booby. I own it. I mean I own it with my cousin and I'm looking for it."

"Does she know you're looking for it?"

"She's looking for it as well."

"I take it then that neither of you has a lead on where it went?"

"I actually don't know what she knows?"

"So you two aren't cooperating," Angella asked. "Any reason why not?"

"You'll have to ask her that question. I only just met her when our grandfather died. It's a tangled story, but the bottom line is she doesn't like me." Hugo paused for a moment, then added, "Actually I said that wrong. She doesn't trust me."

"You give her any reason not to...not to trust you?" Angella asked.

"Not that I know. You can ask her that as well."

Angella studied Hugo for a long moment before saying, "Have to find her before we can ask her. Point us."

"Wish I could. After the Booby was stolen she vanished. No trace."

"You make your living tracking people and you can't ..."

"Pisses me off, you wanta know. But she's nowhere I can find her."

"When was the last time you spoke to her," I asked, getting back into the conversation. "Or knew where she was?"

"The day before the Booby was stolen."

"Let's see," I said, popping my thumb up to begin the backward count to the robbery. "Today is one, yesterday is..."

"Not the bank robbery. The one in Port Isabel where the curator was killed."

"That's well over a year ago."

"That's when she disappeared."

"Foul play?"

"Didn't think so...until this happened. Now I frankly don't know what to think."

"Still want that sandwich?" I asked Hugo sensing he had more to tell us but wasn't yet ready to let it out.

This is where Angella shines. So when she said she was still hungry I fell behind to allow my partner to perform her magic.

TWENTY-NINE

"Tell Professor Demont we're friends of Alice Barninsky. Alice has a message for him."

If there's one thing I've learned from working with Angella it's that she can charm the rattler off a snake when she puts her mind to it. So I hung back, forced my face into a smile—or at least what I thought would pass for a smile—and waited for her to work her charm. My backup plan, should charm not work, was to just go on up. We were armed and they weren't. Simple as that.

"Professor Demont?" the security woman at the desk said into the phone. "Oh, I see," the woman responded to something said on the other end. "Would you please tell Professor Demont he has guests who are waiting to come up."

The security woman had the phone to her ear for so long waiting for a confirmation that the woman with the cute little white dog came in from a side entrance and pushed the button for the freight elevator.

"Pardon me," I said, "is that a Bichon?"

"A Coton. Like our cotton, but it's French with only one 't'. They're a breed from Madagascar. Some ship wreck or something."

The dog was jumping up my leg and the woman apologized, saying, "I'm new to small dogs. My last dog was a German Shepherd and she didn't jump.

It took me a moment before her words clicked into place. "By any chance did you walk the Shepherd on the beach at Padre Island? A black dog?"

"Hydra. Her name was Hydra and we put her down a while back. This one is her replacement. Needed a dog small enough to fly. Do I know you?"

"Wouldn't think so, but we live down there as well."

"So what are you doing here? Live here?"

"Visiting an old professor." Not exactly the truth and not exactly a lie.

I looked over toward Angella and heard the receptionist saying into the phone, "A man and a woman. They say a woman named Alice Barninsky wants them to deliver a message."

"What's the message?" the receptionist asked Angella.

"Here's my elevator," the woman with the dog said. The dog was already inside tugging on his leash. "Got to go. Sorry we can't visit."

"Angella," I called, "come. This nice woman has invited us up."

Without hesitation, Angella turned to the receptionist. "We'll be back down in a few minutes. Talk to you then."

I turned to the dog woman. "Don't be concerned, we're getting off on three." But I did note the floor number she had pushed. Sometimes a coincidence is nothing more than a coincidence. The trick is to know one from the other and right now I was disoriented.

It took a moment before the door to 3M opened a sliver. The woman on the inside, an obvious care giver, said, "You the two on the phone from downstairs?"

"We are," Angella answered. We have a message from Alice Barninsky for the Professor."

"Alice Barninsky?"

"Professor Demont's next door neighbor from his Oakland apartment house."

"I don't..."

"Who is it? Who's out there?" The voice was male, and very weak, punctuated with coughing.

"You've flared up his lungs! Man can hardly breathe as it is and you're here troubling him. Shame on you both."

"We have a message for him from Alice Barn..."

"Give me the message and go away. He needs to rest."

"Who's there?" the voice, now even fainter, called.

"Some people with a message from Alice Somebody."

A bout of coughing was followed by, "For goodness sakes, Jessie, send them back here this instant."

With a shrug and a roll of the eyes Jessie turned and marched across the living room and through a door into a bedroom. Sunlight from the wide window overlooking the river filled the room in direct contrast to the room we had been in where dark blinds were pulled tightly closed.

Demont, frail from whatever sickness he was suffering from, was propped up in bed. The man could not have weighed a hundred pounds. “You know Alice Barninsky? Nice woman. You know she’s in her late nineties? I always thought I’d be attending her funeral, but now it seems it’ll be the other way around. That is if she can get out. How is she doing?”

“She said to say hello,” Angella answered. “She’s looking healthy.”

“At least one of us is. That’s good. Who are you?”

“I’m Angella Martinez. And this is Jimmy Redstone. We’re here to ask you about...”

“About the Golden Booby. Been waiting for someone to come around about that old bird. Heard it was stolen from a bank down in Texas.” A round of coughing, to the point of not being able to catch his breath, followed. Jessie pushed herself in front of me and held an oxygen mask over his noise and mouth. Color returned to his face. He pushed the mask aside and continued his thought. “That is, after it was stolen from a display. I told those kids not to make the Bird public, but they didn’t listen.”

“What kids are you referring to?” Angella gently inquired.

“Grandkids of Professor Simpson Hugo. Actually, that’s the name I knew him as. But in Texas he went by August Villanova. The man lead two lives, it seems. She’s a doctor of anthropology at the University of Mexico in Mexico City. He’s a federal marshal.”

“I assume you mean the grandchildren?” Angella clarified.

“Her name’s Annabelle Neuva and his is Oscar Hugo. They’re the ones found the artifact.” Color left him and the coughing again took hold. This time it stopped before oxygen was required.

"You two better get out of here before you kill the poor man," Jessie warned us.

"Don't be so harsh. This is important," Demont said, scolding his caretaker.

"Kill yourself," she replied, "see if I care."

"That woman cares, I see," Demont commented, when Jessie hurried from the room. "Where was I? Oh, yes, I do believe Hugo wanted them to find it. He used coordinates on another art piece to locate it. Seems that's how it's been found every time. Four times in all and every time with coordinates."

"You mean latitude, longitude coordinates?" I asked.

"Precisely. But once, the first time actually, it was map coordinates to an ancient Pre-Aztecan map. Hand drawn sailing chart actually."

Demont burst into another round of coughing and a moment later when he couldn't catch his breath Jessie came rushing in. "Now you two better go!" She pulled the mask over his face. "His lungs can't take it. I'm surprised he lasted this long. Now go!"

Demont's eyes were closed. The coughing had suddenly stopped and his breathing was now shallow. "Do you need help?" I asked, fearing the worse. "Should I call 911?"

"Not while there's a pulse. I'm a hospice nurse and I'll take it from here. Don't imagine it will be long now. Now please leave." As she spoke she positioned her fingers just below Demont's jaw line.

"Thank him for speaking with us," Angella said from the door.

"Doesn't appear anybody will be thanking him for anything," the nurse answered. "Don't know how he held on this long."

THIRTY

We changed our flight plans and spent the night at the Wyndham Hotel in Pittsburgh directly across the courtyard from Gateway Towers. After dinner we walked down by the fountain and Angella retold the story of the fountain construction and this time I was fascinated by the fact that a fourth river ran below us and alongside the three other rivers. We strolled arm and arm along the wharf that runs almost at water level up the Allegheny. We then crossed one of the many bridges and walked back on the far side passing first the baseball park and then Heinz Field. Paris has nothing on this town.

On our way to the airport the next morning I asked Angella what she had learned from Marshal Hugo.

"Only that much to my surprise I actually enjoyed fries on my sandwich."

"I agree. He told us nothing we didn't already know. He doesn't appear to have any idea where the Bird's hidden and he's run out of ideas on how to go about finding it. Actually, he does have a plan."

"And that is?"

"Shadow our every move. Bet he beats us back to Texas."

"Think if he'd managed to see Demont would Demont have told him what he told us?"

"My hunch says no."

Angella was quiet for several miles, then said, "Think the granddaughter, Annabelle, got to the old man?"

"Doubt it. I'm thinking Hugo killed her and set up the heist himself. Only someone double-crossed him and the Bird disappeared."

"Paco?" Angella suggested.

"Working for someone. Joy Malcom, actually her fake husband Roberto Santiago, is high on my list."

"From his prison cell no less."

"Tell me you're not thinking of paying him a visit down there."

"Not if I can help it. I'm done with Mexico. I've used up my nine lives."

After another pause, Angella asked, "So why did he tell us about the hiding places being coded? That's important."

"Old guy was running out of time I suppose. We were at the right place, right time. And just because the hiding places in the past have been coordinate-coded doesn't mean that will follow this time."

"Jimmy, I think he knows more than he let on."

This time when Angella fell silent she didn't speak until after we dropped off the car and were on our way to the terminal. "You're thinking the hiding place isn't coordinate-controlled this time because...because Paco has the Bird and Paco wouldn't know about the history. Is that your logic?"

"Possibly."

"I've got a different take on it. I think it's fair to assume Paco is the go-fer in all this. Expeditor I think you've called him. He's simply following orders of the mastermind. They've positioned the booby to be hidden a long time. Five, maybe ten years out."

"That would take a serious collector."

"Or someone who knew they'd be watched for many years and who is willing to wait a long while or pass it along to the next generation as August Villanova did."

"I'm thinking you're on the right track, Angella. Here's my take. Bella made the original substitution over in Port Isabel. Hugo found out the Bird was in the vault and killed Belle to keep her from moving it. He then made two mistakes. First, he's not familiar with our part of the country and after checking around he decided to use Paco not knowing Paco's connections."

"The hole in that is Hugo wouldn't have told Paco about the Bird, only that he wanted a package from the vault."

"That brings me to the second, and in my mind, fatal mistake. The Golden Booby meant nothing to Hugo, we know that. He wanted the money. To get the money he needed a buyer. That meant he had to tell someone."

"DePierio?"

"Guy's broke."

"But he has contacts," Angella reminded me. "Mob contacts. Being a Federal Marshal Hugo would know about DePierio's access to money."

"McNaughton told me to use *Marine Savings Bank*, perhaps knowing the bank was set to be robbed. That gave them immediate cash plus a long-term investment. I'm liking where we're going with this."

"That brings us back to Paco. If he was the person to hide the Bird, which from all indications he was, then Paco would, at some point, have to pass along the hiding place to someone."

"Not if Paco sold them all out and cut a deal with Santiago. That all fits!" I said, getting excited. "Paco grew up working for Santiago. Drugs and contraband still move across the border and unless I'm wrong Paco is in the center of the illegal traffic. That would mean Paco still works for Santiago."

"You think Paco double-crossed the folks who planned the heist, hid the Booby, and gave the hiding place to Santiago?"

"Or to Joy Malcom. Same thing."

"So, Jimmy, our next goal is clear: Track down Paco."

***

As it turns out, Paco was easier to find than we had anticipated. Had we not had our phones off on the plane ride to Hobby we would have known exactly where to find him. Our plane from Pittsburgh had come in late and we had to run between gates, barely making the flight to Harlingen. So it wasn't until we were on the causeway to the island when Angella exclaimed, "Jimmy, I'm working my way through my emails and you're not going to like what's here."

"Shoot."

"Poor choice of a word. "Paco was found dead, a bullet hole between his eyes."

"Don't tell me. On the beach."

"Where else?"

"When?"

"Doesn't say."

"Get Tiny on the line."

Tiny answered on the first ring, "I'd thought you'd never call," he said by way of answering his phone. Your plane landed seventy minutes ago. You should be back on the island by now."

"Almost."

"I just sat down for dinner at Gabriella's. Join me. Don't pass go." The line, as always, went dead.

"Who sent the email?" I asked Angella, assuming it hadn't been Tiny.

"Malone. She's asked us to stop by her office *at our earliest convenience*."

I didn't like Tiny's reference to not passing go. The first part of that sentence, as I recall from the hours I sat on my bedroom floor as a child playing Monopoly, was *Go directly to jail*. "I don't like Tiny's message."

"Depends upon when he was shot who she likes for it. Let's just hope it happened when we were east."

"I didn't shoot him, so..."

"How does your lecture go? It's not what you do that counts, it's what they can prove you did."

"I'm beginning to think it's not what I did that counts, but rather what they can frame me for."

"Paranoia has set in big time."

"Only if it's not true, my dear. Only if it's not true."

THIRTY-ONE

As usual, *Gabriella's* was crowded. Tiny was tucked away in a far corner, his back to the door, *Casablanca* playing without sound on a small screen mounted above his head. Angella had commented on how unusual it was for him to meet us in such a public place. Her question only increased my agitation, because in truth I had no answer for her.

He didn't stand, or even shake hands, when we arrived at the table. He simply nodded for us to sit. "Order," he said. "Then we can talk."

After the waiter left, he pulled out his cell phone, touched the screen several times and then handed it to me. There I was, in freeze-frame, sand all around. I touched the arrow and the motion began.

It took several seconds before I realized when this video had been taken. It was on our five-mile hike back to town after our meeting with Tiny a few days back. We had started walking along the highway, but at Angella's suggestion we crossed the dunes and walked along the beach. The portion I was watching had been taken as we crossed the wide beach, the Gulf of Mexico in front of us, Highway 100, actually a two-lane roadway, behind. My agitation level spiked when I realized I was alone in the video. Angella had been cut out.

"This has been doctored. I suppose you already..."

"Just watch."

A moment later I had an assault rifle in my hand, the sight pressed against my eye. My legs and arms were perfectly positioned for stability. Several frames went by without me moving. Then suddenly my head moved slightly backward followed by me taking a step forward in the direction of the water. The video ended. "You had to show us this before we eat? Couldn't it have waited?"

Without a word, Tiny then pulled up another video, this one showing Paco on a beach, water off to his left. Again I touched the arrow and Paco began walking. The water was on his left as was the rising sun. He was obviously walking south, but Photoshopping being what it is he could have been anywhere going in any direction. "Significance?" I asked, as if I expected an answer.

"You don't have to do it, but if you compare the time sequence of this video clip with the time of the one you just saw you'd note that they match almost exactly."

"But Paco's alive at the end of this sequence. If I had shot him, as my video suggests, then he'd..."

"I said the sequences match *almost* exactly. In fact, the Paco video ends two-tenths of a second before your weapon is fired."

"Time sequences can be altered."

"True enough. You better eat that salad and rolls my friend 'cause it may be all you..."

"Redstone! Martinez!" the familiar voice of Lt. Malone rang out. I hadn't seen her approaching our table. "Didn't I ask you to come to my office?"

"Just having a bite to eat," I replied, trying to get my mind around what I had just seen. I had no way to know if she had these videos, but as things were going it wouldn't be long before she did. "Care to join us?"

"This is official. You are both, I mean you and Angella, are persons of interest in the murder of one Billy Jaspers, AKA Paco."

"Can't we just fin..."

"Get on your feet and come with me! You want me to arrest you here, I'll do it. This is a courtesy I don't extend to many people, so I suggest you take it and follow me outside."

Officer Cruz, who I hadn't noticed before, and another uniform I didn't recognize, were standing near the kitchen, their hands resting on their weapons. This was not a good time to resist.

I looked across the table. "Now you know why I didn't wait until after dinner. Sorry, but I didn't expect them this fast. I'll pick up the tab."

"That's good of you. I suppose you'll have our dinners boxed to go."

"Good idea, Jimmy. Glad you thought of that."

At least my question as to why Tiny set up our meeting in a public place was answered. He knew Malone would never entertain a shoot-out in a crowded restaurant.

He had taken a huge chance on me.

***

"You opened my email so you know of Paco's murder," Malone said when we were in her car. She had refrained from arresting either of us with the comment that she hoped we would return the favor. "So here's what I want from you two. A promise of complete loyalty. For most people, Redstone, that would be an easy thing to pledge. But you're not wired that way, I'm afraid. So, here's the deal. The instant you do anything, and I mean anything that I deem breaks your pledge I'm booking you for first-degree murder. If you think for one moment I don't have enough evidence to take you down, and make it stick, then try me out. At best, you'll rot in jail. You'll never make bail, not with your demonstrated ability to move in and out of this country without a passport. At worst they'll fry your sorry butt. You understand what I'm telling you?"

"Yes, boss."

Angella's elbow hit my ribs even before Malone said, "Knock off the wise guy stuff. It gets old fast."

"You got it!" I replied. Angella was right, this wasn't the time nor the place to provoke her.

"We'll talk in my office," Malone said as she parked the unmarked car in front of City Hall.

A few minutes later, when we were all seated, she said, "I understand you were in Pittsburgh. Tell me about who you saw and why you went."

"Nothing to do with Paco's murder, I can assure you of that."

"Let me be the judge of the facts. Just tell your story."

Malone was silent while I spoke, taking only a few notes. I assumed we were being recorded. When I was finished, she said, "So you two were together the whole time?"

"Correct," I answered.

"And you spent time with Federal Marshal Oscar Hugo?"

"We did."

"And with Professor Winston Demont."

"Yes."

Malone reached for something in her desk, possibly turning off the recorder. Then she sat back in her chair, took a deep breath and said, "So here's the way I see it. You leave the island and Paco is found dead, shot between the eyes by a sniper's rifle. You go to Pittsburgh and when you leave, Demont's dead and Hugo's nowhere to be found. All a coincidence?"

"Demont died from natural causes," Angella said, breaking her silence and showing her support for me. "Hugo was very much alive when we left him outside the Primanti Deli. And Paco, well that's a whole different story."

"And what story would that be?" Malone asked, her interest peeked.

Angella glanced over at me and I held my poker face. It was time to allow her instinct to control—at least for now. "We just saw a video of him walking on the beach. Tiny said it was a few tenths of a second before he was shot."

"Go on," Malone said, "that's not much of a story."

"We also saw a video, a doctored video, of Jimmy walking on that same beach. Or at least it was made to appear to be the same beach at the same time. Only Jimmy had an assault rifle in his hands. I suppose that rifle will turn out to be the same type that shot Paco. The video makes it appear Jimmy shot the rifle in the direction of the water. I understand the time marks will line up making it seem that Jimmy shot Paco."

"You have anything to add to Angella's story?"

"My partner's got it all," I said. "Only that I never, at least in the time frames we are talking about, had a pistol or rifle in my hands. The video was Photoshopped is all I can say."

"What do these three deaths have in common? That's the question I keep asking myself. So what's your answer to that?"

"The missing Golden Booby. Paco had it after the bank heist. Demont is the expert on the Booby. Hugo, along with his cousin Belle, are the supposed owners."

"And they are all dead—or missing."

"Seems that way," I said. "Seems that way."

"And someone is trying to frame you for at least one murder."

"And seemingly doing a good job of it."

"Better than you might think."

"What's that supposed to mean?"

"A small fishing boat was stolen last night sometime after midnight over in Port Isabel. The boat was found on the beach shortly after sunrise. Your gun was found in the boat, a round having been fired and a spent casing in the bilge."

Actually, that was all good news. We didn't land until four-thirty and we could prove we were in Pittsburgh last night. Changing our flight was perhaps the best thing we could have done. Perfect alibi. "I suppose you know what time we…"

"That's a given. That's also why your hands are free to move."

"So why the public display back at the restaurant?"

"I want the perp to think his games are working."

"Jimmy," Angella exclaimed, "if your Berretta was used to kill him then the video with the assault rifle must be bogus!"

Angella had overlooked the fact that the time stamp alone made the video bogus. We were in Pittsburgh at that time and with the myriad of security cameras at the hotel and at the airport there would be no doubt.

Then my spirits fell. Time stamps and videos have a way of dissolving if the government, or someone close to the heart of the government, was at the center of this.

To avoid dwelling on that, I said to Malone, "Mind if we examine Paco's file? I assume he's your case."

"Good assumption. Go for it. The only fact of importance is that Paco had the key to the safe deposit box, the one that yielded the Bird, in his pocket. That's how he opened it so fast."

Malone made a note, then said, "Now let me change the subject. The pictures in the camera, you know, the camera that you withheld from me, show the bridge abutment. Tell me what you know about that."

"Angella, mind telling the Lieutenant what we found?"

Malone listened intently as Angella methodically walked through our discussions with Hildigo Francese of the UT Pan American Coastal Studies Lab and his relationship with Dr. Mollie Mayfield, *SpaceX*'s Chief Geologist."

"You don't think *SpaceX* had anything to do with the murder of our diver, do you?"

"If what Hildigo said about tectonic plate slippage is true and most buildings on this island will come down, then anyone with a financial interest down here is suspect. I wouldn't limit it to *SpaceX* necessarily."

"I've heard rumors about the shifting plates for a while now, but haven't put much stock in them. The word always is that the photos have been altered. But the pictures Smith took couldn't have been altered since they hadn't even come out of the camera."

"My guess," I said, "is that Smith showed them to someone who then had him killed and the camera dumped to hide the evidence of the plate fault."

"I'm ahead of you on this one, Redstone. That's what was behind the warrant we served on Philip DePierio. Smith was seen coming out of his suite shortly after he took the photos."

"Obtain anything useful?"

"Can't discuss that at this point. Oh, Angella, thanks for coming clean about the videos showing Redstone and Paco. They were delivered to me two hours ago. Seems someone doesn't appreciate your partner."

"I suspect more than one somebody would like to see him hang for the murders," Angella replied, lost in thought, her usual smile now gone.

THIRTY-TWO

"Where do we go from here, Jimmy?" Angella asked as we drove back to our condo.

"I don't know about you, but my plan is to crash. Covers up to my nose for as long as I can remain in bed."

"For you, that's perhaps six hours, maybe seven at the outside. What's your take on Malone not arresting you?"

"That was never her intention. The ballistics is messed up. Sure my gun was discharged, but Paco wasn't shot with a Berretta from an offshore small craft. Hell, had she not brought the uniforms she would have had dinner with us. It took discipline for her to pass up an opportunity to pump Tiny."

"She would have obtained from him exactly nothing—same as we usually do. So why not wait until we were finished eating?"

"She's not that disciplined. Besides did you ever know a cop who could resist a bit of harassment? Soften me up kind of harassment. Get me to do what she wanted type of harassment."

"And exactly what is that?"

"Stop withholding information from her."

"If that's all she wanted then she won this round."

"Perhaps. But the only thing we gave her was our conversation with Hildigo—and the *SpaceX* connection."

"I don't see a *SpaceX* connection, Jimmy. I truly don't. It's not out of the ordinary to think they would hire the local marine biologist as a consultant."

"Before dawn meetings are always suspect in my mind. They just are."

"I'm thinking you weren't arrested because she doesn't want to tangle with our employer. Or maybe Contentus is protecting you. The more I think of it the more I'm putting my money on Contentus."

"Speaking of Homeland Security, where are they in all this? Tiny's been briefing us, but he's clearly off the reservation. It's been almost two months and we've not been assigned anything. We're not even working on the stolen art case with Viguet. It's as if..."

"As if we've been fired in place. Our paychecks are clearing," Angella reminded me.

"That's about all the contact we've had since...since I came back from Mexico with that money."

"They're pissed. What I can't figure is you solved their problem, yet it's as if..."

"As if HS, or perhaps the CIA, was behind the whole thing and somehow the money not going over caught them off guard. They can't really complain—and they can't really be happy. On another note how about setting something up with Dr. Mayfield for the morning. Let's get her take on the *SpaceX* involvement."

***

At precisely eight o'clock in the morning Tiny's gadget went off. I ignored it the first three times it beeped. But when the sound turned to that of a klaxon my choices became flush it down the toilet or bring the message up on the screen. I still required the big guy to run interference for me, so I hit the read button. TURN YOUR PHONE ON the screen read. NOW!

"You nuts turning your phone off?" Tiny barked when I hit the ACCEPT button on my cell. "Don't answer, I don't want to hear it. Both of you be outside in ten."

I relayed Tiny's message to Angella. "That's crazy! I can't be..."

"Not my decision. Do what you can and if you don't make it, I'll go alone."

"What's this about?"

"Beats me. No need to know I suppose."

"You know, Jimmy, I'm tired of being bounced from here to there and back again with no explanation and only half the facts. Actually, most of the time we don't even know half the facts, nor do we even know who we're working for. I'm thinking..."

"You thinking of getting out?" My question to Angella just slipped out. Obviously, the subject of leaving HS had been on my mind for a while, but at a subliminal level. Now it was on the table front and center.

"If I'm not I should be," Angella called from the bathroom where she was frantically doing what she needed to do to be ready to meet the world. To my eye Angella was always presentable and very much so. "And so should you, Jimmy. So should you."

"Let's stay focused." The problem with that statement is that we really weren't focused. "Almost ready?"

"Start down, I'll catch up," she called. That being her way of telling me to back off.

I checked my phone on the way down and realized sixteen minutes had passed since Tiny's ten-minute order. The hell with it, I was tired of dancing from lines tied to the end of a stick.

A low-slung car was idling at the curb and I bent down to see what adventure awaited. "Get in stranger," a female voice called. "Long time, no see."

The voice was familiar, but the identity eluded me. I could only make out one person in the car, but her face was in shadows.

"Your partner joining us? Or will it be just the two of us?"

"Be down in a moment." Even with the car door open I still didn't know who I was speaking with.

"You can wait in the car, Jimmy. I won't bite."

I have learned the hard way not to climb into cars with strangers. So until I knew for certain who this was, she was in the stranger category. I have also learned that when the bad guys want you in a car you have very few options other than to get in the car. One of those options involved shooting the people trying to kidnap you.

I looked around fully expecting a low-life with a weapon. But all I saw was Angella coming through the door and starting down the few steps to the sidewalk.

Sensing something wrong from the awkward way I was positioned, half standing, half-leaning forward into the car, she stopped and reached for her purse. Like mine, her eyes swept the area.

"You don't remember me, do you?" the driver called. "Washington Post. Abby Johnson. Now both of you get in. Time's not on my side. I'm on deadline."

Abby is Cindy McNaughton's sister-in-law and the Post's chief Homeland Security reporter. We've collaborated in the past and she's never once wavered in keeping me, her source, private. In fact, I may actually be alive today because of her stories on the front page of the Post. Something serious was going on for her to be down here. "Angella, meet Abigail Johnson. She's a reporter..."

"For the Post," Angella said completing my sentence. She bent down to look inside, her hand still inside her purse.

"You two know each other?" To my knowledge they had never met.

"Just from her articles. Pleased to meet you in person, Ms. Johnson."

"Abby. Now both of you get in. We have much to discuss and little time. Angella you better get in back, I don't think Jimmy will fit."

I didn't know how to take that remark, legs or belly, so I just folded the passenger seat forward and allowed Angella to climb in back. When her knees were almost touching her chin I had my answer.

Abby spoke about the weather, the Redskin's upcoming season, the National's past season and a whole host of other topics all in the category of time fillers. This was obviously a rental car but I appreciated Abby's natural cautiousness. That's what makes her good at what she does and is what keeps me alive.

We went south through the town and instead of turning right and proceeding over the causeway, Abby continued straight, stopped at the entrance of Isla Blanca Park, paid the admission fee, and proceeded south until the road forked.

She turned right and drove across the large sand lot toward the point. This is where we had met Hildigo and was as far south as one could go on South Padre Island. Boca Chica is across the ship channel and five miles down the beach is where *SpaceX* is making preparations for building their launch pads.

"Let's take a walk," she said, unfolding herself from behind the wheel and climbing out of the car. "I understand this is the best place to watch the dolphins."

"You'll have to go on out to the point, if you want to do that," I said.

But she had obviously known as much because Angella and I had to hurry to catch her as she made her way along the narrow small sandy beach and up onto rocks that kept the island from being eaten by the tides.

This woman, based in Washington, knew her way around this island as well as I did, perhaps even better. It wasn't a far leap from that thought to the realization that she spent a lot of time down here.

While I hadn't thought of it before, I suppose her being chief correspondent for Homeland Security made her presence on the country's southernmost border with Mexico a natural thing. This was especially true since our country's southernmost Coast

Guard Station stood less than a quarter mile away from where we now stood and HS maintained a facility less than a mile away across the bay. More was happening than meets the eye and certainly more than I was privy to.

Abby proceeded about a hundred feet along the rocks before she turned to us. "I love to come down here and watch the dolphins play as the tides change. Nobody out here other than a few fishermen from time to time."

"You come this way often?" I asked.

"Often enough it seems. With the border being what it is I should move my office down here." Her face turned serious, telegraphing that what she was about to say was of deep concern to her. "Jimmy, you've been a good source for me. Everything you've given has been right on and accurate. Sorry I can't say that about all my sources."

"I don't know if that's good or bad," I replied, not yet knowing where this conversation was going.

"I'll get right to the point. Jimmy, your life's in grave jeopardy. This *mission* you are on, to find the missing Booby is, to be blunt, a fool's errand. Do you know about the video?"

"Video?" I asked, trying to be non-committal.

"Let's not play games here. My job is to ferret out information from people who don't want me to have that information. I've been doing this my entire adult life and I know every, well most anyway, major player in the world on all sides. Trust me when I say I do my job better than they do theirs."

"Meaning?"

"Meaning, when I tell you your life's in danger then your life's in danger."

"And how do you know that?"

"My sources, of course, are private. But they are real and I'm afraid in this case my information is accurate. I've seen the video, Jimmy, of you supposedly shooting Paco. Want to comment?"

"Hell yes I want to comment! And on the record. That video has been doctored. I have not held an assault weapon in months, except perhaps at the range."

"That was my conclusion as well," Abby surprised me by saying. "But the point is, someone with access to technology, and with a good Rolodex, is setting you up. There's some chatter claiming the bank VP was shot with your official weapon. I'm not going with any of this, but others just might."

"So why exactly are we standing out here on these rocks in a location where it would be hard for the powers that be to eavesdrop? You could have given us that information out front of our condo. You talk about this assignment we're on, but do you know it was your sister-in-law, who..."

"Cindy's got herself in a jam. As I'm sure you know, she and Jamison are..."

"Lovers."

"For years, but possibly no more. Jamison, as you know is, actually was, the President's go-to man. Rumors are he screwed something up, but I can't confirm the actual facts. Nobody will talk, not even off the record. In my experience that means it's bad, whatever it is."

"What have you picked up?"

"He may have imparted troop level and ship deployment information to Cindy. Not anything you can't find on the Internet, but at the time it was classified. If he was still in the service he could be court marshaled. Now it's over at Justice, but I doubt if criminal charges will be brought."

"So how does that affect Angella and me?" The thought passed through my mind that if the mighty can fall this fast, it doesn't leave much hope for those of us at the bottom of the feeding chain.

"Actually, what I've told you so far is background, context as they say. What's important about Jamison and in turn Cindy, is that he's way over his head financially. At some point, possibly around two years ago, I don't know actually when, he began making very unwise investments."

"On a General's pension?"

"My assessment is that he wanted to keep up with Cindy, but for whatever the reason this man, who throughout his career has been rock solid, has become, well the word that comes to mind is reckless."

"How so?"

"Most of what he's invested in are military related startups, all of which, I believe have already gone under. Right now his only hope of salvaging anything lies in *SpaceX*. Everything he has left, and a hell of a lot more, is invested in that company. If *SpaceX* is delayed, even by a few months, they'll make a cash call which Jamison can't possibly meet. At that point his financial position in *SpaceX* will be wiped out and he'll be in deep trouble."

This is an area where I have some expertise from my days with the Texas Rangers. "But if Jamison doesn't make the cash call then he's not getting in any deeper. So what's the problem?"

"The money he already put in is secured by the equity he holds in the company, but when he misses the cash call his position goes away and he'll owe a little over fifty million dollars."

"Fifty Million? How the hell...Sounds like bankruptcy to me. Not the end of the world."

"Jimmy, do I have to spell it all out for you? He didn't borrow from the bank. A longtime acquaintance of his, a guy who owns some property down here, name of Philip DePierio, put him in touch with some money people. Long story short, bankruptcy protection is meaningless to drug cartel folks."

"So he'll be found floating in the Gulf is what you're saying."

"Let's get back to the video. My question to you, and be straight with me, did you have anything at all to do with Paco's death?"

"No."

"You being straight with me?"

"For what it's worth, Angella injected, "Jimmy had nothing to do with it. In fact, we were in Pittsburgh when it happened. We were due back, but we...we decided to spend the night."

"Actually, I believe you. So here's what I came to say. This is beyond top secret so if anyone, and I mean anyone, including your friend Tiny, gets a sniff that I told you, I'm done. Do you both understand?"

Here was a woman who spent her life protecting sources asking us if we would protect her. "I understand," I replied. "And will not reveal our source. But if you think Tiny won't know then I have a bridge..."

"I also," Angella broke in, her right hand going up as if she were swearing on a bible.

Abby watched a dolphin family frolicking in the bay, apparently without a care in the world. Without looking back at us, she said, "They ran the video clips for the President as a pretext to authorizing a hot operation."

"The target?"

"You."

"Who's they?"

"Sixty-four million dollar question. They, I believe, is Homeland Security. But understand something, Jimmy. With all the threats to the homeland, real or imagined, the military has been authorized to set up a Top Secret domestic counter-terrorism unit. Code name Liberty Bell."

"I'm a citizen! They can't..."

"They can—and they will. Make no mistake about that."

"I may be a lot of things, but I'm no terrorist. Even if I shot Paco, that's not terrorism."

"You're arguing to the messenger, my friend. Terrorism is in the eye of the executioner. They don't have to explain it to anyone. At least not while it remains a secret operation."

"Publish a story about it. Shine the light on what they're doing. Isn't that what the press does?"

"It's not always as straight forward as that. The story must be vetted by several editors, any one of whom can deep-six it. The Liberty Bell operatives, and I don't know who they are, need only get to one of them to kill the story."

"With your standing and experience..."

"You'd think. But until it's my paper I still have bosses."

"I thought they gave you freedom to print what you want," I snapped, my frustration showing.

"Yes—and no. If I can demonstrate that the story has no holes, that the sources are accurate—and corroborated—then it's hard for them to stop me. But, and here's the problem, this is all highly classified and I have it on background only. Congress doesn't even know about Liberty Bell. So until I get someone reliable on the record I can't publish."

"If Congress doesn't know, then how the hell's Liberty Bell being funded? Special Ops doesn't come cheap."

"Didn't your last operation teach you anything? Stolen art. Actually, anything of high value can be traded, bartered, pledged, sold. You name it, they're doing it. Lots of money changing hands. They hide a ton of shit under cover of darkness—and not all of it legal."

"I suppose that's why they didn't take the forty million when I tried to give it back. I thought DHS just didn't want to acknowledge the money. But it's worse than that. They wanted it funneled to Liberty Bell and couldn't do it on the books. So they...they..."

"They arranged the heist!" Angella exclaimed, putting HSthe pieces together one step ahead of me, "and managed to set it up with the Booby as well."

"I'll bet it worked the other way," I said. "Hugo set up the Booby heist and DHS got wind of it, took over. Paco, we know, works—worked—for the highest bidder. The money I brought back fell into their hands as a windfall. The forty million gave them instant money and allowed them to hide the Bird long term."

"Jimmy, how did you know to put the money in the *Marine* bank?" Abby wanted to know.

"Cindy instructed me," I answered truthfully. "What's their beef with me?"

"Can't be certain, but as far as I can determine they're not at all happy that you came home with that money. Frankly, if you had buried it you would have been better off."

"The mission was a success, what more do..."

"Possibly it wasn't designed to be a success as you define success. As you said a moment ago, maybe that money was destined for Liberty Bell all along. There are a lot of scenarios, most of them not to your liking."

"What about Tiny?"

"He's been trying to retire for years. They haven't allowed it to happen. I know he's helping you, but know this, he's doing so on his own time and on his own dime."

"Does he have access to files?"

"You'd have to ask him directly. But for what it's worth, more people owe Tiny favors than anyone knows. He calls them favors, but in reality it's really bad stuff he has on them. Stuff you go to jail for. A lifetime supply of...of favors. I doubt if the government could ever shut him down."

"Okay," I said, not fully processing what Abby had just said about Tiny. "Time table? I mean for the hit."

"Twenty-four hours at most. And the only other thing I can tell you with any degree of certainty is that the killing will be made to appear accidental."

"It's hard to believe one government agent would take out another. Humans don't eat humans." Even as I said it I knew better.

"They'll use a foreign service, or go freelance."

"You have a name on our side who's in charge of Liberty Bell?"

"Jimmy, I'll tell you what I think, but if either of you ever say I told you I'll shoot you myself—if you're not already good and dead. Got it?"

"Got it," I replied. At this point, Abigail Johnson of the Washington Post and sister-in-law of Retired Marine General Lucinda McNaughton, was not my main concern.

"Jamison," she said, turning her attention again to the dolphins.

"Maxwell Jamison?"

"You know any other Jamison?"

"I can't believe a man of his stature would…"

"You weren't listening. General Jamison is, as they say on the playground, in deep shit. He's been acting strange, that's documented. Maybe they promised to keep his financial backers at bay. From all I've pieced together, the orders are coming from Jamison."

"But he hasn't defaulted yet. *SpaceX* is on schedule."

"I thought we were leveling. You saw the bridge abutment pictures. This island is slipping. *SpaceX* is a straight up company and they're extremely concerned."

"Those pictures may have been doctored. Can't believe anything you see anymore."

"That might be so, and I hope it is. But, and I have this from an impeccable source, until the experts can all agree, *SpaceX* will, on its own, put a hold on building the launch site. They'll make the announcement within a few days. Except they won't provide a reason for the delay other than technical reasons. They'll kill the island by talking about tectonic plate shifts—and the causeway bridge coming down. That they don't want to do."

"Is Angella on their hot list as well?"

"She's not their concern at this point."

"Did I detect a but?"

"She's authorized collateral damage."

THIRTY-THREE

"You buying what Abby said?" Angella asked when we pulled into *Ted's* lot.

I was hoping the pecan pancakes would work their magic and cheer me up, but Angella's question flushed away any thought I had of enjoying my breakfast. "What's in it for her to make that up?"

"The only thing we added to what she already knew was the piece about Marshal Hugo trying to see Demont. I noticed you held back what Demont told us about coordinates always being used in the hide-seek Booby game."

"No need to give it all away. I'm sure she held back information from us as well. It's how the game is played I'm afraid."

"Anything particular you think she held back?"

"For starters, who's coming for me?"

"She most likely doesn't know that."

“If she knows who’s sending the shooter, then she has a good idea who the shooter will be.”

“You are giving her too much credit. She’s a good snoop, but she’s an even better guesser.”

“How will they do it? I mean shot, pushed off a bridge, car wreck, poison. What?”

“You forgot drone, Jimmy. Some agent sitting miles away using a joy stick, dropping one on your head when you’re out on the beach.”

“Paul Revere needs a third number,” I quipped. “Three if by air.”

“There was no air back then. Simpler times.”

“Jimmy!” the excited voice of Joy Malcom broke in. “Just the man I wanted to see. And you too, Angella.” She hurried over and hugged me, holding the squeeze so long that Angella at first rolled her eyes and then frowned. Joy finally pulled back. “Hey, maybe it’s you?”

“What’s me?” I asked, watching as her large smile turned grim.

“The person who shot my good friend Paco. I just don’t know what I’ll do without…Mind if I join you two?”

Before I could answer, she plopped into the seat between Angella and me and immediately leaned forward. “Before you came down here, Jimmy, we had no dead bodies on the beach. Then you show up and people start dying. I hate to say it but I’m starting to think you’re the serial killer yourself.”

“I’m not commenting on that Joy. You know better.”

“Actually, I don’t. Her eyes weren’t dancing as they do when she’s putting me on. “After what you did to my King’s Cup I don’t trust anything you say.”

"I'll say it again. I had nothing to do with the cup going missing."

"You know my lawyer told me not to talk to you. I got carried away." She pushed her chair back and quickly stood. "Tell it to the judge!" she shouted, loud enough for the kitchen help to hear. Then she was gone as quickly as she had arrived.

"Hope the day gets better than this," Angella said as Karen, the owner, approached the table.

"Can't get much worse," I responded, immediately knowing how false that statement was.

"Malcom must be off her meds. She's been in and out of here looking for you. Then when she finds you she huffs off. No accounting for woman of…of a certain age."

I ordered an extra waffle and in answer to Angella's raised brow I said, "Last meal syndrome. Dead man walking kind of thing."

Karen brought the coffee and sat in the seat vacated by Joy. "That woman can be a pain sometimes, but she's essentially harmless," she said in reference to Joy. "Hope your down mood isn't because of her."

"Her, and a whole lot of other folks," I said, not realizing I was wearing my emotions.

"He'll snap out of it as soon as he eats," Angella said, covering for me. "And if he doesn't, I'm leaving him here."

"I can use a dishwasher. Want a job?"

"May take you up on it, you never know."

"If you work hard maybe someday you'll make busboy. Hey, seriously, I'm sure you know about Paco."

"We've heard," I said, hoping not to get into a discussion of what happened.

"I know what the cops think of him, drug mule, all that. But I've known that kid since he was a baby and he's a good guy. Give you the shirt off his back. Guy never had a chance. Did what he had to do to make a living."

"Nobody forced him to deal in illegal deliveries, moving merchandise and people back and forth across the river."

"I beg to differ. You tell me what he could have done. And he's not alone you know. His mother was pregnant when she came to this country, nine months pregnant. She got across the river and the Border Patrol, seeing she was about to deliver, took her right back, put her on the stones over by Matamoras and held her down until she delivered. Then they brought mother and child back across the river to the hospital in Brownsville. The mother walked out of the hospital a week later taking Paco with her."

"At least they got good medical treatment," I said, knowing where this was leading and not wishing to get into a discussion with Karen over the issue.

"Paco was educated in Mercedes where the authorities didn't care if he was a citizen or not. The only work he could get, legal work, when he graduated paid about half the minimum wage. You blame him for running drugs and stuff? I certainly don't." Karen stood. "Sorry to bother you. Your pecan pancakes will be out in a few minutes. Hope they work for you."

"Puts a different perspective on it, doesn't it?" Angella said, knowing how strongly I feel about people doing illegal activities. "I don't condone running drugs, don't get me wrong, but we need to help the folks who were brought here, they have no country to call their own."

Thankfully our breakfasts arrived before I got into it with Angella.

Angella's cell buzzed a few minutes later. "Mayfield just responded. She's on the island and said she can meet us in twenty minutes."

I checked my watch, noted that it was past ten, and said, "Tell her to meet us at the book store, *Paragraphs on Padre*. At this time of the morning we should have the place to ourselves, unless there's a book club or something going on. We'll chance it."

"Ten-thirty at *Paragraphs*," Angella announced.

"Something Karen said about Paco got me thinking," I said, downing a waffle slice with coffee. "We need the investigation notes, including pictures."

"It came in last night. I moved it off your phone into our file and encrypted it. Actually I double encrypted it while you were talking with Karen. If the agency is after us the less they know about what we're doing the better. What was it Karen said that..."

"Shirt off your back. She said he'd give you the shirt off his back."

"Not following."

"The video Tiny showed us last night. Remember how he was dressed?"

Angella thought before she answered, "Something, a colored shirt or jacket or something."

"What color?"

"Actually, if I recall right, several colors. Blue, red, maybe some yellow, can't be certain. Why?"

"We've seen many pictures of him, taken over many years. Always wearing dark T's, sometimes a sweatshirt, but always grey or black. But mostly grey. So why the bright colors?"

"What are you thinking?"

"Just why the bright colors?"

THIRTY-FOUR

Paragraphs On Padre is a delightful bookstore, owned by Joni and run by her and her giant of a husband, Griff, who stands in for Santa when the old man gets delayed at the North Pole. Children and dogs love him.

"Welcome to Paragraphs," Griff sang out when Angella and I stepped through the door. His friendly greeting took the edge off my deep-seated agitation. "You have someone waiting for you. She's over by the local author books."

I walked in the direction Griff had pointed looking for the woman we had seen coming out of the Coastal Studies Lab down at Isla Blanca. Instead, walking toward me was a woman I recognized, albeit from a different setting.

"How are you doing, Jimmy?" she said, extending her hand."

"Lawyer, Maria Reyez Cruz," I said, not understanding why Joy Malcom's lawyer would be hanging around a bookstore apparently waiting for us. "We just saw your client a few minutes ago." Knowing how lawyers bristle when the opposing side talks with their clients outside their presence, I added, "She initiated the conversation, not..."

Ignoring my comment, she said, "Angella, I'm glad you're here as well." Cruz reached out to shake Angella's hand as well. "I think I owe you a big thank you for sending Joy to me."

"You're welcome. You're good at what you do." Angella paused, then said, "If I'm not mistaken, you're Officer Cruz's sister, are you not?"

"Indeed. He's my baby brother. You know him?"

"Worked with him for a while when I was on the force," Angella replied. "In another life it seems."

I glanced around looking for Mollie Mayfield. Not seeing her, and not putting two and two together, I turned to Angella. "Get Mayfield on the line, see if she's still coming."

"I'm your person," Cruz said.

"You?" I exclaimed. "Mayfield agreed to meet..."

"She's not coming. I'm your point of contact. What you see is what you get."

"Are you saying you represent her?" I asked, still working to orient myself. I wasn't doing a particularly good job of it.

"You can't be surprised to learn lawyers have more than one client, Mr. Redstone. Now if you want to talk, talk. If not, I have things to do."

Pointing to the chairs in the center of the store, I said, "Let's sit."

When the three of us were settled, Griff called, "We have complimentary coffee, but sorry no donuts."

I waved my hand in dismissal, but Cruz took him up on his coffee offer. When she was gone, Angella said, "What's a criminal lawyer doing representing *SpaceX*?"

"We're about to find out."

Cruz returned, set her coffee cup on the table and took her seat. "Fire away," she said. Adding, "In your line of work that is perhaps an unfortunate statement. Tell me what you wanted from Dr. Mayfield."

"You can start by telling us why Dr. Mayfield believes she requires a criminal attorney."

"As you well know, my office does more than criminal work. Aren't I representing Ms. Malcom against you for damages relating to the misappropriation of the King's Cup?"

"Nothing's been filed, so I know nothing of the sort."

"Patience, Mr. Redstone, patience. All in due course. But please understand my firm is full service."

"Sitting here today, who are you representing?"

"Ms. Mayfield, of course."

"What's a geophysicist need with a lawyer?"

"What does anyone need with a lawyer?"

I stood. "You want to play games, play games. You're right, I have no patience for this bull..."

"Sit down, Mr. Redstone. Perhaps if you asked me the questions you would have asked Dr. Mayfield you'd get the answers you are looking for."

Angella had remained sitting, her signal for me to do likewise. I sat down. "What's Dr. Mayfield's relationship with the UT Lab?"

"As you probably know, Dr. Mayfield is employed by *SpaceX*. And as you know *SpaceX* now holds a permit to build a launch pad over on Brazos beach. When the pad is finished they plan to launch rockets therefrom. It is *SpaceX* who has hired the lab."

"Can we then assume you represent *SpaceX?"*

"I don't make it a rule to divulge who my firm represents, but that would be a good assumption on your part."

"So I ask again, what was Dr. Mayfield doing at the lab?"

"Specifically, I don't know. But..." Cruz retrieved her cell phone from her bag, fumbled with the screen, cycled through several images, then continued, "Here it is. She turned the screen to face us. Recognize this?"

It was the bridge abutment, but without the shift lines. "I do," I acknowledged.

She then found another image on her cell and again turned it toward us. "And what about this?"

Now the image had the lines and it matched almost exactly the images from the diver Smith's camera, the one I retrieved with the help of Coast Guard Petty Officer Telson. "I've seen that one before as well."

"You give away nothing, do you?" she said.

"And neither do you, Ms. Cruz."

"I take that as a compliment coming from you. Here's what you want to know. *SpaceX,* by way of Dr. Mayfield and that second image, has been put on notice that there is a possible tectonic plate shift going on in this region. If such is the case it would be devastating to a space launch pad. However, after investigation, it is the company's belief that the photos purporting to show the shift have been altered."

"Can't you just send a diver down, take some pictures and determine what's going on?"

"You would think. But we've—our client—has done that now on several occasions. But...but everyone down here has an angle, an interest. For every diver who comes up with the bridge abutment intact there's a diver who comes up showing the rift. Each claims the other diver doctored the images."

"Hey, a fact should be a fact," I said, not understanding how multiple people could doctor images before they came to the surface.

"Think of the world-wide climate change debate. Folks can't even agree on the temperature at the North Pole twenty years ago. Show one side records and immediately they claim the records have been altered. So no, Mr. Redstone, facts are not always facts. Not where big money is concerned."

"Surely, Mayfield has an opinion," I said trying to move forward. "A highly educated guess if nothing else. That's why *SpaceX* is paying her—and the Lab—for definite answers."

"Dr. Mayfield can not say one way or the other with any degree of certainty. Her off the record statement is that there is no plate movement. She's found no other evidence of any movement. That guy, what's his name, Hildigo Francese? An odd one he is. He claims he's seen some evidence of marine life changes but he's not certain if they are due to plate movement or human pollution."

"What's your take?" Angella asked.

"I'm a fire-follows-smoke gal at heart, so I say something is not right down there. If you forced me to bet, I'd bet on the earth shifting. It's always shifting. But, hey, what do I know?"

"Surely your client can go down, watch them work, see for herself and know for certain."

Cruz leaned forward and when she spoke her voice was barely above a whisper. All three of our heads were almost touching when she said, "Several organizations, including Homeland Security, the Coast Guard, as well as the City of SPI, have major vested interests. Since you were down there, the site's been closed. Twenty-four seven guard, the full deal." She sat back, looked around to be certain no one was listening, then added, "As I said, where there's smoke."

"Understood. *SpaceX* have a plan?"

"No choice but to delay the project."

"And just how will that resolve the issue if everything is suspect and you can't get down there in a secure manner?"

She again leaned forward. "They're giving themselves six months. Understand they only require one dive—if that dive can be trusted. They've lined up the world's best underwater team and they'll go down at the first opportunity."

"If it's monitored twenty-four seven how will they ever get down there?"

"Patience is the key. Something is bound to happen to distract everyone. Our team will be ready to go at a moment's notice."

"I hope your client is not planning a major distraction?"

"Heavens no. But down here things do happen."

"What type of things?"

"For one, hurricanes."

"They're more than six months off."

"So we'll wait. But something might happen long before that."

"I'm hearing your client is planning something."

"You, sir, are hearing wrong."

"When will they be ready to go?"

"Oh, the team is here now. The instant the authorities are distracted, the instant that guard is removed, that's when they'll go down and take their pictures. Then we'll know for certain the future of this island."

"What excuse, I mean to the public, will you give when construction stops?" Angella asked.

"It's actually stopped now. Technical difficulties."

"What will you say when you resume construction?"

"Technical difficulties resolved."

Angella then leaned forward, her voice now lowered, "If you don't ever resume then that means..."

"Nothing at all. *SpaceX* will not put itself in the position of being the town crier. One way or another construction will resume. If it's a go then the real launch pad will be built. If the plates are indeed shifting, then the construction will look real, but will be superficial. To the world it will look the same, but trust me it will be nothing but a glorified erector set."

THIRTY-FIVE

Cruz left the bookstore and when she did Griff came over. "I didn't want to interrupt, but a guy named Telson came in first thing this morning, about five-ten minutes before you got here, and asked if I knew where the DHS guy lived. I didn't give out that information, but I did tell him I'd pass along the message. Guy seemed agitated. Here's his name and phone number."

"Thanks Griff," I said, handing the slip of paper to Angella. "By the way, I need a copy of that book I was looking through the other day. The one written by the four authors, the one about..."

"The Golden Booby. Yeh, *Paragraphs.* Right over there." He pointed toward a stack of black covered books. "That book has become a best seller this week."

By the time I paid for the book, Angella had Telson on the phone. He wanted to speak with us right away. He was scheduled for offshore duty in an hour and wouldn't be back to the island for several days. "Tell him to come on over."

"He'll be here in five," Angella called. "Griff, do you know anything about him?"

"Nothing much, except he enjoys island history. He's working his way through Steve Hathcock's history books. Oh, and he was asking about the Singer legend."

"You mean the one where old man Singer buried a lot of his money."

"The ranch's about twenty-some miles north of here. From all accounts, the money may actually still be there, except no one can find the ranch. You want to know more, Steve's the man who can tell you."

"Hi, Rod," I called, when Petty Officer Telson opened the door. He appeared nervous and sat down immediately in a high-backed chair, his back to the door. "Coffee?" I asked.

"Love to, but I don't have the time. Got to get back to my condo and change. I start a ten day duty tour in fifty minutes."

Angella returned to our seats and said, "Well, Petty Officer Telson…"

"Please call me Rod," he replied.

"Okay, Rod. My name's Angella and I'm Jimmy's partner."

"You're the woman who called a few minutes ago."

"Correct. Now what is it you wanted to tell us?"

Telson turned to face me. "The night we dove you told me you were working on the bank robbery, stolen art as well as money."

"That's right," I said. "Go on."

"This may not be worth much but I know in an investigation ever little bit helps."

"Better to put it on the table than not," Angella coaxed.

"Please don't tell anyone where you got this. "I didn't tell Captain Boyle everything and he can be...unforgiving."

"Believe me," Angella said, "Whatever you tell us remains with us."

"Well, here goes. As you know. Smithy and I were condo mates. Our place is almost across the street, up the block a bit. Place called *Beach House Vacation Rentals*. Anyway, when Smithy came back from his dive under the bridge he said he had taken some pretty good pictures."

"He tell you what the pictures were of?"

"He said he saw something unusual and showed them to me. I didn't know what I was looking at, but he said it looked to him like the bridge base, the abutment and pilings holding the bridge up, was separating. He actually said shifting. The abutment was shifting."

"After he told you what he thought, did you agree?" Angella asked.

"I still couldn't tell. Maybe. He said something about plate movement and rumors he had heard. I'm not into that kind of stuff so I frankly wasn't paying that much attention. Sorry."

"That's okay," Angella said, coaxing him on.

"Well, he was always out diving on old wrecks, always looking for treasure, Spanish reales, that type of thing. He was obsessed with getting rich from old treasure."

"Did he ever find anything?"

"Every now and then he'd go on up to the old Singer ranch and come back with a few coins. Not much, mind you, but a few things."

"Did he find them on land or underwater?" I asked.

"Both, I think. Smithy was closed mouth about locations, said that was all he ever had to sell. So he never told anyone where he got anything."

"Let's focus on the camera pictures," I said. "What more can you tell us?"

"He said he was friends with a guy who would pay him big time to keep those pictures from going public. Big time was the words he used. I gathered this was going to be his ticket to becoming a full time treasure hunter."

"So Smith knew the pictures were valuable and was going to sell them to a friend."

"He thought so, yes." Telson stood. "Sorry I can't stay any longer. I barely have time to change and grab my bag."

"One last question before you bolt," I said. "Who was the friend? Know his name, address?"

"Guy by the name of Philip. Last name, DePierio. Lives at the Riveira Hotel. I think he owns it or something. He and Smithy went diving a lot together. According to Smithy the guy knew what he was doing underwater. Gotto go, sorry." Telson then ran to the door and raced to his mostly rusted blue truck. He turned left onto Padre Boulevard and accelerated north. His condo was less than a block away, but every second was precious—especially where Captain Boyle was concerned.

***

I said goodbye to Griff and followed Angella out to the car. She was about to open the driver side door when I yelled, "Angella, stop! Quick, come around over here!"

Two men were closing in on us. They had been standing by the curb on either side of the driveway and began moving forward when I came out of the store.

Angella ran around the car and joined me on the side furthest from the men. Their hands were in front of them and swinging naturally at their sides as they moved. They were either highly trained or totally harmless.

I was betting on highly trained. As they moved closer I nudged Angella toward the front of the car, keeping as much heavy metal between them and us as possible. I had picked out a target on each of them and was ready to draw the instant either of them made a false movement. A sneeze would have done it.

I was certain my partner was doing the same. It was a comfort to know the firefight would be equal, maybe even tilted in our favor because Angella held the highest small arms rating in the Valley. She was deadly at fifty feet and these two were well within that range, twenty feet at most.

The first of the two started up the steps leading to the front door. Then the second one followed. That put them on higher ground, but we still had the car as a shield.

The first guy paused at the door and every instinct said he was going to pivot on his right foot and draw.

But I was wrong. He reached for the door handle, pushed the door inward and proceeded into *Paragraphs*. The second man followed in his footsteps.

The door closed behind them.

I checked to see that they were not still in the doorway waiting for our guard to come down.

They weren't.

We were now both on the passenger's side with the car between the store and us. "Angella, get in back on this side. I'll drive."

"My take, Jimmy," Angella replied, rolling her eyes, "is you're overreacting."

"Those two are professional all the way."

"How do you know? They didn't do anything."

"They did more than you think. They maintained their spacing perfectly and their eyes never met mine, even though they saw every move we made. Two people slinking around a car should have triggered something in them, but it didn't."

"Paranoia?"

"Training. Those two are Special Warfare Command Officers and this wasn't their first mission. I know because I was trained the same way."

"So why didn't they take us, or you, out?"

"Not clean enough. This was a trial run to size us up."

"How did we do?"

"The next time we won't see them coming."

THIRTY-SIX

"I'm living on borrowed time," I said to Angella while I hovered over her watching her make tuna sandwiches for lunch. "There's not a person we can turn to for help."

"That's not exactly correct, Jimmy. And you know it."

"Who do you suggest?"

"Tiny for starters. Your old boss Contentus for another. And hey, what about Levi? You managed to get him out of Mexico. He owes you one."

"Tiny is as disconnected as we are."

"Nobody's as disconnected as we are. You heard what Abby said about everybody owing Tiny. He's on the island for a reason. Use him."

"I can't do that. I can't use..."

"That came out wrong," Angella said. "I just meant, he's here to help, let him help. Who knows his motive? Maybe he feels he messed up with us somehow. Maybe..."

"Maybe he's after that cursed Booby as well. Everyone's following the money."

"Who cares? If he keeps you alive, that's all you should care about. Motive is his problem, not yours."

"I'll call Levi. I forgot about him." It felt to me as if I was rounding up a posse—perhaps a posse of one.

Levi answered on the first ring.

"I was thinking," I began after the normal small talk, "about DePierio and what you said about him."

"What's your question?"

"Why is the U. S. protecting him?"

The line went silent long enough for me to ask, "You still there?"

"I'm here, my friend. I'm here. Okay, I owe it to you. For starters, your government is using him for special ops. Be advised he's one of the best in the world."

"Why him?"

"He's a man, as you say, without a country. He's wanted everywhere, including Israel. Unfortunately, in today's world trained hot operators are not hard to find. But Abrams is special. He's clean. The target disappears without a trace. Your government uses him for inside jobs only. That's my understanding anyway."

"By inside you mean for executions in the homeland?"

"More narrow than that. U. S. citizens. He's part of a super secret outfit called Liberty Bell."

"If it's so secret how the hell do you know about it?"

"I know everything there is to know about DePierio—Abrams."

"You said, for starters. What else you have on him?"

"I told you he's protected. I'm leaning toward his protection being localized."

"You mean by an individual or individuals and not by the government."

"Precisely."

"Name?"

"I'm thinking Jamison." Now the silence on the line did mean he was gone.

Thirty seconds later the device in my pocket, Tiny's communicator, buzzed. I hate to admit it, but I jumped the proverbial mile. Actually I banged my knee on the counter as I came out of my chair.

ROOM 17P ISLA GRAND IN 60 ALONE

"You're not going anywhere alone, Jimmy," Angella said. "You're just not. I don't care who sent the message or why. Stop fussing and eat."

"You're not..."

"This is one time you're not telling me what I'm doing or not doing! Just eat fast. I want to stop in and see Malone on the way."

"I assume you found something of interest in the Paco file."

She turned her iPad around so I could see the screen. "Note the trajectory of the bullet that killed him. From left to right."

"He was walking south. That means..."

"That means the videos themselves actually prove you didn't shoot him. If you had, the bullet would have entered from his right."

"I thought we had already proven the videos were doctored. I mean with the time stamps, the wrong weapon, everything. Whoever is trying to frame me is an amateur."

"Whoever it is they have access to official files. I'm not thinking amateur as much as in a hurry, sloppy."

"This why we're going to see Malone? She's already worked that out."

"That and a few other things."

"What things?"

"No time now, we'll discuss it on the way. But they pertain to the Smith murder, not Paco."

On the way took less than three minutes, so we didn't have time to discuss anything. I was surprised when Angella asked Malone about the warrant on DePierio's penthouse apartment. She wanted to know who issued it. Apparently, the judge's name was not in the Smith file.

"We don't usually put the judge's name in the file," Malone answered, a frown on her face. "Why is that important?"

"A source told us DePierio's being protected by the government."

The frown went deeper and Malone stood, walked to the door, started to open it, then suddenly turned and sat back down in her chair. "That explains it! We got the warrant from a county criminal judge in Brownsville whom we normally use. Our officers hadn't been in the apartment ten minutes when I was informed the warrant had been cancelled."

"Who cancelled it?"

"Who's your source?"

"Must we?"

"You must."

"Guy by the name of Levi ben Yuval. Mossad."

"Mossad?"

"DePierio's wanted by Israel."

"Okay, the call came from the judge who had signed it. He refused to offer any explanation why he had a change of heart. He did say, however, that anything we already had in our possession we could keep and use. That told me he was pissed at somebody and it wasn't us."

"You have anything?"

"Diving tank. We wanted his computer, but hadn't gotten to it yet."

"Diving tank?"

"We took what we could get, is all I'll say on that subject."

"So what were you hoping to find on his computer?"

"Images. We have reason to think the diver Smith showed him pictures indicating the bridge structure moving. Perhaps to blackmail him. There are pictures on Smith's camera, the one you withheld from us by the way, that seem to show the bridge coming apart. Our preliminary expert report is troubling."

"In what way?"

"One expert says the pictures were touched up to show tectonic plate movement. Another expert says the pictures have not been doctored. The third one insists it is impossible to determine because he's seen highly skilled hackers modify documents and photos so well it's impossible to know the difference."

"I thought all that meta…meta whatever…gave you all the information," I commented.

"Apparently, metadata itself, including GPS coordinates can be doctored," Malone explained. "I'm told that usually the pixel count between the original and the added material doesn't match, but someone good can even get that right. What we do know for certain is that the pixel count, the GPS data and the light intensity are all seamless."

"So the probability is that the images on Smith's camera have not been modified."

"It would appear that way, but it's not conclusive."

"By simply looking at the images DePierio wouldn't have had any way to know the difference," I said, "so he would have had to assume the island is shifting. If it's shifting then he'll not be able to sell the hotel and..."

"And that makes him our prime suspect in the Smith homicide."

"Have you issued an arrest warrant for him?"

"Can't."

"Why not?" Angella asked.

"Judge says there's not enough evidence."

"Same judge as before?"

"Same one," Malone confessed, adding, "Makes no difference at this point anyway."

"And why not?" I asked, fearing that I knew the answer.

Malone's face was again in a deep frown, a frown of resignation, of disappointment. "Feds have blocked the warrant."

"And what reason have they given?" Angella asked.

"Refuse to comment is their reason."

On our way out she called, "For what it's worth, whoever doctored the video of you shooting Paco most likely is the same who did the photos."

I turned back to face her. "And you know that how?"

"Can't be many people that good. Not down here anyway."

THIRTY-SEVEN

"What are you doing here?" the subdued male voice asked as the door opened. General Maxwell Jamison was smaller in person than he had appeared to be on the monitors where I had seen him in the past. His perfect posture had given way to a slight hunch and his eyes were hooded. "You're early. The reception is not for an hour."

Tiny is never wrong, but this time he got this screwed up. "I thought…I'm sorry to have disturbed you. I'll just go now and…"

"Oh, if it's not Jimmy Redstone," Cindy McNaughton called from somewhere behind Jamison. "Do come on in. And you too, Angella. You're looking good. Keeping fit, I see."

"Oh, Redstone!" Jamison said, "For a moment I did not recognize you. Yes, do come in. You're late."

"Two minutes," I replied, "but who's counting?"

"I am," Jamison replied. "And I'm not pleased. Who is this?" He pointed at Angella. "Is she a recruit? I didn't know the Coast Guard had girl recruits."

"This is my partner, Angella Martinez. Angella meet..."

Jamison straightened up as if he had snapped to attention. "Of course I know who the hell she is, Redstone. Of course I know. Seen her before. You know, back in the day you'd be doing two hundred pushups, a hundred for each minute you were late. Make that three hundred for not coming alone."

I wanted to inform this aging warrior that this wasn't *the day*, he wasn't a general anymore and I couldn't do ten pushups—well, perhaps ten, but certainly not three hundred—no matter how loud he barked. I held my tongue because Abby had said he might be tapped to head up Liberty Bell and I didn't want to make matters worse than they already were. "Sorry, sir," I replied, not fully understanding what I was apologizing for.

"Help yourself to brunch, Cowboy. And you as well Angella. Max is hosting a reception for the Coast Guard in a little while and we have more food than even they can eat." McNaughton pointed to the far corner of the suite where two large tables were loaded with every imaginable food a hotel could conger up.

"You always overdo the food, my dear. It's expensive and I don't..."

"You asked Jimmy to come up to see you," McNaughton answered, her voice sweet, almost as if she was speaking to a child. "Tell him what you want. You don't have much time."

Showing support for Cindy, I walked over and circled the tables, helping myself to smoked salmon and two hard-boiled eggs.

Not a combination I had ever thought of before, but with a sliced bagel and cream cheese, it filled the plate.

Angella followed my lead and filled her plate with egg salad garnished with tomatoes, a few capers sprinkled around for color contrast. I smiled at the pimento-stuffed olives knowing how much she disliked them.

Last meals were a wonderful invention, and I was taking full advantage.

When we were seated, our plates balanced on our laps, Cindy said, "Cowboy, we saw the video of you shooting that man Paco. The first thing that came to mind was whether or not you got the coordinates from him before you killed him. Tell us you did."

"Coordinates?"

"Don't play stupid Cowboy! Paco hid the Golden Booby somewhere on this island and was delivering the coordinates when you shot him."

"First off, I didn't shoot him. Second, assuming he did hide the Bird somewhere on this island, neither I nor Angella have found any coordinates."

McNaughton stood, "If you will please excuse me, I have a matter I must attend to. Max will fill me in on the remainder of the conversation. It was nice seeing you, Angella. But I must say I'm disappointed in you Cowboy for not delivering the Booby." She immediately turned and walked back toward the bedroom.

"You disobey her at your own peril. Do you understand me?" barked Jamison who was sitting in an overstuffed armchair.

"I do."

"Sir!"

"I do, sir!" I dutifully added, toying with the idea of standing and saluting. Angella's glance settled it. I closed my mouth.

"Good. See to it you step up your performance."

"Yes, sir."

We sat in awkward silence for some time, when Jamison finally said, "I don't recall why I asked…Oh, I remember now. I am told by a reliable source that Padre Island might be moving out to sea. I believe you are well aware of that fact. Is that so?"

"I have seen pictures that seem to suggest the island is shifting. But they…"

"There's a question of doctoring. I know all that. What you will do is dive down, with my camera. The camera over there," he said, pointing to a small desk in the corner. "You are to take that camera and dive down and take pictures. You are to bring that camera directly to me without even looking at the pictures. Is that understood?"

"Yes, sir."

"The camera has an underwater strobe built in so you don't require anything other than diving gear. You should also know that the…the…trigger…is sensitive to your fingerprints. No one other than you can take those pictures. The diving shops are being watched, so when you get back to your condo you will find everything you require awaiting you."

"When is this dive to take place?" According to Abby the bridge abutments were also being watched. Did Jamison know that as well?

"Tonight at exactly twenty-two hundred hours the Coast Guard will be pulled away from the bridge. They, as well as DHS will be gone at least an hour. You are to go down at precisely twenty-two-ten hours and you are to be on shore not later than twenty-two-fifty hours. You are then to be standing in the turn-around at the base of the causeway at twenty-three hundred hours." He again consulted his note card. "A silver Buick will come from the direction of Port Isabel, turn through the turn-around. You are to hand the camera to the person in the back seat. You are not to follow that car. Do you understand?"

"Understood, sir."

Jamison then turned to Angella. I asked Redstone to come alone because I did not want anyone but him to know about the pictures. But since he brought you, I..."

"He didn't bring me, I insisted on..."

"Not important! You are to remain in your condo from the time Redstone leaves until he arrives back. Do you understand?"

"I understand."

"Will you do as I say?"

Angella hesitated for an instant before saying, "I will remain in my condo."

The hesitation was not lost on Jamison, but all he said was, "Take that camera and go. And, Redstone, get it right this time!"

THIRTY-EIGHT

"For people with money trouble they sure live well," Angella said in the elevator. "That food spread alone must have been well over a thousand dollars. I've seen Sunday brunches for a hotel full of people with fewer choices."

"I'm putting the cost at two grand minimum."

"According to Mommy Longlegs, they are hosting some kind of a reception. Maybe the Coast Guard is paying."

"Let's hang and see what we get," I suggested.

Angella and I separated. She positioned herself in the bookstore where she could see the elevator. I did the classical newspaper thing, sprawling in the only leather chair in the lobby, relying on a magazine to provide a modicum of cover.

Sitting in the lobby brought back memories of my early days in police work and I can't say that many of them were pleasant. In fact, I don't recall any that were.

But one thing I learned was that I had to already know the folks that were going up to visit the generals in order for this surveillance to be effective. Or, I had to tape everyone and sort it out later. Which is exactly what I did. These days taping was easy. Turn on my cell and let it run as long as the battery held out, or my patience ran out, which ever came first.

We were rewarded for our effort. Exactly a half-hour after I sat down, Phillip DePierio, AKA Moshe Abrams, formerly of Mossad, walked by. Someone as highly trained as he was should have spotted me, but if he had he was professional enough not to let on.

Of course it was also possible that he was visiting someone on a different floor. My angle made it impossible to see the floor lights.

Not ten minutes after DePierio made his exit, men in the uniform of the Coast Guard began to cross to the elevator. This was the reception McNaughton had spoken of.

I reviewed the video and counted eight in all with the possibility of another two not in uniform. I called it ten.

An hour later they were still up there and nothing of interest had happened in the interim. Angella walked by and disappeared through the front door moving in the direction of our car.

"What do you make of the Coast Guard?" I asked Angella when we were in the car.

"Most of them were young. Very young. I'm thinking new recruits, maybe new folks assigned to the station."

"I didn't see my friend Boyle, did you?"

"Matter of fact, no," Angella answered. "But I did see Telson. Took me a while to place the face. Didn't he tell us he was going off-shore for what I understood to be a multi-day tour?"

"I didn't see Telson," I admitted, pulling my cell phone out and fast-forwarding through the video. "You're right about him being off-shore. I suppose plans can always change."

"It was after the uniformed folks all went up. There were a couple of guys in jeans. Then Telson about five minutes later, but I don't think he went up in the elevator. I think he went back toward the eating area."

I slowed the replay, found the guys I had identified as out of uniform Coast Guardsmen, and then continued to watch.

"There," Angella said. "Stop. Go back a bit."

Sure enough, Petty Officer Telson could clearly be seen, only he wasn't getting in the elevator, he was coming out. "Telson's coming out of the elevator," I said. "But I never saw him go up." I watched a few more seconds and then said, "You're right. He's heading back toward the breakfast room. Maybe that's why I hadn't noticed him."

"Why would he be eating breakfast if they had brunch upstairs?" Angella asked.

"He wasn't part of the reception. Did you happen to note if there's a back way out of the hotel? I didn't see DePierio leave."

"There's always a back way out of a hotel."

"I'm going back in to see what's up. The two could be meeting or maybe there's someone else."

"I'll go with..."

"Stay here. It's hard to get in trouble in a public place. Call Malone and tell her we need to talk ASAP."

"About what?"

"About the threat on my life."

"Malone? You sure?"

"Everyone can't be in on whatever's going down. If she's on their side then there's no chance for us."

"What about Miller Contentus?"

"Keeping him as a last resort."

"You're there, Jimmy. You're already there."

***

I made my way across the lobby and noted that some other guy was sitting in the leather chair ostensibly reading a magazine. Now we had a watcher watching the watcher.

I hurried to the breakfast room only to find it empty. A door to the outside at the end of a short hallway was swinging closed. I ran in that direction.

"Hey, you! Stop."

The voice came from behind me and I glanced back to find a big guy, a guy at least fifty pounds over weight, running after me. He carried no weapon, at least nothing that I could see.

"I said, stop!"

The door snapped closed just as I arrived and I had to stop to push the switch on the wall to release the latch. The big guy was less than five feet behind me when the door finally opened and I ran, actually tripped over a broken paving stone, out onto the pavement.

I saw nothing moving. Anyone coming through the door would have had to be pretty fast to have made it around the nearest building corner. The vegetation was too sparse to hide anything larger than a cat. That argued for someone hiding behind, or under, a car. I turned my attention to the parking lot.

I bent down to see if I could see anything and as I did, a meaty hand grabbed my left shoulder and spun me around.

I was facing the over-weight guard.

"I told you to stop!" he said, as if by saying that I would immediate acknowledge I should have stopped.

"Who the hell are you? And get your fat hand off me before I deck you."

"Hotel security," he announced, reaching his hand under his jacket as if to draw a gun.

Ranger training kicked in without a further thought, just as the government had spent a lot of money teaching me to do. I repositioned my legs, bending at the knees for stability, and with my left hand just above his elbow and my right on his shoulder, I flipped him forward. For added measure, I threw out my leg. His body performed exactly as the physics of the situation dictated, ending face-up on the grass.

"What the hell?" he said, shaky his head to see if it still worked. "You had no call…"

"You're lucky I didn't put a bullet through your head, you punk. Now get your sorry butt up and get lost before something bad happens to you."

The guy slowly stood, looked at me as if memorizing my face. He then took a step back. "I want your name."

"Get the hell out of here before you get hurt!"

"Jimmy," Angella called, "you okay?" She was ten yards away and had her weapon pointing at the so-called security guy. "Federal agent!" she barked. Don't get any closer!"

"I'm fine," I said, turning to the big guy who was now rubbing the shoulder he had landed on. "Get moving!"

Without a further word he turned and headed back toward the hotel.

"Angella, did you see anyone running or coming from this direction?"

"No. Should I have?"

"Don't know."

I told her what I had seen and she responded by telling me what I already knew. There were just too many places for someone to hide, especially when you don't even know who you're looking for.

"What about Malone?" I asked a few minutes later as we walked toward the car.

"Not available until two. But I did set up lunch with that author Hathcock. We're meeting him over at *Coconuts*. According to him they have great sliders—and he says the price is right."

"When?"

"Now. Unless you have something else you'd like to do."

"Did you tell him we wanted to discuss the Singer legend?"

"He said we came to the right guy. He's writing, or about to write, a book on old man Singer and his brother Isaac."

"The sewing machine Singer?"

"One in the same. This should be fun because when I was growing up my brothers always talked about going up island and finding treasure. Spanish reales they called them, the same thing Smith was diving offshore for. Pure silver."

"You think if we gave the generals a map leading to the treasure they'd get off our case?"

"And just where would you get such a map?"

"Draw it like everybody else down here seems to do."

THIRTY-NINE

Hathcock was waiting for us when we walked into the small, mostly open-air bar that doubles as a delightful low-key place to have a light meal. Steve is full-bearded and has the appearance of having just come back from a safari; perhaps he had.

"Please pardon me if I don't stand to greet you," he said when we approached his table in the far back corner, "but I did something to my ankle. I think it happened up the beach a ways when I…I slipped coming down off a dune."

"Where was that?" I asked. "How far up there were you?"

Steve's playful eyes went dark for an instant. Recovering, he said, "I was treasure hunting with…with a client. You know I rent metal detecting equipment and I was out with them."

My initial question was more in the way of being friendly than to gain information, but Steve's manner told me he was hiding something. "Mind telling us how far up island you were?"

"Oh, I'd say between three and eight miles."

"That's a wide range."

"I thought you were here to talk about the old Singer Ranch, not about my treasure hunting. As a general rule I don't announce where I'm going to hunt—or where I've searched. No offense, but that's how I make my living."

"I thought you were a locksmith," I said, trying to figure out what we had here.

"I'm that as well. The best in the Valley I might add."

It was obvious Hathcock wasn't about to discuss his personal business, so if we wanted to get what we came for it was time to ask our questions before he lost his patience. "Just curious, is all. Mind telling us a bit about the Singer Ranch? Is that the same Singer who invented the sewing machine?"

"No, that was Isaac singer, John's brother. John is the one who had the ranch."

"How far north from here?"

"Twenty-six point one miles from the southern point of the island. But I must warn you. If you are looking for it, with hurricanes and things, the island has changed since Singer left just as the Civil War began in early 1861."

"Why'd he leave?"

"He didn't want to take sides. He was living here in Texas, but was born a Yankee. You couldn't be neutral in Texas, that didn't work. So he went north. But…"

"But?"

"But he very likely was a Confederate. But that's another story. He, or one or more of his sons, came back from time to time to retrieve coins from the treasure the father had buried on the ranch. Much of their wealth was in silver coins and they could only safely transport so many at a time."

"So much of the treasure is still up there. Is that right?"

"That's how the story goes."

"What's your take?"

"No one has found anything in years. I'm certain it was there at one point, but it's not there now. No, let me amend that statement. If it's there now it's been moved."

"You mean someone reburied it?" Angella asked.

"Not someone, nature. If I were to guess, I'd say the hurricane of 1867. That 'ole gal ate up the island, leveled some dunes, built others." Hathcock reached into his jacket pocket, pulled out a weathered map and spread it on the table between us. "See here," he said, pointing to what appeared to be a barrier island stretching about a hundred miles, "this is where the ranch was."

"Orient me," I said. "This looks too long to be South Padre Island."

"It's a hundred thirteen miles, give or take. This is what Padre Island looked like before the Mansfield Cut in the sixties. That's when North and South Padre were formed. By the way, as a point of interest, Padre Island is the longest barrier island in the continental United States. As a further point of interest, it was in the running for atomic testing as part of the Manhattan Project before they selected the Jornada del Muerto desert in New Mexico. Sorry, that's what happens when you ask a historian a question."

"Go on," I said, fascinated by Hathcock's love for his subject.

"I'm pointing to the place where the Singer Ranch was. But note what happens when I overlay a recent map of the island." He then proceeded to unfold an even rattier looking map and place it next to the older one. "See here how the island has moved west."

"Why is that?" I said, thinking about what Hildigo had said about the island being in the destructive stage and moving towards Port Isabel even though the camera images showed the plates to be shifting east.

"Technically, the island, the south part anyway, is in a state of destruction. Silt is filling in Laguna Madre faster than the beach is being built up. So, as you can see, the south part of the island is moving west."

"What's that mean with respect to the Singer Ranch?" Angella inquired.

"Two things really," Hathcock responded, the historian in him eager to teach. "First, any coordinates from the eighteen hundreds will be significantly off. Secondly, and this is important even today. The water table is just below the surface. So if you dig down a few feet and put something in the ground the water pressure will move it to the surface. May take a while, but up it will come."

"Surely, Singer knew that," I said.

"John Singer helped build the Erie Canal. He was a clever man and had structures that were watertight. It is my belief he used small versions, perhaps, the size of canning jars to store the coins and other valuables. He must have had a method of securing them in the ground so they wouldn't float away. But that's pure speculation."

Hathcock had his finger on the new map on the far west side of the island. Actually, a bit off the land and into Laguna Madre.

"Is there significance to the location where you have you finger? It seems to be west of where you said the ranch was."

His finger quickly came off the map. "Oh, not really. Just resting my hand there is all."

His eyes told another story, so I noted the exact location where his finger had been. "Anything more we should know?"

"That depends upon what you want to know. The Singers were fascinating folks. The sons were..."

"I think we have what we came for," I quickly said, not wanting to hear another story about some ancient family. "I thank you for your time—and the history lesson. Oh, one more thing? What's the best way to go up there?"

"Beach would be easiest, but then you'd have to get over the dunes and whatever else is there. Not a big problem for someone familiar with this area, but you might have some problems. I'd suggest going up on the bay side. But then you'd need a shallow water boat, a Hovercraft would be best, because of the shifting terrain. Navigation will be tricky. One day it's water, the next marsh, the next solid sand. With care it can be done."

"Thank you, again, Mr. Hathcock. It's a pleasure speaking with someone as knowledgeable as you."

"My friends call me Steve. Please. And, if you're thinking of going on up there I'd be happy to be your guide. Only it would have to be by car. I don't have a boat."

"Thank you, Steve. We'll call you if we need your services."

"Time for Malone," Angella announced when we left *Coconuts*. "Did you learn anything of value from Steve?"

"Made me realize, not for the first time I might add, how little I really know about the world around us. What I learned specifically is that a lot of people keep poking around up there hoping to find buried treasure."

"So are you thinking that with the Singer Ranch being a focal point for people looking to get rich it would be a bad place to hide anything new?"

"That was my thought, yes."

"Yet you look troubled. Not so much troubled as puzzled."

"Paco seemed to be the guy who had charge of the Bird. Paco was killed coming south on the beach. Maybe no connection, but until we have another lead I'm going with Paco hiding it somewhere on or near the old Singer Ranch."

"That's a far leap. There must be a lot of places up there to hide things."

"You heard what Hathcock said about the Singers coming back several times for coins. The old man knew how to build canals, so he knew about water tables and upward pressures. He certainly knew about hurricanes and high winds and shifting sands. Yet, he trusted his treasure to that environment. So he knew what wouldn't move. Paco knew this area better than most. I'm thinking Paco knew Singer's secret."

"Then why didn't Paco find what remained of the treasure?" Angella asked.

"We don't know he didn't."

"Hathcock would have told us."

"What if Paco found it and said nothing to anyone? You know in Texas, the State owns it if it's on State lands. The owner of the land owns it if it's found on their land. In either scenario, Paco would get little, if anything. So he kept his mouth shut."

"Not being a citizen, actually being here undocumented, he couldn't sue anybody. His best bet would have been to take a little at a time and not flash anything."

"Hard to do when Spanish coins are involved."

"Easy for him to take them into Mexico. No questions would be asked. But the truth as far as Paco was concerned was that not even all the money could change his life, such as it was."

FORTY

Malone ushered us into her office, we exchanged hellos, and she excused herself to attend to what she described as pressing business.

We sat for forty-five minutes before she returned. Now she was all business. "Jimmy, mind explaining to me in terms even I can understand why you felt it incumbent on decking a security guard, name's Henry, Aiken Henry, at the Isla Grand? And when he's finished, Angella, you can explain why you drew your weapon."

"He came up behind me shouting and grabbed my shoulder. I did what I was trained to do. Flipped him over."

"Why was a security person chasing you? What did you do to attract his attention?"

"You'll have to ask him."

"I'm asking you, Redstone! What the hell's going on?"

"I was at the hotel because I had been summoned by Jamison."

"General Jamison?"

"Yes."

"Go on."

"I had reason to believe he was about to host a gathering so… so I sat in the lobby to observe. Actually, that's why we're here, we need to…"

"There's time enough for that when we get this behind us—if we get this behind us, I should say. Go on. I still haven't heard what you did to attract the attention of security."

"I went to the breakfast room at the back of the lobby to see who was there. I found no one, but I did see a door at the end of the hall, a door leading outside, closing. So I gave chase. I suppose that's when the security guy came after me."

"You guess or you know?"

"That's when he came after me."

"So you knew who was chasing you?"

"I did."

"And you decked him anyway?"

"I suppose so. He…"

"I know, put his hand on you. That's no call to deck him."

Better than shooting him, I would think. I kept my thought to myself.

"Knowing your reputation I suppose we should be grateful you didn't shoot him."

"That's uncalled for," I replied, trying not to smile.

"But accurate, is it not?"

"I wouldn't say that. As for Angella, she saw him attack…"

"Please allow Angella to tell me in her own words why she felt it necessary to draw on him. Did he have a weapon?"

"As it turns out," Angella said, her voice calm, her eyes soft as if she and Malone were having dinner over at *Café Kranzlers*, "he did not. But at the time I didn't know he wasn't armed. It appeared to me he was attacking my partner. Also, I thought I had seen another guy running, but when I turned the corner all I saw was the guy, Henry, pushing my partner. He wasn't in uniform. I didn't know he was security."

"I don't know the rules you play by, but we don't draw unless it's a last resort. And since you, to my knowledge, are not on an operation, you should not even be thinking of shooting anyone. In fact, I have trouble with either of you carrying."

"Fortunately for us, you don't..."

"Fortunately, for us," Angella cut in, "you don't have to do anything because nothing happened. No shots were fired. The security guy didn't appear to be injured, so all's well that..."

"If he files charges then it won't end so well.

"I can't see as how we..."

Again Angella interrupted me. She wasn't giving me a chance to dig the hole deeper. "Perhaps I was quick to draw. That's not my normal mode." She glanced at me as if to contrast her behavior with mine. "But...but that's precisely why we're here to see you. If we can move beyond this it will all become..."

"Just hope the hotel has enough sense to back down. The guard's only explanation for chasing you, Jimmy, was that he saw you running. He also noticed that you had spent a long time in the lobby watching the elevator. To him, two and two meant you were after someone. He gave chase and you didn't stop. He says he wanted to ask you about it."

"Sorry about the misunderstanding," I said, taking Angella's lead.

"For your information, and this may be unrelated, a guy, oh, I believe you know him, Petty Officer Telson, sprained his ankle rather badly. Hotel security caught it on their cameras and called 9-1-1. He was transported to Brownsville General."

"Did he come out the same door I did?"

"I don't have the footage, but they did say he tripped over something and seemed to roll under a truck parked a few feet from where you nail…encountered Henry."

"You finished with your agenda?" I asked Malone.

"For now."

"Let's work on ours, if you will. We are officially in need of your services."

"Let's hear it. And it better be good."

I outlined the threat on our lives and told Malone what we knew so far. What I forgot to mention, Angella filled in. Neither of us told her about Paco and my theory with the Singer Ranch. Nor did we tell her that we believed the money, the forty million, was in an airtight container in the Laguna Madre ship channel.

"So you want me to believe General Maxwell Jamison, a general who retired with four stars on his shoulder, a man who has distinguished himself in every aspect of life, a man who holds three purple hearts, the medal of valor, and a chest full of other awards, the man the President calls on in times of emergency, has been tasked to take you out?"

"Financial problems. Perhaps blackmail. Who ever knows what takes a good man down. I've seen it happen countless times."

"Not with a four-star general you haven't. Look, I've worked with him. Well, not directly with him, but with men and women under his command. Never once has anyone ever said anything but good about that man. Brusque, maybe. Low tolerance for fools, yes. Stickler for details, certainly. But all of that goes with the territory. I'll be busted back to street patrol. Worse, I'll be lucky to stand guard over the soup cans at the *Blue Marlin* if I even pass along your story. Where'd you come up with something this crazy?"

"Can't reveal my source."

"Makes it even worse. Look, Redstone, my job is finding killers, not babysitting a guy who carries his own gun and can't manage to stay out of trouble. Only DHS can provide the kind of protection you need. This is a job for your friend Tiny."

I wanted to ask her wasn't it better to keep people alive than try to find their murderer afterward, but in my case she had already told me the answer. I kicked my chair back, stood, smiled and said, "Take my picture. Then you'll have a good BEFORE and AFTER comparison for your homicide investigation file."

"If you don't get your butt out of here there won't be any time difference between those two pictures!"

Out in the hall, Angella asked, "Is it Miller time yet?"

"Funny. Funny."

"Want me to get him on the line?"

"If you insist," I said, pissed at the world.

"Make it fast," Contentus barked, "I'm in the middle of something." As the head investigative law enforcement officer in Texas, Miller Contentus always had a lot on his plate. He's held his job through several Governors because he managed to get done what needed to get done without regard to politics and political fights for which Texas is legendary.

I wanted to tell him to call me back when he had a free moment but I might be dead by then. I told him the story as fast as I could, being certain to include all the relevant facts that he would find out anyway when he got involved.

"That it?" he said when I stopped talking.

"That's it," I responded, mentally checking to make certain I had told him everything. "I need major backup."

"If I didn't know you for all these years I'd send someone for you…to lock you up. I don't doubt for an instant your life's in danger, that's not really new news. And I can believe an agent has been tasked with the chore of dispatching you. I'll even buy the foreign agent part. But, and I say this with deep conviction, Jamison does not head up any such rogue operation. I've known the man…never mind…you know the story. It's just not Jamison. That much I know. If you tell anyone what you just told me you'll be put on the mentally unstable list."

"But he has money prob…"

The line was dead.

"What did he say?" Angella asked when I threw the phone down.

"Says I'm nuts for even suggesting Jamison is heading up the operation."

"He said more than that."

"He believes I might be right about all of it, except for Jamison."

"What's he going to do about it?"

"As far as I know, nothing."

"I thought he was a friend."

"Depends on the day. Hey, something came to me while I was talking with Contentus. Let me see the Paco file."

Angella brought the file up on her iPad and handed it to me. My interest was in the coat, or sweater, or whatever it was that Paco had been wearing. Angella initially had said it was colored, blues or reds. But the file pictures showed it to be black and white. Actually shades of grey. "We need to look at that jacket or whatever it is. See it in person."

"What's got you going on the jacket?"

"As I said before, in all the pictures of Paco, we've never seen a jacket—or a covering of any type."

Angella responded by shaking her head side to side.

"What triggered my thought is the color in the first photo. I'm thinking that when that picture was taken some special type of light was hitting the cloth. The later pictures were taken without the special light, so no color."

"Here, let me see something."

I handed the iPad back to Angella and a moment later she said, "Those first photos, the ones with the color, were taken at the crime scene. The other ones were taken at the lab."

"Are you thinking what I'm thinking? At the crime scene they were using UV light, probably a UV LED flashlight, looking for blood and other traces."

"Narcotics also," Angella reminded me. "Let me see what the lab report shows."

It took Angella several minutes before she said, "Here it is. There were trace amounts of blood on the jacket. The technician called them random spots."

"What are random blood spots? Who's blood? Does it say?"

"Slow down, Jimmy. It's Paco's blood and by random I believe they mean not a typical spatter pattern."

"Can we blow it up?"

"Possibly, but we'll need our home computer to do that."

FORTY-ONE

The diving gear and a camera were lying in the middle of the living room when we arrived back at the condo. I mentally kicked myself for not engaging Hathcock to fix our door when we had lunch earlier in the day. "I don't even know why we bother locking the door when we leave," I said to Angella. "Other people spend more time in our condo than we do."

"I was thinking the same thing. Maybe we need two places. One for us and one for all the uninvited visitors."

My cell chirped announcing a call from Jamison. I touched the accept button and McNaughton's voice said, "I'm told you created a ruckus outside in the parking lot this morning. I caution you to be more careful. You'll be pleased to know the hotel's not pressing charges and the security guy's been taken care of as well. Don't ever say I don't have your back."

"I suppose I should thank you," I replied.

"Thanks accepted, Cowboy. Max asked me to give you a message from him. The message is the dive is off for tonight. Your dive partner is...is away. Be a day, possibly two, and the dive will be back on track. You understand all that, Cowboy?"

"I do," I told her.

"Bye for now."

I hung up and relayed the conversation to Angella. "Suits me just fine," she responded. "Just fine, indeed." She hadn't taken her eyes off the computer screen and I walked over to see what she was so intent on.

A blown up version of the original photo of Paco lying face up on the sand was on the display. "Look at this, Jimmy." She manipulated a black line around what appeared to be blue dots and hit a button. The dots expanded to fill the screen and Angella had to reduce the image a bit to make them all fit.

"What am I looking at?"

"Blood drops. The report indicates the jacket was sprayed with Luminol and the photo was taken while infrared light was being shined on it. The blood is Paco's."

"What's your question?"

"It's to...too neat. Too orderly to be spatters, and too consistent to be random. You're looking at the right breast area. There's an identical pattern on the left side as well."

"Usually, a pattern on a jacket front is exactly that. A pattern on a jacket front. So what..."

"Usually patterns are not made using blood."

"Artisans for thousands of years have been using all manner of substances to make dyes, even blood."

"Since it's Paco's blood I'm assuming Paco made the pattern."

"Maybe his killer made the pattern," I suggested, not even convincing myself I was right.

"His killer was a mile off shore, Jimmy."

"An accomplice? A person who found him dead on the beach?"

"You don't believe any of that, do you?"

"Just keeping the possibility alive. Okay, let's assume it was deliberate. We need to decode the message. What did Dr. Demont say about codes?"

"He said the names of certain cities were found and the zip codes from those cities pointed to latitude, longitude coordinates for Port Isabel. That's how the Booby was found this last time. In the Train Museum."

"For starters, then," I said, "let's assume the code is in numbers. We'll see where that leads."

"I've tried that and got nowhere. There are ten rows of dots on the right side and eleven rows on the left."

"Row one," I said, "count the dots."

I found a pencil and a yellow note card and was ready when Angella said, "Four."

"Next line."

"Two."

"Next."

"Four."

It went this way until Angella announced, "That's it on this side."

Before you switch over to the left, let's double check. I read off the numbers, "424509blank568. Do I have it right?"

"Yes."

"What's the blank about? I mean what's really there?"

"Nothing, Jimmy. All the other lines are perfectly spaced, but then the last three numbers are separated by what I believe to be a blank line."

"Okay. Do the left side."

Angella adjusted the image on her screen and while she did so I examined the numbers I had on the card. My first thought was this was a latitude or longitude number. Possibly latitude. But forty-two was far north of us, somewhere around Michigan, Wisconsin.

"Ready?"

"Fire?"

"Five, zero, eight, two, one, seven, eight, blank, five, six, five."

"So the two numbers are: 424509-568 and 5082178-565."

"That's what I get," Angella said, but they mean nothing to me."

"Not lat, long coordinates as far as I can tell. Even if you put a decimal point where the blank is you don't get anything I recognize. As I said, if the first number was latitude that would put you way up north and if the second number were latitude you'd be even further north. The other two numbers would place you in mid-Atlantic or perhaps in the Gulf of Aiden or the Arabian Sea."

"You know the coordinates for the Gulf of Aiden because?"

"The latitude would be wrong. Croatia would be more likely if that were an east latitude. But fifty south is where I spent what seemed a lifetime at the time."

"Back to ground zero, then. We don't even know if these are coordinates, or even if I am reading them properly. I had assumed the dots on the right were independent from the dots on the left. But they could be one long number string."

"Could be, but that makes it even worse."

After spending several hours working different combinations of dots into numbers, and then looking up dozens of different coordinate combinations using Google and Google Maps, I was exhausted. Worse, we weren't any closer to understanding what the dot matrix meant–if anything.

Angella handed me my cell and said, "Call Hathcock and see if he recognizes the numbers."

"Which of the two dozen combinations should I read to him?" I snapped.

"I know you're frustrated, but that's no call to shoot me. Give him the one you first wrote down. It's the most straight-forward set we have."

"Who said anything about shooting?"

"The look on your face gave you away. Paco may have been a clever man, but in the end if this is a code it was meant to be broken."

"Or the person—or persons—who put him up to it gave him the code pattern and he filled in the coordinates using a book or something."

"If there's a code pattern, we're chasing our tails on this one," Angella said, collapsing the displayed file. "One thing I know, Jimmy, if a code book was used, we aren't going to break it in any time frame that works for us. Where's Alan Turing when we need him?"

"Steve," I said when Hathcock answered, "Redstone here. I have a question for you. Got some paper?"

When he returned to the line, I said, "Write two numbers down."

A moment later I said, "Read them back to me. Okay. They mean anything to you?"

"Not off the top of my head," Hathcock replied, "but they appear to be coordinates. They definitely are not lat, long numbers, that much I can see. I don't believe they are GPS either."

"We agree with you on that, but we do think they're coordinates of some sort."

"Okay if I get back to you? I have cases of old land documents, deeds, land grants, that type of stuff. I'll prowl through and see what I can find."

"Time is of the essence."

"Good, 'cause I can't spend much on this at this point. But I'll give it a good shot. Call you when I have something."

"Thanks."

The gentleman that he is, Steve waited for me to hang up first. After all, I had been the one to place the call. That hadn't happened to me in a long time.

FORTY-TWO

Hildigo Francese answered on the first ring. Angella was on the extension phone. "Got a proposition for you," I said, figuring his caller ID had done its job and properly announced who was calling. "You game?"

"That would, of course, depend upon the exact nature of the proposition, Mr. Redstone."

"Call me Jimmy. I want you to take us up the Laguna Madre?"

"How far is up?"

"About twenty-seven miles, I'd say."

"Oh, you're going up to the Old Singer Ranch. Doing some treasure hunting?"

"You can say that."

"You know the land's shifted up there. Those old treasure hunting maps are worthless, case you got one."

"Just out for some recreation. Have some time to kill and I'd thought it would be fun to go up there with a marine life expert.

I checked DHS records," I lied, "and found the Coastal Studies Lab has a HoverCraft."

"You mean you want me to take you up the bay in our boat?"

"That's precisely what I am asking."

"It's against the rules to take passengers."

"Think of us as DHS agents. Think of yourself as the guide taking us up there on a secret mission."

"Well, since you work for Homeland Security and since that craft was given to us by Homeland Security I can't imagine why I can not do it. When do you want to go?"

"Make it nine tomorrow."

"Just a moment I must check my calendar for the day."

For a high tech kind of guy it took him much longer than I would have thought.

"Are you still there, Mr. Red…Jimmy?"

"I'm here Hildigo. Can you make it?"

"That's what took me so long. I had an appointment tomorrow at noon and I moved it. So I'm free to go. This should be fun. The boat is over at the *Port Isabel Navigation District BoatYard.* Meet you there at 9:00. Combination to the yard gate in case you arrive before I do is 36-15-53. The lock for the craft is 1794. We'll top the tank over at the fuel dock. It holds twelve gallons but that gives it a two hundred mile range at normal cruising speed, so we'll have plenty to spare. I always keep two spare five-gallon jugs in the hold to be on the safe side. Unless we continue up to Port Mansfield, there's no other place to fill up."

"See you at nine," I said, cutting off Hildigo's enthusiasm.

"Okay, see you at nine," he answered.

I hung up. Second time in a row I controlled the call. Just say'n.

"Set your clock for five-thirty. Got a long day."

"We don't have to be over to the boat until nine. You planning on a big breakfast? An early morning meeting? What?"

"By nine, we'll be at the Singer Ranch."

"That means we're leaving the dock around seven. But you..."

"Leaving time for gassing up, I anticipate being under the causeway bridge no later than seven-thirty."

"Without Hildigo?"

"Without Hildigo and without anyone who was listening to the conversation."

"What if he hadn't given you the combination?"

"That's why they make bolt cutters, my dear."

"Or your Berretta."

"Or my Berretta."

"You're missing a piece of the puzzle. The coordinates. You don't even know where you're going up there."

"We have over twelve hours before we leave the dock. A lot of stuff can get done in twelve hours."

"But not a lot of sleeping," Angella said, if we have any hope at all of cracking that code."

"Sleep on the boat ride."

"That's an hour, maybe two if we do it right. Besides, I don't want to miss that part."

"Okay, then let's get to work and figure out where those coordinates lead."

"And if we don't?"

"And if we don't, we go on up and look around anyway."

"With no sleep," Angella chided.

"There's always time for sleep."

At exactly midnight Hathcock called. "I believe I found what you're looking for."

"You go through all those file boxes so..."

"I told you I couldn't spend much time with the files. What we're looking for is most probably in there, but that's not how I found it. I was on eBay. I get a ton of old documents on eBay, many of them documents pertaining to land grants in South Texas."

"Steve, it's midnight. Cut to..."

"Hear me out, sir. I've been trying to find the owner of a small parcel over by the Rio Grande River. I believe there's a civil war artifact worth a lot of money. Oh, I don't keep the money, but I do need permission to go on the land."

"Please..."

"I'm getting there. I saw that very same parcel listed for sale on eBay. I'm in the process of bidding now. Auction ends in fifteen minutes. But here's why I called. I was reading the description location and I suppose I knew this but it never registered. I've always traced land by name of a previous owner and by surrounding names. But this little parcel had another set of numbers that looked similar to the ones you gave me. Not similar numbers, mind you, but similar in style. Except the numbers on eBay both start with 4205 and both have an M at the end of the number string. Another difference is the first string on eBay ends with a mE and the other string ends with a mN."

Steve finally took a breath and I wanted to tell him to get it out already. All this M and N crap meant nothing to me. I rolled my eyes and said nothing, knowing he'd finish in less than thirteen minutes so he could go back to his auction.

"The only other difference is there is a period where you have the dash. It took me a while to think of it. Actually the 4205 gave it away. I just couldn't think why I knew that number. You know with the excitement of the bidding and all. But if the M stands for meters and the N and W for north and west, then I know what your numbers are."

"Are you going to tell me, Steve, or is this where we play twenty questions?"

Angella kicked me.

"I'm sorry. This is exciting. Listen, those coordinates are State Plane numbers."

"What the hell are State..."

"One of the many ways land can be identified. The South Texas zone is 4205. So go onto the Internet and find a conversion site that goes from State Plane coordinates to Latitude, Longitude."

While Steve was talking Angella was searching.

"Then when you have the site there should be a place for the zone. I think they call it list. Type in..."

"Found one!" Angella exclaimed. "Okay, I've typed in 4205 for the list. Now which number do I put in for the X?"

"Use your first number. I don't want to say it because I might be overheard. Sometimes my lines get tapped. Don't know why."

Little did he know that cat was already running loose. But it was too late now.

"But add MN to the end. For Y use the second number, but add MW."

A second later the outline of South Padre Island popped up on Angella's screen with a yellow line marking off a large parcel of land. In the upper left corner a flag appeared showing lat, long coordinates.

"Steve," I said, "thanks a million. Say no more. Good luck with your bidding. Hope you get what you want. Bye."

At least I had said 'bye'. That's more than is usually said to me.

"Look here, Jimmy! "These coordinates go right down to the hundredth of a second. That's some accuracy!"

"I'm guessing now, but this is undeveloped land so when these State Grant coordinates..."

"State Plane coordinates..."

"...those State Plane coordinates were drawn to what existed then, not now. Based on what Steve told us, the land has accreted on one side and washed away on the other."

"But, hey Jimmy, they're far better than anything we had before. If Paco drew them in blood they must mean something important."

"He must have been delivering the sweater to his bosses when he was shot."

"If his bosses have access to the murder investigation file, then he actually succeeded. Unless I miss my guess, the Golden Booby coordinates will be stored in a safe place at government expense for a very long time."

"Angella, I think you have it exactly right." She flipped the computer off, stood, stretched her back, took my hand and said, "We have five hours, let's make the most of it. Sleeping I mean."

FORTY-THREE

"Where did you learn to operate a Hovercraft? You're as comfortable on this as if you drove it every day." Angella asked as we left the fuel dock on our way down stream toward the swing bridge that connects the Port Isabel mainland to a small spit of land known as Long Island. Not to be confused with New York's Long Island, this one holds only about a hundred homes arranged around snaking canals. Many of the residents are Winter Texans inhabiting the island only from November to March. Spring Break drives them home faster than the northern winter can thaw.

"Same place I learned everything else. Ranger training. I should have known since DHS gave this to the Lab it would be the new 19XR Search and Rescue version, with the upgraded 135 HP engine. This baby will move out if need be."

"Just don't do anything foolish."

"Do I ever? Hey, don't answer that." I threw a salute to the bridge operator who had the bridge swung open in plenty of time to allow us to move through without circling. "I'm not as familiar with Laguna Madre as I'd like to be and the fishing map I picked up on the dock will help a little, but not to the extent I'd like. But the reason we're using a Hovercraft is because we can lift about eight, nine inches above the water. We still need to be careful of stuff sticking up, but other than that we can step this puppy out if need be."

"Just take it easy is all I'm saying. I want to enjoy the sights. We're in no hurry, are we?"

To tell the truth, I was worried about our phone being monitored and whoever was listening knowing exactly where we were going, what we were doing and what time we would be there. The fact that we're two hours earlier gives me little comfort. "If you don't mind," I replied, "let's save the sightseeing for the trip home. We're running early to throw off any observers, let's not give the time back to them."

"Yes sir, captain." Angella threw the same kind of salute I often threw Captain Boyle and it felt just as insulting. When I didn't take the bait, she said, "No one seems to be following. The only other boats out here are those fishing skiffs over by the edge of the channel."

"Hope they stay away from the money," I said.

"So you think it's still down there?"

"I do. Paco was the delivery guy for all things. The heist was built around the Booby—and Paco. There wasn't much time after the money came into the picture to do elaborate planning. I think the plan was first to secure the Bird, which Paco seemingly did, and then move the money. For a guy like Paco, moving the money is the simple part."

Angella thought about what I said, then added, "We know of only two people other than Paco who know where the stolen money is. The guy you and the Game Warden spoke to on the fishing boat. He was the one pulling the container. And the diver Smith."

"Smith's dead," I said.

"And there's a warrant out for the boat guy. He's gone to ground. So with Paco dead, there's no one going to get to the money anytime soon."

"Now do you agree with me? The money's down there."

"That's where the logic takes me. I agree." Angella got out the binoculars and scanned the horizon.

"With Jamison behind this then we're likely being watched from above. Satellites or drones. My money's on drones."

I increased our forward speed to twenty knots, about half its designed maximum and operated the hover engine. The craft immediately lifted us off the water about eight, maybe ten, inches.

"We're flying," Angella exclaimed. "How fast can this baby go?"

"I'm thinking about forty knots, give or take."

I was holding a compass heading of ten degrees, which gave us a slight bit of easting. An hour later Angella, who had been monitoring her cell, said, "Jimmy I think we're a bit too far east and according to my cell we'll be on site in less than a minute."

I brought the speed down to five knots.

"Something's bothering me, Jimmy. Didn't Steve say twenty-six point one miles from the southern end?"

"That was his number, yes."

"I've been tracking the distance. We're only twenty-four miles from the south end. Actually slightly less, but call it twenty-four. We're off by two miles."

"But this is where Paco's number led us. Twenty-six miles is the Singer Ranch. Nothing really points there. That was a hunch."

"We derived these coordinates as a conversion using a code book, the State Plane chart. Maybe we got it all wrong."

"Wrong or not, we're here. This is the best we have."

"Fine with me. But move us slightly north and a few hundreds west. No sense adding any more error to this puzzle than need be."

We were over semi-swampy marsh when I came off hover. The big machine settled into the muck less than an inch. Of course it's designed to float so it wouldn't sink far. But I had the impression it was being supported by mostly solid sand. "At least the ground is supporting this monster, but be careful where and how you step." We had brought hiking boots so the vegetation wouldn't be a problem.

"Jimmy," Angella called, "I hate to call into question your piloting, but my cell position says we should be closer to the Gulf. "We're off to the west too far."

"According to the reading on the boat, we're straight on top of the coordinates. I'm putting my money with the boat."

Angella had the binoculars to her eyes and was again scanning the surface in a three-sixty radius.

"See anything?"

"Not a thing. I'd think if Paco had been here there'd be tracks, broken grass, some trace."

"Professionals are trained not to leave trails. I'd be dead today if I'd left even one blade of grass, one twig, broken. Paco was a professional. Maybe he wasn't trained by our military, but he was good at what he did."

"Somebody tracked him."

"I like your theory. He was killed by his employer—or by someone with access to his employer's information."

"You're thinking Jamison, aren't you?"

"That's who comes to mind."

"Give me your logic."

She continued to scan the area while waiting for my reply. She knew me well enough to know I hadn't just thrown Jamsion's name out without something behind it. "Starting at the beginning, well, there's never a real beginning, but starting from where we came in, the bank was robbed and Smith was killed on a dive. Assume he was murdered because he had pictures of the abutment suggesting a plate shift. Either real or doctored, we don't know. He uses the pictures for blackmail."

"Who is he blackmailing?"

"For a while now I've been thinking it was DePierio who couldn't afford to lose the sale of the hotel which the pictures would certainly cause to happen."

"But?"

"But think about Jamison. Guy's over his financial head with *SpaceX* so if the pictures are made public *SpaceX* pulls out, or postpones. Either event causes Jamison financial hardship. He orders Smith killed and the pictures brought to him. Maybe he also has blackmail on his mind."

"So, you think he hired someone?"

“I’m thinking DePierio.”

“Under either scenario, he’s your man it seems.”

“It seems.”

“Hey, I just thought I saw movement over there!” Angella pointed off to the east. “Gone now.”

“There are deer out here. Cougars, I mean the kind with claws.”

“Don’t all cougars have claws?”

“Some show them sooner than others. The ones out here are the sooner type.”

“There it is again! Don’t think it’s a deer, nor a cougar. Moves more like a human than an animal. A big human.”

“Whoever it is, knows we’re here, that’s for certain.”

“So why is he moving?”

“Perhaps he was using the same cell phone app as you were and he expected us to land out by that tree. He’s getting repositioned.”

“How did he get here so fast? Couldn’t have left much before us.”

“Spent the night. Unless he was airlifted in, and that would put too many people into the picture. He came by boat.”

“So where’s the boat?”

“Buried. You could be looking at it and not seeing it.”

“That sounds like DePierio. Mossad Special Ops. Working in sand is like being at home for him,” Angella said. “Turn the boat back on, Jimmy, and let’s get out of here. Live to fight another day.”

“Ranger’s don’t run.”

“You’re not a Ranger. Not anymore you’re not.”

"Then he's not Mossad. Anymore that is."

"Jimmy, you have a death wish."

"That's where you're in error, my dear. I have a life wish. We know he's here. The next time we meet him we might not be so fortunate."

FORTY-FOUR

"Jimmy, the last time we were out here, I know it was further south, but same terrain, it didn't end well for you. Got your neck slashed and you're alive now only because of a SEAL rescue. There'll be no SEALs coming for you this time. In fact, no one will come for either of us."

At the mention of my neck, my hand, as it always seems to do, involuntarily went to the still visible, and sensitive, line that runs across my neck and stops just under my ear. On bad days the scar seems to glow pale red. On other days it's just there, a constant reminder of what one man with a knife can do to another. But if you let such things invade your mind you can't function. And I wasn't yet ready to throw in the towel. "The answer then, Angella, is to not let ourselves get put in a compromising position."

"That's what I've been trying to tell you. Fire this puppy up and let's get out of here."

"That's not the answer. We're in it and have to see it through. When this is behind us we can talk about what's next. For now, we'll explore the coordinate area and see what Paco's blood spots lead us to."

"I'm not happy about this, but you're on. Cover me. I'll head out to that dune over there and then you can follow. Good?"

"May be soggy. Be careful where you step. Go!"

Angella stepped off the craft, tested the ground with both feet, gave a quick thumbs up and then ran quickly to the dune.

Nothing moved. Nobody shot at her. All was quiet.

I followed. Same result.

"What are we looking for, Jimmy? What's out there at the location of the Booby?"

"Who knows? But we have to find something. Keep alert for whatever you saw moving."

"I see nothing that could be a hiding place. Whoever it is, he's good."

"He'd be dead by now if he wasn't," I commented. "I'm going on the assumption the Booby location is marked by something. Could be anything permanent. I'm thinking we should have brought a metal detector. Hathcock's the expert in using those things. If we can't locate anything then we'll bring him up here. But the fewer involved the better."

"Especially if we're being hunted," Angella reminded me.

We set up a grid using the Hovercraft as the western boundary and the location that came up on Angella's cell for the eastern limit. For north-south we agreed on a hundred yards, a football field. It was all arbitrary, but no more arbitrary than how we had deciphered the blood spots to begin with.

We found long reeds and walked beside each other poking into the sandy soil. I was doing most of the poking and Angella was doing recon.

More often than not, water seeped to the surface when I withdrew my reed. Twice my reed had hit something solid only to find in one instance compacted shells and in the other a large piece of concrete. We marked the concrete and moved on. It was slow going.

We were almost at the eastern limit of our grid and the ground under us was compacted. I thrust my reed into the hard-packed sand and my wrist vibrated with pain. For an instant I thought it was broken. There was something down there and it wasn't compacted shells. I got down on my hands and knees and began scooping sand. It wasn't particularly difficult to dig, but the reed had gone in about two feet, so a lot of sand, vegetation and shells had to come out.

Soon a ring of rocks began to take form and the hole had to be made much wider before I could discern that we had found the sidewalls of what now appeared to be a water well. Sand was packed inside the ring of stones which was over a foot in diameter, but the sand was loosely packed as if someone had recently filled it in. Without continuing to dig, there was no way to determine how far down the stones went, or if there was water below the sand.

"Angella," I called, "I think we have something. Come look."

"Not a good time," she called, anxiety in her voice. "Better get over here."

I jumped up and ran to where she had positioned herself, getting there in time to see a large man race from our Hovercraft and take shelter behind the same dune that we had used.

Anticipating that the boat would explode, I pulled Angella down. We lay for several minutes with our faces pressed against the cool ground, my body against hers to give her a modicum of protection against the blast.

But nothing happened. I gave it another minute and still nothing. We slowly got to our feet, our weapons drawn, looking for any sign of movement. There was none.

"Whoever it is," Angella said, "he's really good. Can't see where he went, but he's not behind that dune anymore."

"Help me fill this hole and we'll get out of here. In hindsight, we should have started our search over here. This is almost exactly where your cell would have taken us."

"That makes sense because Paco wouldn't have come by water, so he'd have used his cell like I did."

"Any sign of the guy?"

It wasn't a female voice that answered, but it was a voice I recognized. "Put your guns on the ground!" the voice barked. "Both of you!"

I was already down on the ground beginning to push sand back into the well-hole, so my hands weren't near my weapon.

Angella said, her voice calm, "He's armed, Jimmy."

"Redstone, don't move a muscle. I'll take your gun myself. Lady, put yours down and do it now!" the menacing voice of the hotel security guy, Henry as I recall, Aiken Henry, instructed. "Thank you. Now sit over there and don't move while I get his gun. One move and I'll put a bullet in his head!"

Henry took my gun, threw it off to the side, then said, "Okay, now Redstone you dig that hole deeper, say about four feet deep and six feet long. The lady and I will watch."

"I assume you plan for this to be our graves. So if I'm to die anyway just shoot me!" The exercise he'd get digging the grave would do him good. I stopped digging.

"Your assumption is in error. Right now it's a single grave you're digging. Yours. But if you keep this shit up I'll put a bullet through your girl friend's face and then it'll really be a double grave. Now get at it!"

I began digging, making it appear that a lot of sand was moving, but in reality the hole wasn't getting much larger than it was to start with.

It took Henry a while before he caught on. "Get with it, Redstone. I don't have all day. Either you're finished in a half-hour or she's coming in with you!"

Abby had said they wanted me, but it was okay with them if Angella became collateral damage. There was no sense pushing this guy into killing Angella, so I dutifully speeded up the digging process. The well-stones served as a headstone marker so I dug toward the west, the vision of lying for eternity with my boots facing west firmly engraved on my mind.

"You Bitch!" Henry screamed at the top of his voice.

I turned my head in time to see Angella on the ground, her outstretched fingers touching my Berretta. But before I could climb out of the mostly complete grave to help her, his boot came down on her hand and she screamed in pain.

"She's dead if you make one more move toward me!" Henry kicked the gun further away. "I've had enough. Hole's deep enough for what I need. Redstone lay down!"

Water was already seeping into the hole and suddenly his real plan became crystal clear. I'd lie down in the sand and he'd bury me. But I'd drown before I ran out of air. Then he'd haul me out and have someone find me along with the boat I stole. It would be easy enough to chalk my death up to a boating accident. There went my image of lying for eternity with my feet facing the setting sun.

"Lady, get your ass in there! You two think you're hot stuff. I'll show you how hot you are. Get in beside him. Redstone, turn on your side and make room for your woman."

A moment later Angella fell, or was pushed, into the grave, landing on my back and knocking the wind from me. My nose went below the water level and I gasped for air. That was a mistake because water went down my windpipe and set my chest on fire.

Angella slid off me just enough so I could lift my face from the sandy water. Henry was above us pushing sand with his feet. It wasn't going in fast enough for him so he bent down and began dragging his arms in a wide arc, gathering sand as he did so. He was concentrating on our heads and his plan was working. There wasn't enough room for either of us to move our heads and the water was rising faster than we could lift them.

I was gasping for air, desperately trying to clear my lungs. Talking was impossible and with Angella's body wedging me down it would be only a matter of minutes until we'd both take our last breaths.

The sand came down and the water kept rising. Angella was only able to get small amounts of air and to do so she had to force her head upward against my shoulder. As the water table rose, I had to lift my shoulder higher and higher to accommodate her breathing. Angella's head was pushed into the water every time I coughed. I tried to hold my breath but my lungs wouldn't cooperate.

Angella's head came out of the water for shorter and shorter intervals because I couldn't lift my shoulder any higher. She had perhaps a minute, two at most. I would last perhaps a minute longer before the water was higher than I could possibly move.

I fought to turn over so I could clear an upward path, but every time I twisted my body Angella was forced lower. Without sacrificing her I simply could not dig my way upward.

As the sand around us saturated, the water rose faster and faster. Angella stopped pushing her head upward and I couldn't determine if she had already drowned or if she was holding her breath one last time.

So this is how it ends. I'm sorry, Angella. I'm sorry I failed you.

I forced my head up as high as I could make it go, my eyes and mouth clamped tightly shut against the sand, struggling to inhale one final breath. With Angella no longer breathing there was nothing more to be lost by forcing my body to turn over so I could use my legs to open a pathway.

I managed to turn partially on my back, but it was enough so I could kick my left leg upward. Sand fell away, filling in gaps around my body. My second thrust dislodged enough sand to completely cover Angella's head.

My third kick hit something more solid than sand. It wasn't as hard as a rock or a tree, but solid enough so I couldn't punch through.

He's up there! It's him! The bastard's sitting on our grave!

That's when I heard something. Actually, in after-thought, I didn't hear anything. I felt it first through my foot which was in touch with Henry's body. Then I felt a slight shake of the ground.

Not more than five seconds later strong hands clamped around my leg and with one mighty tug I was on the surface gasping for air. I couldn't open my eyes because my head and eyes were encased in a sandy mold.

I ripped the sand from my face in time to see Angella's body lifted from the hole just as mine had been. I assumed by the same pair of hands. More sand poured into my eyes and I forced them to close.

My head fell back and landed, not on the ground, but on something large but soft. A moment later when the mound I was laying on moaned I realized it was the prone body of Aiken Henry. I didn't know if he had been shot, his neck slit or whether he had been strangled. Frankly, I didn't care.

When I next opened my eyes I saw the back of DePierio's head bent over Angella, wet sand flowing from her lifeless body.

I crawled closer, still gagging and trying desperately to blink the sand from my eyes. "Is…is," I coughed and couldn't catch my breath.

"Not breathing," DePierio yelled, positioning his mouth over hers and holding her chin away from her chest. He blew air in twice, then slid to her side, placed his palms on her chest and started to push up and down.

"The Hovercraft has oxygen and a medical kit," he barked. "Bring them both over here. Move!"

There was no mistaking the fact that Mossad Commander Moshe Abrams was now in charge.

And I was only too willing to comply. But neither my lungs nor my chest would cooperate.

FORTY-FIVE

When I didn't respond, he said, "I'll go for the bag. You press on her chest as fast as you can."

I continued crawling toward where Angella lay. "Stop worrying about your eyes! Close them! Get over here!" I forced myself forward and suddenly his hands grabbed my wrists and yanked me close to Angella. He positioned my hands where his had been and commanded, "Push up and down. You know what to do, now do it!"

I got on my hands and knees, my eyes pressed closed ignoring the pain of my scratched corneas, and followed his instructions. My CPR instruction of years ago kicked in and I compressed and released Angella's chest as fast as I could, all the while gasping for breath and forcing the pain from my scratched corneas out of my mind.

Angella still wasn't breathing when DePierio returned with the oxygen. He quickly had the mask over her nose and mouth and pushed me out of the way.

I fell back, finally able to take normal breaths without coughing. I dug through the bag and found a small eye wash cup and sterile water. A minute later I was able to see, albeit blurry.

"I got a heartbeat," DePierio called, "and it's coming on strong. Your partner will be fine. A little sand aspiration. She's breathing, but is in discomfort. In my part of the world we live with this all the time. Oxygen often does the trick."

"What's sand..."

"Nothing that can't be fixed. If the oxygen doesn't work, then we'll get her to a hospital and they can clear it out."

Angella's eyes were closed, her breathing shallow, her color pale. Blood pressure on the low side of normal, but pulse was high at 101.

"I've seen worse," DePierio said. "But I won't lie to you, I've seen better. The way this works is that if the sand just scratched the bronchia a little then she'll recover quickly. If it's worse, then medical intervention is called for. I think this is minor, but we'll know in a moment or two. Wash her eyes with that sterile water before she starts rubbing them."

"FYI," I said, "that guy Henry over there's still alive. Heard him moaning."

"Hand me the medical kit."

DePierio dug through the large compartmentalized case, first pulling out a syringe, then screwing a needle to its end and finally holding up a vial of liquid. He carefully inserted the needle into the vial, drew several CCs into the syringe and handed it to me. "In the butt. Go through his pants. Not the best technique, I admit. But he doesn't deserve any better. He'll be out for hours."

Angella moaned, tried to sit up but fell back. Her color hadn't improved, but it hadn't deteriorated either. DePierio ran to her. "Hurry up. Knock that guy out. I need your help over here."

"What am I injecting?"

"A sedative. It'll keep him down until we get out of here. Need your help here with Angella!"

I rolled Henry onto his side and shoved the needle through his jeans into his right thigh, using more force than was required, my anger at him burying us alive taking control.

DePierio had administered something to Angella and the death gray of her face showed a slight improvement, but not much. A check of her vital signs indicated that she was holding steady.

"Not good," DePierio said, telling me what I already knew. "Need to get her to the hospital."

"You have a plan?"

"The Hovercraft is the fastest way. Get the gurney over here, forget the wheels. We'll get her loaded on."

I moved as fast as I could back to the boat, separated the gurney from its mobile base and made it back to where Angella lay on the wet sand. Her eyes were now open, her breathing had improved slightly, but she was clearly in pain. "You're on your way to the hospital," I said to her. "You'll be there in no time." I wanted to kiss her, tell her I loved her. Hold her hand. But all that could wait. The mission right now was to get her loaded onto the gurney, carried to the boat, and delivered to the Brownsville hospital alive. I concentrated on the mission, all other thoughts erased from my mind.

Once Angella was stabilized inside the Hovercraft, DePierio asked, "Are you okay to drive this? You'd be wise to have a doctor check you out as well."

"I can hold it together for an hour or so," I answered, not as certain as I tried to sound. My lungs hurt and my vision had not cleared much beyond when I first rinsed my eyes. But at least it wasn't getting any worse.

"I'll set the coordinates for the bridge. Just stay up off the water and don't hit anything. Once I see that you're on your way I'll call for an ambulance to meet you at the dock."

"How will you get home?"

"Same way I got here. You certain you can drive this thing?"

"I'll manage. It's a straight shot."

"Listen to me, Redstone, and listen well. For the record, you made the call for the ambulance. You were up here alone with her. What you tell them about why you went, why you hijacked the boat, all of that, is up to you. My name is not to appear in any of this. That clear?"

"Clear. What do I tell them about how she was injured?"

"Make up something. She fell in a hole, anything. Get DHS to cover you. They usually do."

I bent and kissed Angella's forehead. When I pulled away, wet sand and shell pieces coated my lips.

"Ready to go?" DePierio called. He was standing next to the steering console.

"Ready as I'll ever be."

Almost immediately the big engines came alive. I moved to the console, DePierio threw a salute and stepped from the boat.

I moved the shift lever to forward, pulled up on the hover control, and the boat lifted from the sandy marsh and flew over the vegetation toward open water. I steadily increased the speed until the meter read fifty.

We were flying down the bay, but the ride was flat and comfortable.

***

The next several hours were a blur. We weren't exactly unknown to the hospital staff and one look at my red eyes and the sand still sticking to various parts of my body convinced the intake staff that I had to be admitted along with Angella. They wanted me to undergo a bronchoscopy, or some such thing and I was in no condition to argue.

The good news was that other than a now very sore throat, I was pronounced good to go. Angella, on the other hand, was released on the condition she rest and do nothing to increase her breathing rate. Sleep is what they wanted from her. Sleep and a prescription lozenge. No one believed my story that she had fallen in a hole and I ingested sand trying to pull her out.

On the way back to our condo, Angella, her throat hurting even more than mine, didn't want to talk. But she did want to know why DePierio came to our rescue and why he was out there in the first place.

"I can only answer some of your questions," I began, also hesitant to challenge my throat. "Some is conjecture, some fact, and some, well, some is what I was told."

"I'm listening," she rasped.

"Fact: Aiken Henry was sent there by someone he called the General. Fact: I was to be found drowned with no evidence of foul play. Fact: You were collateral damage, but if so, you were also to be found drowned same as me. Fact: We guessed right about the coordinates. Someone, I'm thinking, Paco, dug down there, either inside the well or just along the outside of it. Fact: the water in the well is fresh, not salt."

"The water I swallowed was salt, Jimmy. That much I know."

"The water seeping from the ground might be salt water, but the water coming out of the well is definitely fresh. Okay, put a question mark on that fact. Speculation: DePierio and Henry were working as a team. DePierio was the leader."

Angella started to say something and I held up my hand. "Hear me out on this. I don't know if this next statement belongs in the Fact category or not, but it certainly was told to me. DePierio said he was also sent by a general to kill me."

"Go on."

"DePierio didn't kill me because he said he owed me a big one. According to him, I saved his life in 1980 during Operation Bright Star. He's accurate that I did save a life, actually four lives, in the Gulf of Aqaba. But I don't specifically remember his name. I was with the 101st and Israel and Egypt were performing secret operations together. This was just after the Peace Accords were signed and things were still a bit rough over there. He said the weather was too rough and they had called off air rescue. He says I went back for one last pass when I found him."

"Well, did you? That's something I'd think you'd recall."

"Perhaps I did. Look, I was young then. A guy was missing, I couldn't just let them take me back to a nice safe bunk. But I really don't recall if who I pulled out that night was DePierio, Moshe Abrams, or some other guy."

"How did he, or they, get up there so early?"

"Came the night before, by kayak. Buried the kayak. That's how Henry will get home when he wakes up."

"How will DePierio explain us getting away?"

"Surmise: DePierio will claim Henry bungled the job and that we got free and captured DePierio. DePierio will report to the general that we captured him but that we were injured and went to the hospital. They'll believe his story because they want to believe his story."

"If I were Henry," Angella said, her voice now almost gone, "I'd head north or maybe south across the border. What I wouldn't do is go anywhere where Jamison is."

"He's not smart enough for that. I don't think he knows who he's really dealing with. But he's about to find out."

I had one more question and Hathcock, I knew, would have the answer. "Tell me," I said, when Steve came on the line, "about the water system up by the Singer Ranch."

"What is it you wish to know?" he replied, eager, as always, to help.

"Is it possible that old wells exist up there? Fresh water wells?"

"It is a certainty there are wells. There is, or to be accurate, there was, a fresh water stream, or lake, under the island. There reportedly were wellheads every mile along a north-south axis.

I've never seen them personally, but I believe they are up there, now buried. They're most likely still functioning."

I thanked him, hung up, and for the first time all day, I smiled.

"Jimmy, what's that grin for?" Angella asked. "Finding fresh water can't be all that important to you."

"It's not the water, it's the markers."

"Explain, please."

"If there exists a set of hidden wells, then they can be used as land markers because they can't move. We know where one of them is. Lot's of people most likely know that one."

"Jimmy, something I read once might be helpful. This was a cattle ranch. They drove the herd north and south. As I understand it, they placed the watering stations a day's drive apart."

"That's right," I said. "My father would tell stories about cattle drives from Texas up through Fort Worth and then north. As I recall, they moved roughly ten miles a day."

"That's what I recall from what I read. Ten, maybe twelve miles."

"But, and this is the key, if we simply select another well then all we need to know is how far away from this one it is."

"You thinking of hiding something?"

"You never know when a hiding place will come in handy. A place we both know. Pick a number, say from one to five."

"I'll go with two."

"Pick a direction. North or south."

"South."

"Our magic number is two-south. Remember it."

"Answer me. Are you planning to hide something?"

"Plans come and go. But if the occasion arises, we're all set—and we won't require shirts with bloodstains, or secret disappearing ink codes. Now stop talking or your throat will never get better."

FORTY-SIX

I hadn't seen my life pass before me when I was face down in that watery grave. I don't know why, I just didn't. But somewhere around three in the morning I came out of a dream, not the dream of falling from planes, or of being chased by a vicious creature, or even of missing classes and flunking school; but rather a dream where I'm being searched for my identity and I apparently have none. I'm nobody at all. I have no name, no home, no friends, no records. I just don't exist.

I sat bolt upright, my mind racing, focusing on nothing. Then it hit me that by all rights I should be dead. Angella, who was breathing noisily beside me, should be dead. But we weren't thanks to a paid assassin who disobeyed orders because he believes I saved his life.

I thought about that for a while and came up dry. What's to be gained by him lying about me saving him?

I was just getting back to sleep when a sound startled me awake. I listened intently for a long while and heard nothing more. I tried to get back to sleep but couldn't. My mind raced even harder. Something troubled me about the whole incident beyond the fact that I should be dead.

Then it came to me as clear as could be. Where was DePierio while Henry was burying us alive? If they were partners as he claimed then they would have been working together. Yet I had only heard one voice, felt one presence. So where was DePierio? There were precious few hiding places and for two people to move around undetected by Angella and me didn't add up.

If DePierio knew all along he was going to save us then why wait until we were mostly dead to do so. Two possibilities came to mind. The first was that he hadn't arrived until just before he knocked Henry out. The second was that he only found out, or realized, that he owed his life to me while Henry was shoveling the sand into our watery graves.

I selected the first option, but that would mean Henry and DePierio came up island separately. Possible, I suppose, but it didn't feel right. I opted for the second option.

Enough of this. I slid out of bed, took a long hot shower, even longer than the one I had taken when we first came back from the hospital. There are times when I've felt so violated that no amount of soap and hot water will scrub away the desecration. This was one of those times.

Angella appeared in the bathroom. "Save some hot water for me, Jimmy."

"Sorry if I woke you," I replied, stalling.

"I've been tossing and turning for hours."

"Feeling any better?"

"A bit, I suppose. But not great."

"Voice sounds better. Less raspy."

"Magic of drugs. Now get out of there before all the water's gone. I feel so...so abused and...and at the same time thankful. I don't know who DePierio really is and I frankly don't care. Thank God you saved his life."

"If I saved his life," I said, accepting the towel she was holding for me.

"You have doubts?"

"You know me and coincidences."

"But he knew you were in that Operation..."

"Bright Star."

"He's the right age. That's a fact. Sometimes coincidences do happen."

Tiny's communicator was on the bedside table and it was now buzzing. The clock read five-fifteen. I wasn't ready to deal with Tiny, or with anything for that matter. So I ignored it.

A moment later the screen went red signaling a message with the highest priority. If I didn't read the message within thirty seconds the device would begin a series of annoying beeps which would grow louder and more annoying every thirty seconds.

I caught it just as the first beep began. The message read: GET TO MALONE-NOW!

It was five-thirty in the morning, early even for a dedicated detective. But Tiny usually didn't steer us wrong. I retrieved my cell and hit Malone's number.

"You have thirty minutes, no, make that twenty minutes, to get yourself to my office. Bring a toothbrush."

"How about a heads up on what this is about?"

"God help you if you can't figure it out! Nineteen minutes and counting."

"Hot water's gone," Angella said when I rejoined her in the bathroom. "Pass me the towel, please."

I repeated Malone's message for Angella, and added, "What's up now you suppose?"

"Doesn't sound good. The toothbrush part worries me."

"You doing okay?"

"As well as can be expected. Lungs hurt when I take a deep breath. I couldn't possibly chase anyone if my life depended on it."

I didn't want to say anything to Angella at this point, but I had the definite feeling that our chasing days were quickly coming to an end. "I'm locking up the Berretta. I'd sooner leave it here than trust it to their custody. You want to do the same?"

Angella checked her communicator, then replied, "No message for me. Malone wants only you. I'll keep my weapon with me."

We walked into Malone's office at five forty-five, actually five minutes earlier than her deadline. Two cups of coffee were positioned at the front of her desk and she had a third clasped between her hands as someone who has just come in from cold would do. Except it was in the sixties outside.

"Your timing is impeccable, Redstone. The City Prosecutor is due in his office at six and my plan is to deliver that file to him first thing." She nodded in the direction of a large stack of papers, not yet in a binder. The stack was delineated from other similar stacks by the word REDSTONE scrawled in black marker across an otherwise blank piece of white paper.

"Okay if I look?" I had nothing to lose by asking.

"Knock yourself out."

I pulled the pile toward me and flipped over the sheet with my name on it. The next several pages held the standard housekeeping stuff about me. Name, address, phone numbers, employment history type of stuff.

Then there was a white page with yesterday's date written on it. The notation was made by the same person who had written my name on the first page. Possibly Malone herself.

I turned that page over.

"Jimmy!" Angella exclaimed. "I didn't..." She snapped her mouth closed and for good reason.

There I was jabbing a needle into the left buttocks of one Aiken Henry. I guessed the picture had been taken by DePierio, but I couldn't be certain. But I was certain I knew what the next picture would show. I wasn't surprised then when I removed the picture of me injecting Henry to find a picture of him lying on his back, his eyes rolled back in his head.

A series of pictures followed showing the Hovercraft sitting on the sand flat, and then me at the helm heading south on the bay. None of the pictures showed DePierio or Angella. Further down in the stack were images extracted from the video of me shooting the assault weapon and Paco walking on the beach.

"Anything you care to say?" Malone was sitting back in her chair her face masking her thoughts. "Remember, anything you do say can and will be used against you."

"Off the record?"

"Nothing's off the record, Redstone. You know better than that."

"I didn't see photos of the site," I said, hoping to gain as much info as I could. "In fact, I didn't see any crime scene photos. The ones in here are not official."

"Correct."

"Let me guess. They came from a drone, or a satellite, and these are all you have."

"I'm not going to answer any more questions. Is that you injecting Henry?"

"Is that Henry?" I asked. Two could play this game.

"That's Henry and he's very much dead."

"So where are the crime scene photos?"

"That's not your business. Care to comment on what you see there?"

I couldn't deny it was me in the pictures, so there was no point saying anything. "You do know the video of me shooting into the Gulf was altered. Do you not?"

Malone didn't answer, so I continued, "I assume you received these from the same source." Still no response. I added, "For what it's worth, you should assume these have the same veracity."

"At least with the video you immediately denied the accuracy of the images. Here I haven't heard a single explanation."

"Off the record?"

"You heard me."

"Then we have nothing more to discuss." I stood to leave, my coffee mostly untouched.

Angella threw me a curious look, but fell in behind me.

Halfway down the hall Malone rushed past me, slowing just enough to whisper, "Back parking lot, five minutes, I'm driving."

I took solace from the fact the official police clock read six-twenty and to my knowledge my file was still on Malone's desk.

FORTY-SEVEN

I thought we were taking another trip to the end of the paved road, but the unmarked police car turned off near where the diver Smith was killed. “Here’s what we have, Jimmy,” Malone began when the car stopped, “Henry’s not dead.”

“I thought as much,” I said, “from the lack of site photos and early tox reports.”

“But you will be arrested. They’re going before the judge right about now as a matter of fact.”

“You serious?”

“Afraid so. We don’t have much time, so let me play it out for you. The warrant will be issued, uniforms will be dispatched to your condo, and you will be arrested. For goodness sake don’t resist. The folks coming for you don’t know this is staged. You’ll be arraigned this afternoon, the preliminary hearing will be set two days from now. You’ll be released on minimum bond.”

“How much will…”

"Don't worry about the money. A friend of yours will post it."

"Since when do you arrest and arraign all in one?"

"We need you on the street tonight. You're going to dive down to take pictures with the camera Jamison gave you. It's too late to change that, and the fact that we will actually have arrested you demonstrates to whoever is trying to pin this on you that your protection has been stripped away. In their eyes you're now vulnerable and because your bail could be revoked at a moment's notice they have no time to waste."

"How the hell…"

"There's a lot going on and frankly the less you know the better. DHS, FBI, CIA and a whole lot of other agencies, many I didn't even know existed, are involved. President's being briefed, the whole nine yards. Your job is to answer the bell."

"My life's on the line and I'm not supposed to know what's going on."

"From what I've been told, you're lucky to be alive. Both of you. DePierio saving you has thrown their plans into disarray. Whoever is behind all this doesn't know Henry lived and this is our opportunity to catch them improvising."

"I thought your job is to keep me alive, not throw me to the wolves."

"Hate to break it you, Redstone, but keeping you alive is your responsibility. The way I see it, either you're up to it or you're not."

Time to change the subject. "Any special reason you chose this place to talk? It's a crime scene."

"I suppose because it's on my mind. We sent another diver down, a shipwreck guy from Corpus, not connected to anyone down here. Started a little after midnight last night and finished around four. Almost didn't find what we were looking for but the guy is good. Really good. Has underwater metal detecting, everything needed to find what he calls treasure. I call evidence."

"What you call things usually depends upon where you sit," I said.

"You a philosopher now?"

"That's what coming back from the deceased will do to you. So what were you looking for?"

"Evidence DePierio was diving down there at the time of the murder."

"What kind of evidence proves where a diver's been?" I couldn't think of anything. Footprints, fingerprints, blood, all useless.

"He has a special Mossad issued diving tank. Actually, he has two. I don't know what's so special about it, but he won't dive without it. We found one in his quarters at the *Riveira* when we executed the warrant. We had reason to believe he left the other one down there because the foreman positively identified him as coming out of the water while Smith was down there."

"I assume you found the second tank down there?"

"That we did. And with his name on it. And this time we have a judge that will issue the arrest warrant. Last time we tried the evidence was good, but not conclusive. Now we have him almost to a certainty."

I was more confused than before. "You've known since the day of the murder that DePierio was on scene. So what has changed?"

"He wasn't wearing diving gear when the foreman saw him. When interviewed he claimed to have been out kite boarding and his rig broke. Suspicious, but not impossible."

I thought about the guy I saw poking in my trunk the night I went down with Telson. Maybe it was DePierio looking to see if we had retrieved his gear. "The tank you found could have been lost any time," I said, playing defense lawyer. "I don't see..."

"Marine growth, Redstone. Dr. Francese will testify to exactly how many days that tank was down there. And without any prompting by us as to the significance of the tank or the time frames we are looking for, he pinpointed the number of days the tank had been in the bay. Matches exactly to when Smith was murdered. Francese says he can get it to within an hour if we require it that close. Guy's a piece of work. We're charging DePierio with Capital Murder."

"Capital Murder?"

"We believe he was paid for his services."

"Who paid him?"

"That. Redstone, is why you'll be out on bail this afternoon."

I must have been running on a tape delay or some such thing because I wasn't ready for Malone's next words.

"You're diving partner tonight is none other than DePierio."

"You've been eating bad mushrooms if you think in some fit of comradery he'll confess to being hired to kill Smith."

"Not my plan, Redstone. But if he confesses, all the better."

"Why not use a medium? Maybe a séance? You have as good a chance that way."

"Don't get testy, Redstone. I suppose that's something Angella can do while you and your buddy DePierio are down there communing with Neptune. Now both of you get out, I have work to do."

***

Getting home from the sand flats is relatively easy. Walk a mile south to the Convention Center and wait for *The Wave.*

"I don't know if it's smart for me to walk, even a mile, Jimmy. My lungs hurt when I breathe."

"Okay. Stay here and I'll go get the car."

"There's a place to sit over there," Angella said, pointing to what appeared to be a mound of concrete dumped off to the side of the wide hard-packed sandy area.

I walked with Angella, not wanting to leave her alone until I knew she was settled and comfortable. Normally, she would have waved me away, but her breathing difficulties were taking a toll. I pulled out my cell thinking I'd just call a cab, which is what I should have done in the first place.

I looked up in time to see a large man appear seemingly from nowhere. He was about a hundred yards away. My initial impression was that it was Aiken Henry. Too tall.

DePierio? Two heavy.

Tiny! Just right.

"Imagine meeting you two out here on such a nice morning. Enjoying yourselves?"

Tiny's eyes said he was toying with us, so I played along. "We're the walking dead. Or is it dead men walking?"

"Take your pick, but you might want to pay attention to improve your chances."

"For a guy working outside the system you're really well wired. You knew about my pending arrest. That's local, so tell me how you knew."

"Time for that later. If you're not arrested soon our target will smell a rat and close it down. They've worked hard to pin this on you." He reached in his pocket and pulled out what appeared to be a lens cap. "Here," Tiny said, holding it out to me, "put this on Jamison's camera when you get back to your condo. Take off the filter that's on there now and replace it with this one."

"What exactly am I doing this for?"

"Stop with the questions already. Just do as I say."

"I'm being used as bait in a scheme to trap a person, or persons, unknown and you want me to blindly follow your instructions? Not going to happen. We both almost lost our lives less than twenty-four hours ago and frankly I'm done!"

I was now on fire and about to unload even further when Angella intervened by placing her hand on my shoulder. She then turned to our handler, or better yet, our former handler. "Tiny," she said, her tone calm, but serious, "we understand the need for secrecy. But you've gone beyond the limit on this one. We can't function if we don't know what's going on."

The big guy checked his watch. "Okay, but I only have time for the short version."

I nodded.

"First, I have a question. How did you select which bank to put the forty million in?"

"I don't really recall. I..."

"Didn't you discuss the money with McNaughton?" Angella asked.

"I don't...actually, yes I did. I forgot about that. McNaughton suggested the *Marine* bank."

"It's one of the few banks on SPI with safety deposit boxes," Tiny said. "How she knew the Bird was in that bank I don't yet know. But the fact is it appears McNaughton is behind the heist."

"McNaughton? Is that what this is about? Catching McNaughton? I thought...I thought it's Jamison, not McNaughton, driving whatever's going on."

"DHS believes its Jamison. He's setting McNaughton up for the fall. It's been narrowed down to one of the two." Tiny checked his watch. "Listen, that device you're holding isn't a filter, if you must know. Well, it is a filter, but it's very much more than that. This device is as sophisticated as it comes. There's a camera in there as well as a transmitter."

"You didn't pick this up at *Wells Electronics* or even at *Radio Shack*. This is Company stuff. I thought you were off the reservation."

"Once a Company man, always a Company man," Tiny replied, the twinkle back in his eye. "They own you for life. Kapish?"

What he didn't say caused me pause. They own you for life and if you don't die in the line of duty you'll always die of natural causes—with the Company controlling the causes—as well as the timing. "As a matter of fact, I don't Kapish."

"So this has been DC run from the beginning?"

"Pretty much. Things get real tricky when top folks like McNaughton or Jamison go bad. And that's all I'm going to say on the subject. But you must know this. Jamison may or may not be behind the big bird hunt, but we know he's also heading an operation to take out selected operatives in the homeland without regard to whether they're foreign or U. S. citizens. The camera lens and transmitter are designed to record him in action."

"If he's working for the government then why record his actions? I'd think no one would ever want to trace that type of operation." Didn't the IRS investigation teach these guys anything?

"There's a major flaw in your thinking, Jimmy. Major and critical."

Speaking of being off the reservation! Executing U.S. citizens at home without due process is as illegal as it gets and there can be no lawful order. None! If Nuremberg taught us anything, it taught us we'll all receive lethal injections. "Here, take it," I said, pushing the lens back toward him. "Angella and I are out. O-U-T! Out!" If we were being recorded I wanted the record to be clear.

"It's much too late for that, my friend. What you don't know is that Jamison has not been instructed by the Company, or by anyone in our government for that matter, to do what he appears to be on the verge of doing. The money from the Booby Bird is designed to support illegal operations. The money you brought back from Mexico is an added bonus."

"You know that to be true? How?"

"It's true. Trust me, it's true. Jamison is very much rogue on this. The first four-star ever to betray his country. He's going down. Kapish?"

I wish I did understand, but I didn't.

FORTY-EIGHT

While we waited for *A-Taxi* to come pick us up, Angella said, "I don't claim to know what's going on, but it would make more sense to me if DePierio and Henry were up there as a team."

"That would imply that burying us alive was a charade to make me think DePierio saved my life."

"A charade that went way too far. Jimmy, I was within seconds of...dying."

"I thought of that. If it was all an act then why go to all that trouble. All they had to do was have Henry hold us at gunpoint and then DePierio ride in on his white horse and save us. Simple and clean. That's what Special Ops folks are taught. Make it fast and simple."

"Here's a thought. Hear me out on this. They went up there as a team with the mission of killing you as Abby said. I'm collateral damage and once I saw who was there that sealed it for them."

"Then why…"

"I'm getting there. DePierio didn't at first know you were the one who saved his live in the Sinai—or the Gulf of…"

"Aqaba."

"Gulf of Aqaba. But something triggered his memory. Something you said. Some vision he had. Something. You didn't remember his name, if in fact you ever had it. If I know anything about the way our government handles Special Ops he wouldn't have had yours, ever."

"So how…"

"He called, or more likely texted, someone who confirmed your name for him. That could be why I—and you—almost died. He waited for confirmation. When it came, he went to plan B."

"There're holes in that scenario, but I'll accept it. I'm thinking about who he could have called."

"What about Levi?"

"Levi's Mossad. Levi's not his friend. Someone else."

"Jamison would have fast access. And that fits."

I grabbed the communicator and texted Tiny. YESTERDAY MORNING 8-11 DID DEPIERIO CALL OR TEXT ANYONE?

I showed the message to Angella. She nodded her approval. I hit the send button.

We were in the back seat of the taxi almost back to police headquarters before the communicator buzzed. TO JAMISON 9:16. J TO D 9:22.

"Six minutes," I said. "It took Jamison only six minutes to find that I was the one who saved DePierio."

"Thank God it only took six minutes, Jimmy, or we'd both be gone." She shuttered and pulled me close in a rare display of public affection. Her voice low, she said, "Tell me, Jimmy. Please tell me this is not all we have to look forward to. I'm not sure I can..."

"Is your car parked in back or out front?" the driver called.

"In the front. Right over there. This will be fine, drop us here."

"Now what do we do?" Angella asked on our way back to our condo.

"Await my arrest. And then hope all goes according to Malone's plan."

"Sounds like it's going according to General Jamison's plan if you ask me."

"According to his plan we'd be buried alive. So I suppose it can't be worse than that."

No sooner had the door to our place closed when someone pounded on the door. "Police," a voice shouted. "Police business. Open the door."

When I did, Officer Cruz greeted me by saying, "I have an arrest warrant for one Jimmy Redstone." Knowing full well who I was, he still asked, "Are you Jimmy Redstone?"

"I am."

"You're under arrest. Place your hands behind your..."

"Must I. I present no danger of..."

"...back. Anything you say can and will be used against you. You are entitled to a lawyer and if you can't afford one..."

I stopped listening. The next couple of hours would be a choreographed *piñata* with me taking the beating and I wasn't anxious to find out what would spill out when I broke wide open.

The indignity of being booked, fingerprinted, photographed, strip searched, and placed in a cell are real, even if the whole thing is scripted make-believe to everyone else. Normally, felons arrested for murder would be held in the county jail but because of the charade, I was being kept locally on the island. Thank goodness for that because the experience would have been even worse had I been in a Brownsville cell.

It was late in the day when I was hauled before a judge for the preliminary hearing where bail was to be set. Judging from comments made by the jailers about putting me on a great diet and how all too often the key gets lost, I fully expected the judge not to have been given the script.

But he had, and the hearing lasted less than ten minutes before the gavel came down and we all stood to watch the old man scurry from the bench. To the horror of several people in the courtroom, bail had been set for the murderer.

Even though this was all going according to plan, it took another hour and half before I was released from the city's custody. Lunch had consisted of one slice of what can best be described as a tired-looking piece of cheese between two slices of cold Texas toast. I was tired, hungry, and angry.

I wanted to go home and sleep.

Angella had other plans. "Jimmy, I know what they gave you for lunch, so let's stop at *Tom & Jerry's* for a steak. It'll be quick and hopefully will help erase that I'm-going-to-shoot-the-first-person-who-crosses-my-path look you're wearing. Then you can get a few hours sleep."

I glared at her. "What's up with a few hours?" I demanded. At that instant Angella was no longer my partner, but rather an obstacle to be overcome.

"It's seven now. We'll be out of the restaurant by say, eight. You're meeting Hildigo and diving on the bridge at two."

"Hildigo? Where the hell did that come from? And why the hell two in the morning?"

"You know that boat contraption parked over by the Hovercraft? The one you commented on."

"Big kayak looking thing I couldn't figure out what it was?"

"It's a diving platform. Somehow it inflates to seal it. Belongs to the Lab. Anyway, Hildigo is taking you down. I set the time. Jamison wanted ten, but I knew you'd be exhausted. Five hours sleep is better than one."

"The hell with him! Ten hours is better than five. We'll do it in the morning."

"It's set for two. That's been cleared with the Coast Guard. There's just a small window. A nice dinner, five hours of sleep, you'll be ready to go. I've seen you do it before. Once more and..."

"You seem happy I'm doing this. What gives?"

"Not happy, Jimmy. Resigned to it. Better diving with Hildigo than DePierio. If Abby's right, your life's on the line. The sooner they arrest Jamison the better. And besides, right now the SPI police are involved. They're doing surveillance. Piss them off and there's no telling what will happen."

Regardless of whether or not she had a good point, if I knew Angella I knew we were going to get a steak and I was going to get five hours sleep. End of story. "I suppose Jamison knows Hildigo through their mutual connection with *SpaceX*. But I thought Jamison wanted the camera shots to be unbiased, no chance of manipulation."

"Hildigo hardly posses a problem in that regard Jimmy. That's what you're there for. You are taking the pictures and they are going directly to Jamison."

"Let me get this straight. Jamison trusts me to send him undoctored pictures of the bridge abutment while at the same time he's running an operation to kill me. You smell the same rat I do?"

"Big time. That's exactly why we need to have Malone in the loop."

FORTY-NINE

As per instructions sent to Angella, she dropped me in the turn-around portion of the causeway bridge on the SPI side of the bay. From there it was a short walk to the sand flats on the north side of the bridge. Fishermen typically waded out from this point, but two in the morning is early even for the most ardent of them. I saw no sign of Hildigo so I walked a few feet out into the unusually warm water. The tide was in, and abnormally high, so the water quickly came up to my knees.

Still no Hildigo. Actually, no nothing. Not a vehicle crossing the bridge, not a boat on the water that I could see, not a drop of wind. The water was photograph flat, having no dimensionality. I was dressed in a shorty wetsuit and wore neoprene booties to protect my feet. I waded out further until the water came chest high. I understood the camera to be waterproof, but I was taking no chances so I held it high.

A kayak suddenly appeared from behind the first bridge abutment, almost directly south of where I was standing. In the dim light from the bridge surface I could make out a single person in the boat, which seemed to be moving without any visible means of propulsion. I began walking in that direction and as the distance closed it became clear that the boat was not a kayak but rather the strange vessel we had seen tied up next to the Hovercraft. The cover was now off and it appeared to be an extra wide four-person skiff with a very pointy bow. Hildigo was alone in the boat.

I took one step too many and suddenly I was in water over my head with no bottom I could touch. I swam back toward the edge of the sand bar, still keeping the camera above water.

"Don't worry about the camera," Hildigo called. "It's waterproof. Get up on the bar and I'll pick you up."

A moment later I was sitting directly behind him. The boat was actually roomier than I had expected.

"You'll have to show me which abutment we are to dive on. I was only told where to pick you up and that we would be photographing one of these bridge abutments. I assume it will be the one from the photographs we've seen."

"Go across the bay toward Port Isabel. Almost to the center of the bridge. I'll tell you when to stop."

Hildigo bent forward, twisted one of several dials mounted in a small panel in front of him and the boat began to move forward. I heard no engine noise and he didn't seem to be steering.

"This is all most strange," he said. "I must say. Most strange. And you leaving without me in the Hovercraft was most disappointing. That could have cost me my job you know. But I filed a report saying I loaned it to Homeland Security. You're covered."

"That was certainly decent of you, Hildigo. I hope I can return the favor."

I wanted to ask him what medications the medical bag on the Hovercraft typically held, but that would only raise questions that he didn't need to be part of.

The boat glided smoothly and swiftly through the water with what appeared to be a minimum of effort. That's exactly what I would expect from the design. The specs that I had seen said that when it was submerged it had a forward speed of over thirty knots.

"Next one," I said realizing we were already almost to the highest point of the bridge. The next section is one of the sections that had been replaced in 2001 when a heavily laden slow-moving barge hit the bridge. Eight people had died that night when vehicles they were riding in fell into the bay. Three survivors were pulled from the water.

"Which side are we diving on?"

"The far side."

"Then I'll stop over here and we'll deploy the cover. The top is designed for underwater use and makes the platform unstable on the surface."

"What can I do to help?"

"Not much. This puppy is fully automatic. Everything works from a few buttons on this panel. I just set the lat, long coordinates, or GPS if you wish, and off it goes. I can also set the depth up from the bottom we want the platform to maintain. It's equipped with underwater communication and an air trap that allows for loading and unloading small cargo, such as a person, no matter what depth we are at. I haven't explored all the bells and whistles yet, but next week a few of us are going out for sea trials." Hildigo was understandably excited about his new toy. Quite frankly, so was I.

"Okay," he said. "I'm going to deploy the top and make us water tight. This will take a few minutes." He then reached forward and flipped a switch.

I expected something to burst out around us, but nothing seemed to happen.

The boat began to rock slightly and then it became clear that from all around us a giant beach ball-appearing apparatus was rising. It took several minutes before I realized that we were now inside a small dome.

"On the surface this looks like it couldn't cut through the water at all. But trust me, once it's underwater the system shapes the dome for maximum speed. It's patterned after the shape of the dolphin and uses their sonar system for navigation. It's really neat."

"How many times have you been out in this?"

"Twice. But only in the bay. In a moment a door will become apparent. Actually it's an air lock. I don't profess to understand how this all works, but the inside will fill with oxygen from equipment built into the hull. The oxygen is generated from sea water and the pressure will remain constant regardless of how far down we go, or how long we remain down there. NASA's been working on this for years and this is only the fifth one delivered. *SpaceX* actually paid for it. The neat thing about this platform is that you can set it for any coordinates you wish, like anywhere in the world, and any depth, say five feet off the bottom, and it will take you there. From what I understand it can remain down for over a year."

"Depth is unimportant out here in the bay, so I don't understand why we're using this," I said, trying to figure out how much he knew about the operation I was on.

"I'm just following orders, Agent Redstone."

"Whose orders?"

"A general. Actually a retired general."

"Jamison by any chance?"

"Yes and no?"

At first I didn't appreciate what he had said. Then I said, "What does yes and no mean?"

"A woman general came to see me. Tall woman. She said she came on behalf of Jamison. I don't recall her name."

"Does McNaughton ring a bell?" Something was really wrong here.

"Certainly does. That's her name. I have a photo on my cell." He reached into a hold and retrieved his phone. A moment later I was looking directly into the eyes of Lucinda McNaughton.

"That's McNaughton all right. And she's the one who ordered...asked...you to use this...this diving bell for the pictures?"

"It certainly was."

I sat in the boat, the air beginning to pressurize around us, trying to process what I just heard against everything that had happened since the great bank heist.

Then it came to me clear as could be. Tiny had been right. Retired General Lucinda McNaughton was running some off-the-books operation and it wasn't Company authorized. DePierio was working for her and while he did so he was, as Levi ben Yuval had said, untouchable by the Mossad. Abby had said there was friction between Cindy and Jamison. Only Abby had it backwards as to who was off the rails.

I replayed my conversation with Jamison and realized what it was that had bothered me at the time. The man was in the throes of senility. Whether it was Alzheimers or something else, I didn't know. But I was positive McNaughton had taken full command and was doing things in the name of Jamison.

I grabbed my cell to call Angella.

"Throw it overboard, Redstone! And yours as well, Hildigo!"

I didn't have to look behind me to know it was DePierio speaking. The air lock door was being held open by the muzzle of a Glock. He was sitting in a kayak with the words *UB Captain Rentals* stenciled on the hull. The kayak was most likely stolen.

My cell phone followed Hildigo's into the salty bay. "What now?" I asked.

"Request permission to board your craft."

Hildigo was too frightened to answer so I said, "Permission denied."

"Doesn't work that way. The man with the gun makes the rules."

"So do as you wish."

"Just trying to be polite is all," he said as he came through the small opening. "The three of us are going down there and taking those pictures Jamison so dearly wants. After that you'll see."

I didn't think there would be an after that, but there was no percentage in telegraphing my thoughts.

"How much longer will it take this contraption to be ready to go?" DePierio asked.

"I...I...think about...five more min...minutes," Hildigo forced himself to say.

"Redstone, you got the camera? From what Jamison tells me it's set for your fingerprints and only yours. I don't believe him on that, but that's what he said. So you'll take the pictures."

"Right here," I said, showing him the camera.

"I'll take it."

He examined the camera as if he had never seen one before. He unscrewed the substitute lens and examined it closely. "I've seen filters before, but this one...well this one seems...much too heavy for its size."

"It's not my camera, remember? Maybe that's what checks my fingerprints."

"Why would you be touching the lens?"

"Good point," I replied. "You know we're in salt water, there's turbulence, it's night, we're shooting through a window. All that combined could cause distortion." I couldn't think of anything else to add.

"Was it on here when you got it?"

"Most definitely," I replied. Why he trusted me to give an honest answer only he knew.

DePierio continued to study the lens, then screwed it back on the camera. "Harmless enough," he finally pronounced.

"It's ready for us to submerge," Hildigo announced a few minutes later. "Be careful that air lock is securely closed. I'm told the outer skin of this puppy is impervious to cutting, tearing, you name it. But because it's some sort of a membrane, the inner surface can be easily damaged. So please be careful moving around. I suggest you remain seated."

"Just get this thing moving and stop talking! You sit in front, Redstone, where I can keep an eye on you."

When the three of us were sitting, Hildigo locked the air chamber as instructed.

"Now take this to the dive site," DePierio instructed, "and be quick about it."

"If you have the exact coordinates it will make it much easier," Hildigo replied. "Otherwise. I'll have to activate the underwater camera and turn on the lights in order to steer. That will take much longer."

"Sorry," I said, "but mine went overboard with my cell."

DePierio pulled a note card from his pocket and handed it to Hildigo who then studiously dialed coordinates into what appeared to be ancient input dials, much like those used on a bank safe. I would have thought something as modern as this would be controlled by a laptop, or even an iPad. Some designer had a sense of historical dignity—or simply distrusted iPads.

A moment later we were moving, but because we had no vision to the outside it was disorienting.

"I'll turn on the underwater lights when we submerge," Hildigo said, as if anticipating my next question as to how we were going to take pictures if we couldn't see out.

"Hildigo?" DePierio said.

"Yes."

"Do you want to come out of this alive?"

"Of…of course…I do," the kid stuttered.

"Then from this point on you will do exactly as I say, nothing more, nothing less. Just treat me as the captain and you'll be fine. Understand?"

"I…I…understand, sir."

"Good. Now relax and enjoy the ride. You too, Redstone. We need good pictures from you and that fancy camera."

It didn't take very long and our underwater office stopped moving. Hildigo said, "We're here."

"Okay," DePierio responded, "turn on the lights. Redstone, you take whatever pictures you're going to take. I'm told that camera can transmit from underwater. Don't believe it myself, but, hey, technology marches forward."

"Hildigo," I said, turning around on my bench to face him. "Open the window."

"Is it okay if I open the window?" Hildigo asked.

"Do what you must," DePierio replied. "But don't go getting cute and do something foolish."

The window was beside Hildigo and I moved back to his bench. I held the camera against the small porthole like window and began shooting. The fact that I couldn't get a clear look at the abutment didn't stop me from shooting over a hundred shots, using every angle I could muster. After about ten minutes of twisting and turning I announced that I was finished.

Jamison, or whoever, should now be able to make an informed decision as to whether or not the tectonic plate is indeed slipping and sending South Padre island out to sea.

"Okay, Hildigo," DePierio said, "Redstone's finished. Take us back to where I tied up my kayak so I can get out of here."

I glanced over at Hildigo to be certain he had heard the singular pronoun. It was clear to me that DePierio had no intention of allowing us to leave the diving platform. Not alive anyway.

FIFTY

I was about to tell Hildigo not to comply with DePierio's demand because we would not be getting out of this machine alive if he did. I'd much rather take my chances at depth because then his options were very much limited.

But Hildigo was ahead of me. He had dutifully dialed in the coordinates for the short return trip, which in essence would mean tweaking the least significant digit of the longitude number by one or two thousandths. Instead of turning the last dial, he turned the first dial from nine to seven and hit the enter button.

Then the young scientist did the totally unexpected. He reached over and touched a switch labeled LOCK.

"What'd you just do?" DePierio demanded, sensing something wrong but not knowing what it was.

The skinny doctor, who looked more like he belonged in a children's classroom than in an underwater submarine facing a world class villain, stretched to his full height and turned to face DePierio. Looking him straight in the eye, his voice defiant, Hildigo said, "I locked the coordinates and turned off the radio. If I don't get out of here, neither do you."

I was proud of the kid, but his bravado wasn't going to serve him well with a guy such as DePierio.

"We're moving!" DePierio exclaimed. "I can feel it. But we're not going up and, in fact, we should have been there by now! Where the hell..." He looked at the control panel and it only took an instant before comprehension spread to his face. By changing the first number from a nine to a seven Hildigo had programmed coordinates somewhere in the Atlantic. "Where the hell we going?" DePierio demanded, his command tone subdued.

"East," Hildigo said. "Pretty far east."

What he didn't say was that the platform was still programmed to be less than a foot from the bottom, so unless we got out very soon, the depth would prevent us from getting out at all until we surfaced.

"Unlock this now! I want this platform on the surface."

"Won't! And only I have the combination."

"You son of..." Before DePierio finished his sentence, his emotions took command and he stabbed Hildigo in the right side with a knife he had been holding. The stabbing happened faster than I could react and the kid fell forward smacking his head on the control panel. He rolled off the bench and lay unmoving on the floorboards.

"You did it now," I said. "He's our only hope of getting out of here alive."

"Shut the hell up, Redstone!" DePierio stepped to the control panel and began twisting dials. Nothing changed. He grabbed the radio, but it would not come on.

The navigation display was the only readout that seemed to be working. The depth, which had been at twelve feet under the bridge, now read forty and was continuing to increase. The last few digits of the latitude and longitude numbers were changing fast. We were clearly on our way out to the Gulf of Mexico and then on to the Atlantic. While oxygen and pressure might not be the problem, food and water soon would be. I expressed that fact to DePierio and then added, "It's up to you, my friend. It's all up to you."

"What's up to me?"

"How you...all of us...actually die. And die we will unless you do something, and do it soon."

"You want a plan, I'll give you a plan!" The desperation in his voice betrayed his bravado. DePierio knew he was trapped.

"So what's your plan, my friend?"

"Kill you both and then cut my way out of here. You heard him say the bubble's vulnerable from the inside."

"And then what?"

"You think I can't surface and swim to shore? Is that what you think?"

"We're now at seventy feet and falling," I replied, pointing to the depth gauge. I didn't know for certain whether we were or weren't being tracked, but I did know the chances of him going up seventy, now seventy-five feet, without oxygen bubbles forming inside his body and killing or severely crippling him, were not high. "We've been at pressure for a while now and..."

"I'm a master diver, Redstone. I don't need a lecture on the frigg'n bends! In fact, I don't need any lectures from you at all. So shut the hell up!"

"As you like it," I said. "You're in command."

DePierio sat quiet, making no move to open the air-lock underwater hatch.

"I think," I began, hoping he would listen rationally instead of lashing out, "you'd better understand that if Hildigo dies you'll be tried for murder. That is, assuming we get out of here alive. I doubt if your current protection will hold."

"You think I'm worried about your government. That's a joke. They'll call it work place violence or some such gibberish."

"So what are you worried about, if not the government?" I asked, realizing we were now negotiating.

"Ben Yuval, among others, has a mandate from Israel to execute me on site. When my protection's gone he's coming for me. There's no place on earth I can hide from that…that trained killer. If my guardian angel abandons me it won't make one bit of difference how many people I kill. They can only assassinate me once."

A classic stand off. And the longer it lasted the less likely Hildigo or I would survive. I needed to play for time and to work on a plan. "Mind if I tend to Hildigo? He's our key to going to the surface safely."

"Knock yourself out. Just don't do anything stupid."

I turned the young scientist over. His wound was no longer bleeding and his breathing was regular. He moaned once and I thought he was coming around. Then he passed out again. I examined the slice in his side and determined that no organs were cut. That was good. "He's alive," I announced, not that DePierio cared. "But there may be internal bleeding and most likely there is. If we surface soon at least a homicide wouldn't be added to the counts against you." I let that sink in, then added, "Now would be a good time to surface, give yourself up."

"To what end?"

"Maybe we can work something out," I said, putting the finishing touches on a simple plan that had the lure of working.

"You have something in mind? Let's hear it."

"I assume you have information valuable to the American government. Is that a fair assumption? I mean information of immediate benefit to them."

"That's a fair assumption. Go on."

Now came the leap of faith. Something Tiny had said about no American general ever becoming a traitor was playing in my mind. Because I believed Jamison himself was in mental turmoil it then was a simple step to think of McNaughton. "Let me also assume," I said to DePierio, "that you, under direction of whatever government you are working for, want us to believe General Jamison is behind various nefarious plots to kill certain individuals. Is that assumption also correct?"

"Go on," DePierio said, not committing one way or another. But his attention told me I was spot on.

"But by my assessment Jamison is well-along the unfortunate path to senility. Therefore, as between him and McNaughton I'm betting it's McNaughton who is behind all this. Am I getting hot?"

"Go on."

"Not until I receive a confirmation."

"Confirmed."

"Okay. So here's my plan. We surface. In exchange for your continued protection, you do two things. First, inform the CIA of exactly what country you work for and what your mission is. You will agree to work with the CIA as a covert agent."

"And the second condition?"

"Tell me exactly what you have on McNaughton that is so bad she'll do your bidding as she's been doing."

"What makes you think..."

"U. S. generals simply don't go rogue. They just don't. I take that as a fact. So whatever you have is...shall I say...pretty bad."

"And I have your word that if I give you what you want, I'll be protected?"

"You do." I wasn't certain I could deliver on any of this, but I didn't see any other way. On the other hand, DePierio's negotiating position was even worse than mine. We had to get this submarine to the surface and we didn't have a lot of time to waste.

"And how will you get us to the surface? That guy's out for the count." Indeed Hildigo was again unresponsive.

Another leap of faith. "I know the code." I was relying on human nature here. Hildigo had given me the combination to the fence and to the Hovercraft. I was betting one of those, probably the one to the Hovercraft, was the one used on this diving platform.

"Prove it. Unlock the controls."

"You nuts? Not until you hand over all your weapons. Glock and knife first."

DePierio hesitated.

"Hildigo dies, all bets are off. I may be able to convince them to do a lot of things, but killing an innocent civilian is not one of them."

DePierio's eyes went to the gauges, which now showed depth to be eighty-five feet. This puppy was moving east much faster than I thought possible.

DePierio laid his knife on the bench followed by his gun. "Now turn around, hands up."

"What the..."

"Do it! That way we won't have surprises." He came up clean. "Sit down back there, turn around, face back, and don't move." When he did as instructed, I said, "Now tell me exactly what you have on McNaughton, leaving out nothing."

"Take us up first. You get nothing until this tomb starts upward."

He had a point and there was no percentage in arguing. I entered the gate code. The LOCK light flashed several times, but remained on. I tried the Hovercraft code and the same thing happened.

"How many codes are you going to try before you give up?" DePierio called. "You're guessing. This thing will lock up permanently if you're not careful."

I stopped listening to him, preferring instead to concentrate on the code. But he had planted the seed. Systems as sophisticated as this usually have a two or three-times-and you're-locked-out-permanently protocol. I might have already tripped the lock out. Or this next try might be my last. Or the time after that. I couldn't imagine having more than five tries. Three was my guess.

I studied the Hovercraft code and noticed the last digit of the five-digit code was a two. Did the Hovercraft arrive before or after the diving platform? I had no way to determine. So perhaps the code ended in a three—or a one—depending on the order of arrival.

I searched my memory to determine if I recalled any other toys the Pan Am Lab had. Then I recalled that Hildigo was often out in the bay with a large flat-bottomed powerboat. Angella and I had walked past that boat on our way to the Hovercraft. The diving platform had been tied up at the slip beyond the Hovercraft. But I couldn't recall if there was a slip between the Hovercraft and the platform. If there was, it was empty.

If the order of the slips held the key to the code then Hildigo, the extremely organized, actually compulsive, person that he is would have set a *one* for the flat bottomed boat, *two* for the Hovercraft and a *three* or a *four* for this vessel depending upon which slip it was in.

My visual memory is usually pretty well defined so I replayed Angella and me walking down the dock in the early morning light. There had been two DHS ultra fast chase boats tied up at slips one and two. Then the flat-bottomed Lab boat at slip three followed by the Hovercraft at four.

So the question became 1795 or 1796.

Was I over thinking this? Probably, but I had to select between *five* and *six*. But only if the lock mechanism accepted three tries. And only if I was on the right combination track to begin with.

Amazing that no matter how smart you think you are, life often comes down to luck. I was on a roll, what with DePierio suddenly remembering me from a time when it had appeared to him that his luck had run out. I was going with…*six*!

I entered the numbers slowly and carefully, checking each several times. Now was not the time to get careless. I dialed in the six, checked it three times and then pushed the enter button.

The LOCKED light flashed once. Twice. Then it turned off. Another lucky day.

We were in business. "I'll take the platform up to twenty feet to show you I can operate it. Then I want to hear the whole story. Not just what you know about McNaughton, but who killed Smith and Paco. Who orchestrated the heist? All of it."

"And if I don't?"

"If you don't I'll…I'll turn you over to Levi."

"Take us up."

I first changed the longitude input to the number now showing on the position readout so that we would hold position and stop going east. I then set the depth to twenty feet from the top. I didn't feel any change in our motion, but the depth numbers slowly began to decrease.

"To save time, you can start your story now," I said to DePierio, who, I could see was thinking of taking over command. "You're wasting valuable time thinking of overpowering me. The only way you'll get out of this alive is with my help. The old adage, sinking ships drown all souls is still very much viable."

Something was giving DePierio comfort in stalling. To change the status quo I reached over to the control panel and saw that we were only up to forty feet below sea level. I dialed in forty. The meter stopped moving. "Here we stay until you give me what I want. I relocked the console and turned to him. I'll make it easier on you. Who planned the robbery?"

"I really don't know that. At first I thought it was McNaughton because she was interested and seemed to know Paco. But the more I've thought about it, the more I think it was a professor from Pittsburgh. My sources tell me the old man who smuggled it into the country had promised him a piece of the Bird. Seems everybody wants a piece of that Booby."

"What was McNaughton's role in all this?"

"I don't know how or why she got involved. I think Paco came to her, but I'm uncertain. She asked me to work with Paco. I was to get a share. It is my understanding that the Bird was put in the deposit box by the granddaughter of the old man. A woman named Belle. Don't know her last name."

"Who killed the diver Smith?"

"I did, but no one will ever tie it to me."

Little did he know that Detective Malone already had a warrant for his arrest. But that was his problem, not mine. "Why? I mean, why kill a city diver?"

"He came to me with pictures of the bridge. Pictures he claimed proved that the earth under the bridge abutment was slipping. He told me the tectonic plate was moving and that my hotel could never be sold. Truth is, if I can't unload the hotel I'm in deep financial trouble to a bunch of very bad people. All the protection from McNaughton, or anyone, won't help. I wanted to make the pictures go away, so I went down there to grab his camera and things got…messed up."

I took another leap of faith. "But you knew there was a hundred million dollar Bird in the bank you were about to rob. The hotel is literally peanuts compared to…"

"If I don't pay up before the week ends I'm a dead man. It'll take years to get the money from that Bird. You can't just sell it on EBay you know."

"And Paco? Who shot him?"

"I have no idea. But if I were a betting man I'd put my money on that marshal guy from Pittsburgh. Marshal Oscar Hugo I believe his name is."

I made a mental note to see if Hugo had flown back to SPI from Pittsburgh in a time frame that fit. That information shouldn't be hard to track down. That is assuming we made it to the surface.

Then I recalled Tiny's communicator and I flipped it open. The cryptic message said: CAM FUNCTIONAL AT DEPTH

Unless I missed my guess that meant that whoever was monitoring transmission from the filters I screwed onto the camera was recording everything that was being said. That changed my plan a bit. I didn't want the information on McNaughton made public. "That brings us to McNaughton," I said to DePierio. "Oral is not acceptable. I want it written."

"That wasn't the deal."

"It is now. What do you care?" I found the notebook Hildigo always carried and relieved him of his pen. The kid moaned, tried to open his eyes, but fell back into whatever state he was in.

"Here, start writing," I said to DePierio.

It took a good fifteen minutes and several pages before he handed back the notebook. I ripped out the pages I wanted and threw the notepad at Hildigo's feet.

"You ready to go on up?" I asked. "Anything further you want to add?"

"Ready as I ever will be, Redstone," DePierio responded.

The next thirty minutes took a lifetime as the diving platform slowly rose. As my mind played back recent events, the tectonic plate movement answer came to me with sudden clarity. Nothing was moving at all. Smith's underwater camera, as I now recall, didn't have a filter over the lens. Whether by design or not, I don't know. For close ups that he normally took it worked fine. But what he had captured at a distance through salty and turbulent water was the original bridge abutment in place where it had always been. But when TEXDOT rebuilt the bridge after the sections fell in, the new abutment was placed just to the east of the old one. The blurry images on Smith's camera of the new abutment superimposed on the old one made it appear as though the abutment was shifting. Could have been an elaborate hoax to extort money from DePierio or an honest mistake. We'll never know.

Agitated, I turned around to refocus my thoughts and as I did so I realized there were several large pockets built into the dome structure surrounding us. Several of the pockets held various pieces of equipment, most of which I didn't recognize.

I probed further and found that four of the pockets held single person life rafts, each packed in a small container.

A new idea took shape. An idea I liked. Then came a second idea, one I liked even more. The ideas were not mutually exclusive. In fact, they complimented each other rather nicely.

Suddenly, the motion of the platform changed from dead calm to gently rocking. The depth gauge now read zero. I pulled one of the life raft containers onto the floor and carefully opened the hatch door. The water of the Gulf of Mexico was relatively calm with a light breeze blowing. The sun was just below the horizon, throwing its first light to reflect off the surface. Always a great sight. And, of course, it felt good to breath fresh air.

I pulled the tab on the raft container and threw it into the sea. True to form the outside shell popped open and in less than thirty-seconds the raft was fully inflated. "Okay, DePierio, out!"

"But..."

"Captain says overboard, you go overboard!" I pointed his Glock directly at his head. "Didn't special ops school teach you never to disobey the captain?" I dropped the painter into the water. "Now get moving before the life raft gets away."

I moved back from the small door and watched as DePierio moved to the opening, sat, sucked in the fresh air, and without another word slid into the water. Boarding the life raft wasn't going to be easy, but with his training and physical conditioning he'd have no real problem.

My eye still on DePierio, I reached for Tiny's communicator and typed in the coordinates of where we were. Then I added, ABRAMS IN RAFT. INFORM LEVI PROTECTION IS GONE.

The reply was almost immediate: ANTICIPATED YOUR ACTION. LEVI'S ON HIS WAY. I suppose great minds think alike.

I responded with: DIVING DOWN. WILL PROVIDE NEW COORDINATES IN ONE HOUR. ARRANGE PICKUP FOR BADLY INJURED PASSENGER. I WILL BRING PLATFORM BACK TO BASE.

I set the coordinates to take the platform straight west at an arbitrary depth of twenty feet.

The first part of my new plan now executed, I was moving onto the second part, doing something for myself.

What I hadn't put in the message was that on my way home after Hildigo was airlifted from the platform I planned to retrieve and relocate a package from the Laguna Madre ship channel. A very special package indeed. I knew exactly where it would go. Singer Ranch, location two-south would do very nicely. If it was good enough for old man Singer, then who am I to complain.

Before I closed the hatch I threw a salute to DePierio who was sitting glumly in the life raft drifting slowly away. "Don't fret," I called to him, "they're coming for you."

"What about our deal, Redstone?" he yelled. "Is this how you repay someone who saved your life?"

"We're even, my friend. We are very much even. One life for one life. Only I performed first."

***

Other Books by David Harry

Jimmy Redstone / Angella Martinez Series

the Padre Puzzle

the Padre Predator

the Padre Paranoia

the Padre Pandemic

the Padre Poison

General Fiction

Standard Deviation

Soon To Be Released

(Under the name of David Harry Tannenbaum)

Out Of The Depths

Thank You

As always, I want to thank my editor, Marvilyn Miller, who not only painstakingly corrects my spelling errors, but who also keeps the plot honest and the characters real.

And a big thank you to Steve Hathcock, the man who knows everything there is to know (well, everything worth knowing) concerning the history of Padre Island and the environs.

Communications

David Harry can be reached at authordavidharry@gmail.com

For information on upcoming books and other items of interest, please go to http://www.davidharryauthor.com. You can follow David Harry on Facebook: davidharry and on twitter: david1harry.